By JODI PAYNE

Creative Process

With BA Tortuga
Heart of a Redneck

COLLABORATIONS
Refraction

Published by DREAMSPINNER PRESS
www.dreamspinnerpress.com

By BA Tortuga

Published by DREAMSPINNER PRESS
www.dreamspinnerpress.com

By BA TORTUGA

Published by DREAMSPINNER PRESS
www.dreamspinnerpress.com

Heart of a Redneck

JODI PAYNE   BA TORTUGA

Published by
DREAMSPINNER PRESS

5032 Capital Circle SW, Suite 2, PMB# 279,
Tallahassee, FL 32305-7886 USA
www.dreamspinnerpress.com

Heart of a Redneck
© 2018 Jodi Payne and BA Tortuga.

Cover Art
© 2018 Alexandria Corza.
http://www.seeingstatic.com
Cover content is for illustrative purposes only and any person depicted on the cover is a model.

Mass Market Paperback ISBN: 978-1-64108-037-8
Trade Paperback ISBN: 978-1-64080-524-8
Digital ISBN: 978-1-64080-539-2
Library of Congress Control Number: 2017919425
Mass Market Paperback published November 2018
v. 1.0

To our wives.

Chapter One

IT WAS a beautiful day. The sun was bright, and a light breeze ruffled Gordon's hair as he got out of his Jeep Wrangler. He opened up the back, pulled out a heavy, square cardboard box and a bag with two bottles of wine, and then headed into the restaurant.

He stopped and set the two bottles of wine on the bar next to a man bent over some paperwork. "Hey, Oscar."

"Hey, boss." Oscar was the manager at Delmara. Gordon had hired him many years ago, not long after he opened the place. It had been Oscar's brilliant idea to add tapas to the menu, and look where they were now. Oscar was constantly proving himself more valuable.

Gordon had asked Oscar if he'd be interested in running his new farm-to-table place, Gaia, when it opened a year ago, but Oscar had turned the job down.

He said he knew what he was good at and it wasn't yuppie tomatoes. Gotta love him.

"Oscar, these two bottles are for Mr. White. He has a reservation tonight and requested them specifically. The first one is on the house because I want him to sponsor part of the spring mentoring fundraiser. Make sure he gets his usual table and Becky as his server."

"Got it. And is he bringing his... er...."

"Date. Call her his date. Remind Becky." Becky had a few other choice words for her, he knew. He understood; after all, the woman, drunk at the time, had loudly accused Becky of flirting with White the last time they were in. But Becky would be fine. White liked her and tipped well, and she liked her bread buttered.

Oscar laughed. "I'll do that. Oh, boss? Don't forget that the ladies' room has a...."

"Got the tile." He pointed to the box under his arm. "But I need to make that call. I'll go do that right now. Thanks, Oscar."

Gordon hurried back to his office. The fucking special-order tile in that bathroom was costing him a fortune, but scheduling the work would be easy at least. His tile guy was also a buddy, and always easy to bribe with good beer. He closed his office door and dialed.

"Yo, sugarbutt. How goes it?" Colby answered him with a low drawl that reminded him of incredible whiskey poured over sugar cubes.

He put the box down on his desk and collapsed into his desk chair, grinning. "Hey, Colby. Listen, I need you to come by and install that replacement tile I ordered for the ladies' room at Delmara. You got time this afternoon? I have a beer with your name on it."

"For you? I'll make time." Colby laughed, utterly unashamed about wanting his beer. "You might have to have me dirty, though. I've been loading my truck with tile boxes all morning, and I'm covered in ceramic dust."

That was Colby, always coming off a hard day's work somewhere. "Please. Do you ever show up clean? What time will I see you?"

"Is four too late? Then I won't have to run off."

"Four it is. The bathroom stall has been taped off for a week. It can go one more day." He still needed to head upstairs and change. He spent nearly every evening front of house, and he had a VIP coming in tonight, so he needed to be on time. Oh shit, he needed to pick up his suit at the cleaners. Okay, that errand was next.

"You'll have to let it cure twenty-four hours anyway." Something crashed, and he heard, "I swear to God, y'all. You break those tiles and I will personally rip off your heads and shit down your neck."

"Oh, listen to you go all boss. Should I let you go?"

"Yeah, yeah. I got a reputation to uphold and shit. See you at four, man."

Gordon laughed. Colby's voice had dropped a whole octave. "Your secret is safe with me. See you at four."

A raspberry sounded, and then Colby hung up on him. There was something about Colby—this genuine joy when it came to anything from working to shooting pool to watching a movie—it made the guy fun to hang out with. And Gordon needed some fun once in a while. He loved his job, but it could really eat up his personal time.

Still grinning, he put his phone back in his pocket. He cut open the box to check out the tile he'd ordered. It was the right stuff. He'd just leave it on his desk for Colby. He took a second to look through the mail Oscar had left for him. Bills, bills, and more bills as usual, but also the package he'd been expecting—the newest addition to his porn collection. He left that on his desk unopened and headed out to the bar.

"Hey, Oscar, I have to run out and get my suit, and I'm going to stop by Gaia and make sure they're good for the weekend. I'll be back by three. Colby McBride will be by around four to see about the tile. Send him to my office when he gets here?"

"Oh, great. Will do."

"What do the reservations look like?"

"We're packed, boss. Tonight and tomorrow, both."

"Nice."

"He'll be out by six, right?"

"I'll make sure he is." It wasn't a lot of work; it'd be okay. They could hang out and have that beer after Colby was done. Damn priorities.

"All right, I'm off." Gordon brushed the wrinkles out of his shirt and headed out the door.

God, this gorgeous day. No wonder they were expecting a packed house. People were out everywhere. Nothing was as good for business as the promise of springtime.

After a long winter, there was nothing quite like coming alive again.

Chapter Two

"McBride? You get that utility room floor done?"

"Would I be out here looking for my draw if I didn't, man? Y'all know I do good work." *Come on, motherfucker. Pay me. I got to tile a bathroom and see my man.* He reckoned it didn't matter a bit whether Gordon knew he was Colby's. That was just details. Eventually he would make Gordon see him as more than a beer buddy.

If he could start his weekend with a check in one hand and a beer in the other, he would be a happy little cowboy. He'd started one job, picked up supplies for another, and trimmed out the third. He was a busy man.

Thank God for that.

"You're the best guy out there," Lou admitted grudgingly, handing over his draw. "And I gotta say, you will work for money."

"I'm good that way." He pocketed the check after peeking to make sure all the numbers were there. "Thank you, sir. I will be on the Williams's job come Monday. Should take me a day and a half, give or take."

"Then you'll work that Best Western?"

"Just the lobby fireplace, man. You can get any asshole to slap down twelve-bys on the rooms." He knew what his happy ass was worth, and it was worth more than mindless tile work. He liked to be pushed some.

"Just the lobby." Lou rolled his eyes like dice. "The owner's wife has ideas."

"Faboo." Something else he was pretty good at was talking to folks. He liked people, so for the most part, people liked him. "I can talk to her Tuesday afternoon or Wednesday, huh? Let her show me what all she wants."

Lou snorted. "Oh, I'm sure she'll love whatever you have to offer. Try for Tuesday, yeah? I want you done over there by Friday. I've got a couple of big jobs I've bid on for the week after, and there might be some design work on one of them. I could use you."

"Just call." Lou paid on time and, so far, didn't seem to be too much of a dick, so Colby gave the big man priority. "Have a good weekend, sir."

"You too, cowboy."

He tipped his gimme cap and headed out to his F-250, then hauled his butt up into the cab. "Okay. Let's get this show on the road."

Colby cracked his window, turned Luke Bryan up loud, and put on his sunglasses. Damn, he did love to have him some springtime, even if it came later up here than it did back home. The snow was gone, the trees were budding, and the sun was making promises that it might be time to grill out wearing nothing but his cutoffs.

Between the weather and his music, the forty-minute drive from the worksite just flew on by. Traffic into town was pretty heavy but moving, and it wasn't long before he was pulling into the lot at Delmara. He saw Gordy's Wrangler, looking a damn sight cleaner than any Jeep he'd ever seen back home. Figured. That Wrangler probably hadn't seen a dirt road in its life. He parked right next to the shiny Jeep, tossed his sunglasses on the seat, grabbed his tool belt, and headed inside.

"Ah, Mr. McBride." Gordy's manager waved him over to the bar. Hell if he could remember the guy's name.

"Yes, sir. Mr. James called. Says he got a job for me?"

"Yes, but he wants you to stop by his office first. You remember where you're going?"

"Think so."

"I'll buzz him. You can head on back."

He headed through the restaurant to the office, thinking that the tile floor in the hall probably ought to be replaced. It was pretty beat-up.

Gordy's office door opened before he even had a chance to knock. "Hey, man. Come on in."

"Hey, honey. You wanting me to get to work on that bathroom, huh?" *Look at that hot motherfucker.* Colby did like him some stud.

Gordy closed the office door. He turned around, and Colby got a good view of his five-o'clock shadow and his crazy green eyes. "I'd really like to take a break now, but we open in two hours, and those ladies aren't going to like you in their bathroom much."

"I live to serve, honey, and your fancy-assed customers might be took aback by my Wrangler butt."

"They're not that fancy. You're just that cowboy." Gordy laughed, blond bangs falling in his eyes. He swept them away the way he did, one hand carding through them and then that little toss of his head. Gordy gave him one of them weird-assed man-hug deals, bicep popping through his shirt like some high-dollar Popeye. "Thanks for coming by. Now get to work."

"Bossy old man," he teased and opened the office door real quick before Gordy could react. "You put the tiles in the bathroom?"

"Oh shit. No, they're on my desk." Gordy picked up the box and handed it over. "Here. And don't make me hound you for an invoice like last time."

"Yeah, yeah. I'm on it." He grabbed the box, nodded, then made his way to the bathroom. He was going to have to set up his wet saw to trim around the toilet....

Before long he was lost in the steadiness of the work, setting the tile, making sure everything was just so, and the time just flew by.

"Hey, looking good in here. Not that I would expect anything less." Gordy set a cold bottle of beer down on the floor next to Colby. "We open in a half an hour, you close?"

"You know it. I'll pop in tomorrow afternoon and grout it before y'all open." He grabbed the bottle and downed half the brew. *Oh, hoppy goodness.* One thing about hanging with a restaurant guy? You didn't have to drink so much Coors Light.

"That would be great. Really appreciate it. Come on up when you're done if you want. I need a shower, and I have to put on a tie for a VIP tonight, but I've got some time to hang out. Back elevator's running again." Pretty neat that Gordy owned the building and lived two floors above the restaurant.

"Spiffy! Sure." *Man in a suit. Yay.* "I got to go load my truck. You got a sign for this stall? Someone steps in here on this thin-set and they'll slide and hurt themselves and ruin my tile job."

"Can't have that." Gordy winked at him and then looked around. "Oh. I thought there was a rope and… yeah. I'll get Oscar to set something up in here. Do your thing and then come on up. Door'll be open."

"Yessir. I'm on it." It took him two trips to load up the truck and get his shit locked in his toolbox. He finished his beer on the way and took a second to wipe his face off.

Lord have mercy, he was filthy. Good thing he'd warned Mr. Fancy Tie before he showed.

He headed around to the back of the building and took the stairs instead of the elevator. The stairs were more convenient anyway; the fire door on the third floor opened up right next to Gordy's front door.

He let himself in, as he had done many times before, and was overwhelmed as usual by the size of the damn TV in the front room. He kept telling Gordy to move it to the back wall, but the guy was as stubborn as a hog on ice. Otherwise, though, the apartment was comfortable and not nearly as showy as Gordy could probably afford to be if he wanted. Everything was new and shiny, but the couches were comfy, and the decor was basically gay bachelor pad. Framed Stonewall poster on one wall, rack of DVDs, mostly porn, under the TV, the usual. Broadway soundtracks lined up next to the stereo.

"That you?"

"No, sir!"

Some ancient rock band was on the radio. Gordy always had music going. Colby just shook his head.

Gordy came out of the kitchen still in his jeans but nothing else except the two bottles of beer he was carrying.

"You get mugged on your way up?"

"What?"

"You lost your shirt."

Gordy laughed, holding out one of the bottles. "Have another beer, cowboy. Your jokes aren't funny yet."

"Now, now. Ain't it you that ought to be having another one so I start getting funnier?" Lord have mercy, he did love to look at that man. He could watch Gordon James wander around his so-fancy condo for days.

Well, maybe not days. That would lead to long-term blue balls.

"Yeah, that's never worked. There's no hope for you." Gordy took a swig of his beer. "Oh!" He pointed to the coffee table. "New porn in the mail."

"Lord, honey. Don't you know that's all on the computer now?"

Gordy shook his head. "That's vintage, my friend. The early bareback stuff. Low edit, tons of fucking. That's not your cheap internet thrill. You should borrow it."

"Low edit—what the fuck does that even mean, man? Seriously." Tons of fucking he got.

"No cuts? No kissing and then cut to the money shots?" Gordon sounded a little snooty about it. Like this was something everybody knew but Colby. "You know, the whole scene—foreplay to finale."

"Not all of us are conness... connoisseurs and shit. Me? I like a nice long bout of on-screen fucking. That way if your mind wanders...." He did love to tease.

"Your mind or your hand?" Gordon snorted. "I'm with you, the longer the better." He drew his words out, and they had a little heat and a little growl in them. "Mm."

"Listen to you." He'd like for Gordon to listen to his happy ass, just for a second, just long enough to prove that he was man enough to rock Gordon's world.

Gordon laughed. "One of these days we should hit the clubs in Denver. You get over there much?"

"Once a month or so. Depends on whether I have to run over for a specialty tile in the afternoon. That makes it easier." And he got to dance. Damn, he did love to two-step.

"I think it's been—God, I don't know—maybe five or six weeks since I've been there. I used to go every Sunday. Last few weeks I've been watching a game or bad movies with this tile guy on Sundays. Or losing at pool. I'm still waiting for that chance to redeem myself, by the way."

Few weeks? It had been three months. "Oh, now. I'll play you any time, but you ain't got redemption coming."

"I might if you'd drink anything stronger than beer."

"Country don't mean dumb, Gordy." He winked over. Some things were real important—knowing when to drink and when to make a bet were two of them.

"Nope. And apparently a college degree doesn't make a man wise either." Gordy winked right back at him. "Oh, speaking of wise. Have you got a couple of work days open in the next week or two? I'm having a new shower installed in the master bath, and I want to do something kind of modern and flashy in there with the tile after. I told them I knew a guy."

"Yeah? Sure. We got lots of options. I'll bring a few things over—wood-grain tile is huge right now. I did a bath the other day with glass pieces in the grout line. It looked like diamonds or some shit. Too fucking cool."

"Glass? How cool is that? Must take forever to do, though, huh?"

He shrugged, took a long swig of beer. "Depends on what you want. They have some strips you can lay in. You do know a guy, after all."

"Yep. A very reliable guy that does top-notch work. Thanks. Just let me know when you can show me the samples." Gordy finished off his beer. "Drinking before work. Good thing it's not full-on summer yet." He set his bottle on the coffee table. "I need a shower. You want to hang out and watch the cable or whatever, go ahead. I might even have some food in the fridge."

"You mean you're not worried about your virtue?"

Gordon snorted and tossed Colby the remote. "Don't drink all my beer, cowboy." He headed down the hall toward his bedroom.

One day, man. One day I will have my shit together enough and I will make my move. Colby watched that tight little ass as Gordon disappeared into his bedroom.

He could be patient. In theory. Really he could.

He hoped.

Chapter Three

GORDON STARTED the water and got into the shower, even more ready for that renovation now that he had Colby on board. They'd be tearing this thing out early next week and installing something big enough that he could actually move around, and then Colby could get in there and make it a great space to spend some time.

He grinned and ducked his head under the spray.

Worried about his virtue. Ha.

As if he had any virtue to be worried about.

Even if he did, that cowboy wasn't making a move on anyone. In the few weeks since they'd really started hanging out together, Colby hadn't asked him for anything. The man didn't seem to care what game they watched, which bar they hung out at, what beer he was drinking, nothing. He was all "sure, man," and "good deal." Even dinner was "I could eat," not what or even where.

He was just... easy. Easy to work with, easy to hang out with.

Easy on the eyes too.

If he and Colby didn't have a professional relationship—well. He'd be all over that perky little ass. But you don't shit where you eat, right? Keep business business and pleasure in Denver.

He finished scrubbing and got out, turning his thoughts to work while he shaved. He had White in the house tonight, and he needed to make sure that was a good impression. He wanted that sponsorship.

It didn't take him long to dress. Sharp suit, shiny shoes, silk tie, and he was good to go. He took one last look in the long dressing mirror in the corner of his bedroom and grinned.

Still got it, Gord-o.

He headed back into the living room and found Colby leaned back on his sofa, sacked out, beer bottle dangling from limp fingers—and froze.

Oh.

Gordon watched Colby sleep for a second, admiring... something. Something other than the way Colby's jeans stretched across his hips or how dark his lashes were where they rested just above his cheekbones. Definitely something else.

Maybe how the cowboy's boots were leaving smudge marks in his carpet.

He exhaled, only just realizing he'd been holding his breath, and took a couple of steps forward. Jesus, Colby always smelled so good after work.

Gordon reached for the bottle and slid it from Colby's fingers before he dropped it.

Colby's eyes popped open. "Shit. Sorry, man. It was quiet, and you know me, I sleep when I can."

"Jesus Christ!" Gordon jumped back. "You scared the crap out of me."

"Sorry!" Colby grabbed his wrist, the motion quick as a snake, and kept him from toppling over the end table.

"Whoa! Shit." Gordon grabbed hold of Colby's forearm with his other hand and got himself upright, laughing. "Cowboy's trying to kill me."

"Bah. You were fixin' to go ass over teakettle. I just saved your life."

"Yeah, sure. After your eyes popped open like a fucking zombie back from the dead." Gordon shook his head and smoothed out his tie, grinning. "Giving me a fucking heart attack."

"You look good, man. For real. You clean up real nice."

"Thank you. Got a VIP to impress." He straightened up and squared his shoulders with the compliment. Preening like an idiot for Colby.

"I better get down there." He dumped his keys on the coffee table. "Just drop those on the desk in my office whenever you take off. No rush."

"Yeah? I'll go ahead and measure your bathroom, then, man. So I know what I'm talking about, design-wise."

"Oh, perfect. Thanks. Catch you later." *Or maybe I'll catch you asleep on my couch again later. Not a bad image.* Grinning, he headed out the door and trotted down the stairs to go find Oscar and get the doors open.

Chapter Four

FUCK TRAFFIC.

Fuck traffic and people with more money than sense.

Colby headed west on 119, climbing into the mountains, the stress fading from him as the number of cars started falling away. He turned up the satellite radio and started singing along, but the real peace didn't come until he'd gone far enough that his phone didn't have a signal.

Oh. No texts. No phone calls. No bullshit. Just him, the mountain, and a case of beer.

Colby drove until the road petered out, and then he pulled over and got the four-wheel drive set and drove some more. He rattled and clattered all the way, bouncing on the seat as he headed up and up until he found just the place.

He never knew how he found the right place to stop, but he managed to find a good one every weekend, trusting his soul to lead the way. This was why he'd ended up here in this high-dollar town—the mountains. Shit, he'd fallen in love on first sight. The way the aspen leaves shook, the columbines growing out of that last lingering snow.

The mountains didn't judge, and they didn't tolerate fools either. You fucked up, you paid, easy as that.

One day maybe Gordon would come, see this. Maybe start to understand that he was more than a beer and a tile guy. Maybe start to look at him like he was worth seeing.

Colby hopped out of the truck and stretched, his back popping like mad. He had his gear, his sleeping bag, cooking grate, his chair, and he'd set up camp here in a bit, but first?

He grabbed a beer from the cooler and leaned on the wheel well, staring out at the trees. Fuck yeah. He let himself breathe deep, all the shit from the week—good and bad—fading off.

Chapter Five

GORDON HAD a zillion pairs of shoes. He had so many that they had their own closet. He had a shoe closet. It was ridiculous. Stupid. Nobody needed that many pairs of shoes, including him.

But he sure liked them.

After his shower he'd pulled on a pair of jeans and a button-down, standard uniform for him for pretty much everything except evenings at Delmara. The only thing that changed were his shoes.

He finally decided on a pair of Cole Haan suede oxfords and sat on the edge of the bed to put them on, grinning at the bit of dusty bathroom floor he could see.

That was going away. In a couple of days, it would be something fantastic. Colby was in Denver early, picking up his special-order tile, and was on his way back right now. He'd texted Gordon a picture of the boxes in the back of his truck.

He got up and had a look around the bathroom. The new shower was zero entry and glass on two sides, and plenty big enough for Gordon to have a party in it. He'd like to have a party in it eventually, but for now he was just thrilled he'd be able to turn around without smacking an elbow into something or brushing up against the wall.

He had a lot of work to do today, and it started with confirming his appointment with one of the potential architects on the Delmara renovation, and looking over the numbers the bank had emailed him to try to put together a dollar figure he could live with.

Then it was going to be nearly two hours of interviews for spring and summer waitstaff, a meeting with Chef to finalize the seasonal menu, and his usual Wednesday head-to-head with Oscar.

It was spring. He loved spring and the promise of packed restaurants and long workdays. He lived for it. If Delmara was busy, he was a happy camper. If it was swamped, he was over the moon and ready to get to work.

But first, coffee.

The soles of his oxfords were slippery on the carpeting in the hall, reminding him of those patent leather Mary Janes his sister wore on Easter and Christmas. His dad used to take a key to the bottom to scuff the soles up so she wouldn't slip and fall on her ass in church.

There was no way he was taking a key to these babies.

He usually just made two cups of coffee, but today he'd made a whole pot, figuring Colby would probably want some if he didn't stop for Starbucks or something on the drive back from Denver.

You never knew with Colby. Rumor was, the man loved a strawberry Frappuccino every now and again. Gordon couldn't imagine anything more vile.

He set two mugs on the counter and poured himself a cup.

His phone beeped, and he glanced down and smiled when he saw Colby's name and *sbux?*

Gordon laughed. The little fucker.

gr skim latte, ex shot thx. text when here I'll help unload

He decided to drink the cup he had in his hand anyway, taking it out into the living room.

By the time Colby arrived, Gordon had settled on his architect and was elbow-deep in budgeting. The renovations were still nearly a year away, but these things took planning, and he didn't intend to go into debt. He wanted the cash on hand. He had a spreadsheet from the bank on the coffee table and another one up on his iPad.

"Hey, you. Coffee and a slice of that lemon cake thing you like."

Gordon accepted the coffee and grimaced at the Frappuccino in Colby's hand. *Gross.* "You need a hand with the tile?"

"I got the first boxes up here. I'm gonna set my saw up downstairs like last time, if that's cool. It makes a mess."

Was that an answer?

"Sure." He set his coffee down on the table and dug into the lemon cake, breaking off a big bite. "So... don't need help, then?" he asked, still chewing. He held the little bag with the cake in it out in case Colby wanted a bite.

"This is enough, thanks. I'm good right now. I'm gonna get to it. Remember, you can't use it for a couple days. I need everything to set just so."

"Haven't used it since the weekend. I have the other one in the hall with the tub in it." Gordon watched him. Colby's work clothes were as beat-up as ever, but he was clean and smiling, rested. He looked... great.

Mmm. Really good.

Gordon swallowed and turned around to pick up his coffee again. Damn, that cowboy had been making him twitchy lately. He'd been thinking. He'd been wondering.

Hell, he'd been fantasizing.

It was time to go work downstairs in his office, obviously.

He closed the cover on his iPad and gathered up the paperwork and his coffee. "I'm gonna leave you to it, then. I've got some interviews and stuff I need to be boss-in-the-office for. You good? I'll come up and see how things are coming along after I'm done with all of that."

"I am totally cool, man. No stress." Colby's grin bloomed on his face. "You're gonna love it."

Had Colby been standing that close a second ago?

"Yeah. Yep. I... know I will." Gordon cleared his throat. Later. He'd make a move later, something subtle, and see how it went over. He tried to remember what a subtle move was. "Gotta hop."

He gave Colby a quick nod and headed out the door.

At least he knew his bathroom was in good hands.

LORD, HE did good work.

Colby stood and looked at the shower, just beaming. Look at that. He'd used a wood-grain tile that was gray, and set in deep emerald-green glass accents. Gordon would be pleased.

His phone buzzed, and he pulled it out of his pocket. Well, look at that. Right on cue, Gordy sending him a text.

Interviews longer than expected. U still up there?
I am. Looks good.

Come and see. Admire. He didn't get a response, but a couple of minutes later, he heard the apartment door open and close. "All right, I'm coming," Colby heard Gordy call from the bedroom. He appeared in the doorway. "Brought you a beer—whoa."

Gordy slowly reached toward Colby to hand off the beer, but his eyes were on the shower. "Are you kidding me? Look at this!"

"I know, right? That green makes it." He took the bottle and drank deep.

"My God. It looks like a grown man that gives a shit showers here." Gordon leaned against the vanity, taking it in. He reached around behind Colby and turned on the other overhead light in the shower. "This is hot, man."

"It is." He did good work, and he knew it. "Damn near as hot as me."

Gordon let out a low laugh, and Colby felt the brush of breath on the back of his neck. "Not even close, cowboy."

"No?" *Oh please.* He wanted to know what that taut body felt like against him, how they'd fit, pressed together.

"No." Gordon's voice dropped even deeper, and he slid out from behind Colby. "Not at the end of the day. Not when you smell like you do. Like good work."

"Tile dust and sweat." He was hard as a rock and just about ready to get down on his knees and beg. Colby turned around, intending to ask for what he wanted, when he found himself lip to lip with the hottest son of a bitch on earth.

Gordy took the kiss, wrapping a hand around behind Colby's neck and holding him there, a firm tongue forcing its way in and sweeping through Colby's mouth.

Praise Jesus. He blinked, and his eyes went wide as he hummed low in his chest, fingers hunting Gordy's hips so he could hold on.

Gordy made a hungry sound and turned them, kicking the bathroom door closed and pressing Colby up against it. He shifted his mouth to Colby's neck and licked Colby under the ear, pressing his thumb under Colby's jaw to lift it.

"Fuck yeah." Lord have him, the world spun. He burned, his heartbeat going a mile a minute.

Teeth scraped along his jaw and lower, biting at his shoulder. Gordy's hot hands jerked his shirt loose and pushed up under it, then slid over his belly and around to his back, fingers tucking in under his waistband. He returned the favor, tugging at Gordy's button-up, hungry for skin.

"Hang on." Gordy growled and let go of Colby long enough to help with the top couple of buttons, grab the back of his collar, and yank the shirt off over his head. He tugged the sleeves loose and tossed it.

"You." Gordy pushed at Colby's shirt again and then went after his belt.

"Uh-huh. Fuck, I want you, honey. Bad." He stripped his shirt off, then got his hands on Gordon's chest, his eyes crossing at the heat.

Gordy fought with his belt buckle but won, opened his jeans, and then kissed Colby again. "Want you," he said and went in for another, deeper kiss. "Want to fuck you, cowboy. You feel so good."

"Now is good." He opened up, letting himself drown in the heady kisses.

"I hear that." Gordy got a little rough, taking him by the hips and turning him, and Colby had to throw his hands out to catch himself against the door. But gentler hands pushed into his waistband and guided his jeans and briefs down over his hips, baring his ass.

He wasn't no virgin, and he knew what he needed, so he pushed back with his ass, making his offer clear as the ringing of a bell.

"Mmm. That's right. Very nice, cowboy." Gordy groaned and gave one of Colby's cheeks a solid smack. "Hold that thought." Gordy dug through a drawer in the bathroom vanity for a bit; then Colby heard the sound of his zipper and a low moan.

Gordy made his way back to him, jeans riding low, popping the top off a bottle of lube.

"Fuck yeah." He'd waited so long for this, and it felt almost like a dream, except it was sharp and real.

He got a grunt in response, and then it was all about cool lube and pressure, Gordy's finger pushing right inside. Gordy was standing close, hot chest bumping into his shoulder blades and rough denim against his skin.

"I've been watching you. Wanting this," Gordy whispered in his ear.

"Good. Take me, honey. I been needing to know."

"Yeah?" Gordon added a second finger and swirled them as he pushed them deeper.

"Yes." He spread a little wider, his jeans biting into his thighs and driving his need a tiny bit higher.

Gordy shifted behind him and his fingers fell away, replaced quickly by the thick head of Gordy's gloved cock, pressing impatiently against his hole. "So. Now you know."

"Tell me more." He bore back, his lips pulling away from his teeth at the amazing burn.

Gordy's fingers dug into one hip and one shoulder as they came together, Colby's ass fitting right up against Gordon's hips. Gordon exhaled heavily, breath catching the hair at the back of his neck. "Plenty more."

"Fuck yeah." That was what he needed, just this, right now.

Gordon started moving. He held Colby by the hips, and after a couple of long strokes he took up a nice steady rhythm. "God, you feel so good."

All Colby had was a long moan and a nod, because all his blood was down south and he was high as a fucking kite.

He felt Gordy shift behind him and lean away, half thrusting now and half tugging Colby's hips back to meet him. Everything was focused. Gordy was riding on a train shooting down the express track. It wasn't romance; it was the best fucking kind of getting off.

Romance was for people who didn't need like he did.

"Harder, man. I want to feel you next week."

Gordon groaned, the sound so deep it could have come from three stories down. "Your wish…." Gordon hammered into him, their bodies crashing together.

Lightning slammed along his spine, settling in the base of his balls, and he cried out, a short sharp bark of pure need, and he gave it up, pouring his fucking soul out.

"That's it. Fuck, yes!" Gordon's fingers scrabbled against his skin and found a grip again, and his breath was coming in sharp, rattling pants. "Colby—you…?"

"Yeah. Fuck yeah." Hell, he'd just desecrated Gordy's wall.

"Thought. So." Gordy's voice was tight, but that throat opened right up as he came, shouting loud enough for his voice to ring off the new tile. He went still, balls-deep or deeper, and shook for a second before letting Colby's hips go.

He stood there, panting like a hot dog.

"Fuck, cowboy." Gordy let out a low grunt as he pulled out, then moved away to ditch the rubber and wash up. He glanced over in Colby's direction a couple of times from the sink.

Colby shot him a grin and resisted the urge to tell Gordy that he didn't intend to turn into any more of a stalker than he already was. "That did not suck, my friend."

Gordy gave Colby another look, but this time he was grinning too. "No, that did not suck." He tucked his dick away and zipped up his jeans as he made his way back over. "At all."

Gordon moved right into Colby's space and kissed him, and damn, that was fine as frog hair. Colby had known Gordy would be able to fuck his world up with those kisses. He'd known it.

"I'm going to have to get a shower and get to work." Gordy gave Colby's bare ass one more squeeze before he stepped away. "It looks fucking amazing in here. How much more time are you going to need? You plan to finish today or… do you need to come back?"

"I'm done for today, honey, but I have to come back for grouting." He shot Gordon a wicked grin. "I'll do some of that on hands and knees."

Gordy laughed out loud, bending over to pick up Colby's shirt and then his own. "I like the way you think, cowboy." He handed off Colby's shirt with a wide grin. "Wiggle those jeans up, you're blocking the door."

"Picky picky picky." He cracked up, getting himself put back together, at least a little bit. "I'll see you tomorrow, buddy. Don't work too hard."

"No such thing." Gordy winked at Colby, then pulled on his shirt and scooted by him to disappear into the bedroom.

Colby cleaned himself up and made sure his worksite was neat and tidy. He could hear his daddy in the back of his head. *It don't matter if no one ever notices. The work makes the man, and we got our pride.*

By the time he was done, Gordon was gone, but the keys to the apartment were on the coffee table with a note that read, *Lock up, cowboy.*

Colby grinned, stretching up and feeling a pleasant ache to remind him of their afternoon delight. Yeah. Yeah, he could do that.

Chapter Six

AFTER HIS run, Gordon dropped into the little coffee shop up the block for a latte. It was his regular Sunday morning routine, and he didn't even have to order anymore. Jocelyn gave him a wave as he stepped through the door.

"Morning." He headed up to the counter but didn't get too close because he probably stank from his run. It was getting warmer, and his shirt was pretty soaked.

"There you are. We thought maybe you weren't coming in!"

Gordon grinned. He loved this town. "Yeah, I'm running late today." Delmara had been busy as fuck last night, and then he and Oscar'd had a drink after the doors closed to decompress. He'd slept in.

"Anything to eat?"

"No thanks." He was at fighting weight, and he planned to keep it that way.

He waited all of two more minutes, paid for his coffee, and sipped it on the way back to his apartment.

He glanced at his watch as he headed up the stairs, wondering if it was too early to check in with Colby. He usually had to wait out the morning since there wasn't any cell service in the mountains. Colby would sleep in and then had to break down camp. But it was almost lunchtime already, so Colby might be in the truck.

Gordon keyed in and scooped up his cell phone from the table by the door on his way back to the bedroom. Call the cowboy, get a shower, see if there was a game on.

Not that they'd watched more than ten minutes of a game in months—it was just habit now. Background noise. Gordon didn't even use it as an excuse to get Colby to come over anymore, didn't bother to look for Texas teams or anything. He'd learned a while back that all he had to do was ask.

Colby hadn't ever said no. Gordon just had to respect his work schedule, and that door swung both directions anyway.

He sipped his coffee while he waited for Colby to answer.

"Hey, honey! Happy Sunday!"

He did love that, how Colby always sounded happy to hear his voice. "Hey there. Headed off the mountain?"

"Yessir. I'm damn near in civilization. You interested in some fried chicken? I can pick some up."

So much for fighting weight. He loved fried chicken. "Sounds great. Get some mashed potatoes too? I've got beer, and I scored most of an apple pie off Chef last night."

"Will do. See you in half an hour." The phone clicked off, leaving him grinning and shaking his head. *So easy. Here, Gordon, have some fried chicken. And my ass.*

Hm. Or maybe his mouth. The man had some serious skills.

By the time Colby arrived, Gordon had showered and dressed in some ancient but soft jeans and an even softer designer T-shirt that looked practically as old as he was. It wasn't; he'd just bought it last week. Ridiculous what you could pay for a T-shirt.

The cowboy was wearing jeans and a tank top that looked like it was held together with a lick and a promise, the whole thing just serving to point out all that bare tanned skin.

Gordon looked Colby over, head to toe, not bothering to hide his appreciation. He figured he should try to hold off the hormones for a little while. Conversation could be a good thing, right?

Then again, Colby knew what was up. There was always time for talk, and he hadn't had his hands on the man in a week. He'd even been too busy for a quickie in his office before the restaurant opened. He did like those moments. He got off a little on a dusty cowboy.

"Smells good." Gordon met him at the door, holding it open for him. "Looks better."

"Mm-hmm. Howdy, honey. How's it hanging?" Colby set the bag of food down and shut the door behind him, locked it.

"Crazy week. What else is new. I'm telling you, Colby, it's not even really spring yet. If this is any indication, by summer it's going to be insane. Oscar and

I are talking about hiring more seasonal staff than last year." He'd be flush on his budget for the renovations by May—early June at the latest. He couldn't help the way the joy tugged at his lips, and just let himself smile. "It's going to be great."

"Rock on, buddy. I like to hear that." Colby grabbed his waistband and tugged, hard.

Gordon grinned as he stumbled forward. "All right, then." He bumped chests with Colby, trying to get him off-balance, which pretty much never worked, and then kissed him, biting at the cowboy's lip.

Colby tasted like coffee and mint and something that was unique to the man himself.

"Long week?" he asked, snaking an arm around Colby and grabbing his ass. "I want your mouth, cowboy."

"Do you now?" Colby winked at him, happy mischief like a light in his eyes. "Works, as I am passing fond of sucking you off."

Gordon shook his head, moving his lips down Colby's neck to one bare, tanned shoulder. "I'm well past fond of it myself."

He bit down, jonesing on how Colby jerked, bowed in his hands. Fuck, that was delicious. Too bad Colby's tan was nearly dark enough to hide the marks.

He nestled a knee between Colby's legs, with just enough of a rub to get him interested, and chuckled. "I feel that, Colby. Did you forget to jerk off up there in your mountains?"

"It was raining this morning. Too cold for it. I was afraid it would freeze."

"You are too much, cowboy." Gordon snickered. He slid a hand up under Colby's top and rolled one nipple in his fingers, then pinched it. The man liked to whine about it, but Gordon knew Colby loved that sting. He started to back up toward the couch, gently tugging Colby after him.

Colby followed right along, working Gordon's jeans open like a master cockhound and fishing his dick out before he sat.

He was surprised by his own moan. Colby was shameless, and Gordon fucking loved it. "Don't have to ask you twice, do I?"

"You can, I don't mind, but I know what I like."

Yeah. He knew what he liked too. He pulled Colby down for another kiss. He'd never thought of himself as much of a kisser, but something about the cowboy just made him want to taste.

Colby opened up, settling between his legs on the floor.

"Mmm. Yeah." His cock ached with anticipation. He knew it would be good, and he knew it wasn't going to take Colby long to wind him up. It was almost embarrassing, but everything about Colby made him want to shoot on sight.

Colby eased away from their kiss, hands hot on his thighs. "Mmm. You smell good, honey. Make a man hungry."

He shifted, easing his hips forward and sinking back into the warm leather couch. Then he reached out and combed his fingers through Colby's hair.

"Do it."

ONE OF the major perks of fucking a guy who was always dropping by covered in tile dust or mud was that his desire for a much larger shower had been completely validated, and made for yet another excuse for Gordon to get his hands all over Colby.

In fact, he was feeling pretty smug as he worked the shampoo in Colby's hair into a lather.

"Damn, that's nice, honey. Makes my eyes cross."

"Glad you like it." He hoped Colby was just enjoying the touch and not ready for another round, though. Gordon played a solid long game, but he didn't recover as quickly as that happy little cowboy could.

He pressed Colby under his incredible rainfall showerhead, loving how the soap washed straight down over Colby's shoulders. Bright white suds against rich tan skin. "Rinse."

Colby arched and rinsed off, stretching up tall, the long spine popping and cracking.

"Mmm." He could watch that move a hundred times a day, all those muscles going tight at once, that belly going flat. "You creak like an old man, McBride." Gordon leaned into the spray and gave him a quick kiss.

"It's not the age, it's the mileage."

"I hear that. Those tires are wearing in well, though." He reached around Colby and shut off the water. "I could stand here all day with you, under that water and admiring the classy, sophisticated tile job in here, but my stomach is growling."

"Lord, yes. I could eat a water buffalo and chase it with a couple zebra."

Gordon shook his head and handed Colby a fluffy towel. He'd just add that to the long list of things he'd never heard anyone say in his whole life. Nobody he'd ever known talked like Colby. Then again, the cowboy wasn't like anyone he'd ever known, so it suited him.

"Just the idea of mashed potatoes is making me drool." Could he have wine with fried chicken? Was that weird? Colby would laugh at him, but that was all right.

"They should warm up like a dream." Colby dried off, then wrapped the towel around his middle.

"You need some sweats or something?" Sometimes Colby brought something in with him, sometimes not. He hung his towel over a bar next to the shower and headed into the bedroom to find something to wear.

"I got shorts, but thanks."

Oh. Shorts. That meant he got to watch that long, lean body basically unhampered by clothes. Nice.

"I like shorts." But he was going for this pair of sweats that he liked because they sat low and hugged his ass and made Colby stare. He pulled them out of a drawer, and he swore he felt the ghost of a touch on his ass, but when he looked back, Colby was getting the world's oldest pair of red workout shorts on.

"Those things are practically see-through, cowboy." He grinned. "Not that I'm complaining."

"I don't wear 'em to work, honey. They're for being lazy."

"Like I said, I wasn't complaining." Gordon stepped up behind Colby and bumped into him to get him moving. "Fried chicken. Beer."

"Mashed potatoes. I'm on it." Colby headed out, whistling lazily, the tune random, happy.

"So, what have you got lined up for this week?"

He followed along, feeling damn good himself. Shoot the breeze, have some dinner; he was getting to really like Sundays.

Chapter Seven

LORD HAVE mercy, he'd had a day and a half in eight hours, busting his hump for his pennies. Then Gordon had called and needed him to come out to the restaurant and replace tile on another stall in the damn ladies'.

Colby pulled into the parking lot of Delmara, waved at the manager guy, and got to work. Seriously, Gordon needed to tell these girls to stop plugging up the pots so that things had to be retiled.

Of course, more work was just that. More work.

Soon he was whistling away, blocking out more blue tile than you could shake a stick at.

He was getting close to wrapping up when his phone buzzed in his pocket.

upstairs on a call, want you when you're done
u got it honey

He was all over that. It would make for a good end to a long day.

Gordy didn't need to tell him it would have to be quick. It was a Friday, springtime, very busy, summer coming... just like last summer.

Still, he'd take it, and then head up to the mountains for a nice weekend.

When he finally made it upstairs, it was pretty obvious Gordy had been waiting for him. Gordy hopped off the couch as he let himself in.

"Hey, honey, I'm"—*Oh, look at that fine son of a bitch*—"here."

"Jesus, you have a way of making the day better just by walking into it."

"Thank you, sir," he said, walking right up to Gordy, lifting his face for a kiss.

"That's what I'm talking about." Gordy took him by the chin and kissed him, smiling into it and pulling him closer with his other arm. "Mmm. I'm getting to like the taste of ceramic dust." He started working on Colby's T-shirt, pulling it out of his jeans.

"One of these days, I won't be nasty when I come to visit you."

"Call me kinky, but I just do not care." Gordy kissed him again quickly. "No, that's not it. I do care. I love it." Gordy lifted Colby's hat off his head, tossed it, and then tugged his T-shirt right up and over his head. "I could throw you in the shower if it's bugging you."

"I'd have to put my nasty kit right back on. No worries." His cock was waking up, no question about it. It was standard operating procedure where Gordy was concerned.

Gordy's fingers made quick work of his own jeans, and he let them fall before kicking them smoothly out of the way. His bright blue trunks followed. He kissed Colby one more time, and Colby knew he had his mind set. "Bring it on, you filthy cowboy," Gordon leaned in and whispered hotly in Colby's ear, and then he fell back into his leather couch with a sigh, tugging Colby with him.

Colby ended up between Gordy's legs, cradled between warm, muscled thighs as their naked bellies slapped together. *Oh hello.* He could eat Gordy up with a spoon. "I swear to God, honey, you do it for me."

Gordy slipped a hand between them and gave one of Colby's nipples a sharp pinch. "It's hard to be humble."

"Uhn." He told himself one day he'd be all suave and shit when Gordy did something like that, but he was totally lying.

Colby felt Gordy's fingers in his hair, and then Gordy tightened them into a fist for leverage, pushing Colby's face down into his lap. He shifted, spreading his knees wider. "That's it."

"Greedy bastard." He nuzzled in, sucking in a deep breath that filled his lungs with Gordy-flavored air. His belly drew up, went so tight it hurt, and his mouth started watering.

When Gordy's cell started to ring, it startled them both. Gordy had a special ringtone set up for the restaurant, and they both groaned, realizing that the boss really had no choice but to pick it up.

"Well, fuck."

"Sorry, babe, I have to."

"Yep, I know."

Colby moved out of the way, and Gordy got up, dragging his phone off the end table. "What's up, Oscar?" He listened for a bit, looking confused. "I have no idea. Yeah, I guess. Put him through." Gordy looked at Colby and mouthed, "Lawyer," then shrugged.

"Hello? Yes, Gordon speaking. What? When? Oh. God." He went quiet, just listening for a bit, and then he moved back to the couch to sit. He sighed. "Well, we talked about that, but I didn't realize she'd.... Yes, sorry. Yes, I can.... I don't know about tonight, but I'll.... Okay. I'll call you when I get in and we can.... Right. See you tomorrow."

Gordy hung up the phone and stared at it. Jesus, he was looking kind of wrecked. That had to be bad news.

"Honey, what can I do? Did someone die? Do I need to get you a plane ticket or drive you some-where?" Whatever Gordon needed, he'd figure it.

Gordy leaned forward to slide his phone onto the coffee table and then reached for his jeans. "Yeah. Someone died, and it's... complicated. There's a bot-tle of Jameson in the kitchen."

"Okay. Okay, hold up." He dragged his jeans on too, because... well, just because. Some things de-served better than naked, he guessed.

He went to fetch the bottle and two glasses. No one said he had to drink any, but he could sure pretend.

When he got back, Gordy had buttoned up his jeans and was pacing. He poured out for Gordy, who came right over, picked his glass up, and sipped it, then gave it a swirl and looked at Colby. "Thanks. Lis-ten, I really appreciate that you want to help, but there isn't a damn thing you can do. And... you're not going to want in on this circus anyway."

"Okay." He'd examine that odd dull pang of hurt later. Now wasn't the time. "You want me to head out or hang here? I'm easy as pie."

Gordy was already picking up Colby's T-shirt for him. "I have to work tonight. I'm sorry, we can pick this up another time." Gordy had gone cold and didn't look Colby in the eye as he handed off the shirt. He turned away quick and took another sip of his whiskey.

"Sure, man. I'll finish that job tomorrow. No sweat." He got his shirt on and grabbed his boots. He could put them on once he got the door shut behind him. "You know where to find me."

He didn't wait for an answer; he just headed out and yanked his boots on. Maybe he'd head up to the mountains, make a fire and drink a little, have his Rocky Mountain high. There was a reason his back seat was filled with his backpack and sleeping bag, after all.

Really, he needed to get himself a dog.

Chapter Eight

GORDON WAITED for the door to close behind Colby and then refilled his glass. It pained him to send Colby off, and a piece of him was fighting hard to run after the man. But there was just way too much to sort out, and Gordon meant it when he said Colby wasn't going to want anything to do with this.

Maybe he never would, but Gordon couldn't think about that right now. Nor did he want to know why that even mattered to him. That was another complication he didn't have time for.

He headed toward the back of the apartment and his bedroom. He needed a shower; he needed to get a suit on and be thinking clearly. He didn't need to be concentrating on this right now—what was he going to do? It wasn't like there were any decisions to be made.

He stripped and turned on the shower, let the bathroom steam up a little before he got in. He worked shampoo in and rinsed it, twice like he always did, and then the conditioner. Habit, autopilot. He was ridiculous about his hair. Always had been, even as a kid.

His brain hit on that thought, then skittered away like cockroaches under the light. He couldn't go there. Not right now. He couldn't.

The voice on the other end of the line, though. That was something he couldn't deny. Dry and brusque—not callous, but distanced, professional.

"I'm sorry to inform you... sister... suicide.... Olivia... guardian...."

He hadn't been given many details. Just as well. He wasn't sure he could have heard them even if he had.

He hadn't really been close with his sister since he moved to Colorado; the time difference and the distance, his business, her work—there was always some excuse not to communicate. Still, it wasn't like he'd fallen off the planet. Emma could have called him, right? If she was feeling that alone? If she was feeling that hopeless? Before she decided there was no other option.

Or he could have been a better big brother and kept in closer touch and maybe....

He sucked in one deep breath after another, a band of stress squeezing him right across the chest. *What the fuck?* Was he having a heart attack? He didn't have time for a fucking heart attack.

He needed to book a flight to Boston. Round trip for him and a one way back to Denver for Emma's little girl. How the fuck could Emma leave her daughter? How could she leave everything? Gordon remembered agreeing to be named Olivia's legal guardian. It was one of those conversations you have with family and you say yes because it's the right thing to do, but you never expect to… and then the call just… came, and what the hell was he going to do now?

Think about it later. Maybe on the plane. Maybe.

He had a restaurant. He had to go downstairs and be suave and debonair and not out of his mind with this weird-assed mixture of panic and pain. Right now he had to pull it together. It was that simple.

He finished shaving and scrubbing and couldn't procrastinate any longer. He wrapped up in a towel, finished in the bathroom, and dug his iPad out of his briefcase. The red-eye was booked solid, but there was a direct flight at eight in the morning. He decided to book it one way and just for him, not having any idea how long he'd be back East.

Then he got dressed and got on with it. His best suit, shiny shoes, and a stylish tie. He could do handsome with the best of them. All he needed was an attitude adjustment to go with it.

"Pour me a quick taste of something," Gordon said as he approached the bar. His bartender, Liam, was a good find. He had a fantastic smile and was popular with everyone, though hopelessly straight. Probably—no, definitely—a good thing for Gordon.

"You got it, boss. Run your hand through your hair, man. Straighten it."

"Oh, thanks." Gordon squinted at himself in the mirror behind the bar and fixed his hair. "Always looking out for me, Liam," he teased. Normal, right? Business as usual. He had work to do.

"You know it." A shot of something that tasted like spiked lighter fluid crossed the bar, giving him some liquid courage.

"Yep." That was absolutely disgusting but burned just right. "I'm not going to ask what the hell that was, but the next time I need a slap in the face, that's what I'm talking about."

When Oscar said they were going to be packed, he wasn't exaggerating. The place was filled to capacity by six thirty, and they were working on clearing a two-hour waiting list an hour later. There was a while there that Gordon was helping expedite in the kitchen because it was just that crazy. He spent at least forty minutes behind the bar with Liam, and the rest of the time, he was making rounds and schmoozing.

Things started to normalize around ten and got much quieter by eleven. Gordon strolled over to Oscar to get his take on things.

"First big night of the season. Any mishaps? I caught the backup in the kitchen, but I thought that was pretty tame, considering."

"One of the new waiters bailed, but Mickey warned me he wouldn't last, so we had coverage."

"Good. Hell, if he couldn't handle tonight, he'd be eaten alive when we open up the patios in the summer." Nothing wrong with trial by fire, as far as Gordon was concerned, and waiting tables was certainly not for everyone. Still, most people liked him as an employer. He tried to be progressive and offered health benefits and vacation. He expected a lot in return, he knew, but it worked.

"Listen, Oscar." He'd been putting this off all night, using the excuse that they'd been too busy to talk, which was good enough until now. "I have to head back East for a few days, and I really need you to cover. Are you available? I know it's last-minute and all."

"I'm available. Everything okay?"

No. Not at all. But he'd downplay it for now, until he really understood what the hell happened. "Death in the family."

"Sorry to hear."

"I'll call over to Gaia and make sure they're set too, but if you have time to check in over there, I'd appreciate it."

"Consider it handled. Do what you need to do. I got this."

No doubt he did. It wouldn't be easy on his own, though. At least it was early in the season. The summer crowds could make Delmara an absolute madhouse to manage. Thank God for Oscar.

Things had quieted down enough that Gordon was confident he wasn't needed anymore, but he figured he'd hang around at least until closing, just in case. It wasn't that far off.

He closed his office door and looked over the supply catalog he'd picked up that morning. Gaia was really new, and everything was fairly modern, but he was just about ready to sign the final paperwork on the renovation here. It was nearly ten years old and needed a facelift in places. He was going to jazz up the bar, renovate the main dining room, and put in a raised platform that could be used as a stage for live music in the winter and support three or four tables for two when not in use. And he wanted a big fireplace on the far wall. He wanted new lighting too, but he was going to have to play with the budget.

His phone buzzed, and he pulled it out of his pocket, only realizing he'd been hoping it was Colby when he was disappointed it wasn't. He ignored that call, thought for a second and then dialed, but after a few rings it went to voicemail. Either Colby was ignoring him or he'd gone off to the mountains. Or both. There was really no way for Gordon to know. Colby was good at disappearing when he wanted to, and Gordon had done a pretty good job of driving him off.

Once the restaurant closed, he checked on Oscar and Liam once more and then went on up to his apartment. He was not a guy who usually had crises; he was generally very much in control. He was really good at just making a decision and fixing whatever the issue was. He was the boss.

His apartment felt empty tonight. His sister hadn't ever been in it, so the feeling was kind of confusing to him. Emma was the last of his family—well, except for little Olivia—and most of his friends either worked with him or were fellow business owners, and equally busy. But even so, he didn't get lonely much. Thinking on it now, that was probably because he was always busy, and if he wanted company, certainly since he'd met Colby, he was rarely unable to find it.

He found his suitcase in the back corner of his spare room. Jesus, the room was a complete disaster and was about to have a five-year-old sleeping in it. He had work to do before he got on that plane.

Chapter Nine

COLBY CAME down off the mountain feeling like a new man. He'd woken up with a brutal hangover that he'd shocked out of his system with an ice bath in the little pool the river had made.

His balls might never drop again, but his head felt way better.

Time to sneak into the restaurant, grout, leave a bill, and head home. Tomorrow could be reserved for laundry and watching bad kung fu movies on Netflix.

He pulled into the parking lot, telling himself that the reason he parked three slots down from Gordy's SUV wasn't that he was an emotional fuckmonkey who was pouting because he was shown the door. Gordy'd never made promises or nothing, and he needed to respect that. Although... surely they were friends and shit, right?

"Oh, for fuck's sake, McBride. If you want to be a titty baby, you can go to Denver and wear hot pants."

He wasn't even sure what hot pants were or why titty babies would go to Denver, but saying it made him feel better, so he took it.

He grabbed his tools and the grout, went up, and banged on the door. "Let me in, y'all. I got shit to do."

The manager dude answered the door. "Sorry, I was in the back. I'm Oscar." *Oscar!* That was the name. "Mr. James is out of town on some family business, but he said you were totally on it. Come on in."

"Thanks." *Out of town? What the actual fuck? Damn it.* He should have stayed and made himself irritating. Damn. It. He needed to call Gordy, but first the bathroom needed to be finished. He knew what was important to Gordon James, and the restaurant was at the top.

"You know where you're going? There's doughnuts and coffee and shit on the bar. Help yourself, and I'll be in the kitchen if you need me."

"No problem, man. I'm cool." *Work first, make with the worry later.*

He opened the bathroom door, checked his lines. Everything looked set, and all he needed to do was grout and clean. Easy.

Then he'd call Gordy and see what was what. Tile was easy; Gordy was not.

He snorted. Shit. Gordon was a turd, but there was something about the man that did it for him.

It was more than the biceps that busted out of his T-shirts and his broad-ass shoulders. It was definitely more than the fancy suits he liked to show off in, though those were definitely a draw. And it was more than Gordy's wild green eyes or a husky voice on the phone asking him to come over.

There was something that made him wish. Something that made him want to ask for more, and that was a rare fucking bird.

But at the moment, Gordy was... somewhere, on "family business" with a family Colby didn't even know the man had. The more he thought about it, the more the things he didn't know about Gordon James started to pile up.

Still, whatever it was, whatever the problem, he was Gordy's friend, so he'd call like a grown-up. That was him, grown-up, all adult, not just a busybody who desperately wanted to know what the actual fuck was up.

The grout went down quick enough, and after he'd cleaned and put all his tools away, he carefully put back the red rope across the stall door the way it had been when he arrived. He poked his head into the kitchen before he headed out.

Oscar looked up from whatever paperwork restaurants needed doing. "Done already?"

"I am. I'm fixin' to get out of y'all's hair. When y'all open Tuesday, everything should be right as rain."

"Right on. Boss'll be happy. Thanks for coming back in."

"I live to please." He didn't even choke over the words as he headed out, his hangover headache whispering at him again. *Go home and shower, or call Mr. Turd on the way?*

Well, his man was always telling him how much he liked Colby dirty.

He made the call, tossed his phone on the dash, and backed his truck out of the parking lot. It rang three times before Gordon answered. "Colby? What's... uh. What's up? Everything okay with the tile?" Gordy's voice sounded like he'd been shouting for hours. Rough and dry.

"The tile is fine. I was calling to check on you." *Jesus Christ, the fucking tile.*

"Oh. Well, I just landed a little while ago. It was a smooth flight. Oscar told you I had to leave town, huh?"

"He did. You... you okay, man?"

"Sure. Just waiting for a taxi." The weighty sigh on Gordy's end of the line could have sunk the fucking *Titanic*. "You're not picking up on my state of denial, are you? I'm not good at this, Colby."

"I'm not even sure what this is. I just know my good friend is upset." Was that so damn weird?

"I'm not upset. I haven't let myself think that hard about it yet. Hang on. Let me get out of this damn line." Colby heard traffic and street noise and random voices for a minute before Gordy came back. "Sorry, just too many people over there. I'm just... I'm back East. My sister, she... died. Suddenly. I have some shit to deal with, and I'll be back in a few days."

"Oh, honey." *Oh, how bad did that suck?*

"I did try to call you last night. Too late, obviously. I got your voicemail."

"I was up in the mountains. No signal. Is there anything I can do to help?"

The long silence made Colby wonder if he needed to repeat the question. Just as he was about to ask whether Gordy had heard him, Gordy cleared his throat at him.

"Yeah, actually. You mind doing me a favor? I wouldn't ask you except... well, the poor thing lost her mom and all."

He was maybe gonna need a map to follow that train of thought.

"Not at all. Just point me and shoot me." Maybe Gordy was drunk. Losing a sister would make him drink.

Hell, he'd tied one on yesterday and he hadn't even known it was because Gordy's sister'd died.

"Okay. There's a full-size bed in that little bedroom across from the master at my place. I need you to run out and buy some bedding a five-year-old girl would like. And maybe a couple of stuffed animals or something. And curtains. Can you hang curtains?"

Not drinking. High maybe.

"I can totally hang curtains. You want to tell me what's up?" He was trying to figure out what the fuck a five-year-old girl had to do with anything.

"Sorry. Sorry, I'm working on, like, no sleep here. My sister's daughter—my niece? She's.... I'm her guardian, so she's coming back to Boulder with me. Olivia. So listen, Oscar can give you the key to my place and some cash."

"I can do that." He leaned against the truck, shock rocking him.

A little one.

A little girl.

Damn. Gordy wasn't the daddy type.

"Thanks, man. That room—I mean, I cleaned it up mostly, but it's no place for.... She's just going to need something to smile about." Gordy cleared his throat again. "Right. I can't do this right now, okay? I gotta grab a cab or I'll be late to my appointment with the attorney. We'll catch up when I get back."

"If you need to talk, I'm—well, you got my number."

"Yes, thanks. Talk to you soon." Gordy's end of the line went dead.

Okay. Okay, little girl. He knew this. He had nieces. Nieces and sisters, both. He just needed to call Patty and talk to her.

Whoa. Poor Gordy. Poor little wee one, losing her momma. How hard did that shit have to suck?

Okay. Okay. First, home. Then shower and food. Then phone calls. He could do this.

Colby sighed and pulled into the parking lot where his travel trailer lived. "Shit marthy, God, I love you, man, but you got some shitty timing."

He parked and grabbed his ditty bag. He needed to do some damn laundry and get to work.

Chapter Ten

HEADING TO the offices of Lancer, Harmon, and Yates straight from the airport might not have been the best idea, but it was the only one Gordon had been able to get his head around. Get there, have the conversation, get the work done. That was just how he did things. Dive in, make a plan, move on. Do business.

As it turned out, meeting with Chuck Harmon gave him a plan, but it wasn't as cut-and-dry as Gordon was hoping it would be. It wasn't just signing papers. Chuck had given him a short lecture on how guardianship worked, and then given Gordon the address of the probate court, where they had an appointment the following afternoon. Just a formality, Chuck had explained to him, but the court had to approve his guardianship in person.

He'd gone right to his hotel afterward, taken a shower, and crashed. A long night's sleep, some breakfast, and half a pot of strong coffee had helped some, but not enough. And this morning he was off to meet Olivia for only the second time in her short life. The first time she hadn't been even two yet.

He looked in the mirror and smoothed out his shirt, which he had neatly tucked into his jeans, and finished off with a black belt. Chuck had suggested that he lose the tie to meet the girl, something about being less intimidating. Chuck had also suggested he buy the teddy bear that now sat on his bed. Apparently, his complete lack of experience with children was glaringly obvious.

He stuffed his wallet in his pocket, grabbed the bear, and headed out the door. Nine in the morning be damned, he wanted a drink. But that was a slippery slope he didn't have time to go sledding.

The sleek black car was waiting for him, a huge man filling the seat. As soon as he walked up, the guy moved to get out, and Gordon waved him down. "I got it."

Gordon opened up the passenger side door and slid into the back seat.

"Mornin', sir."

"Good morning. You know where I'm headed? I think it's some place in Arlington. I can find the address if you don't have it." He tossed the bear onto the seat next to him and found his seat belt. He didn't know much about the neighborhoods around Boston, but he sure remembered the way people drove out here.

"Yes, sir. Chandler, I got it."

"Great." Chandler. He'd been to the address before. He remembered that friends of his parents used to live there. But he was sure they'd both passed years ago, so this was probably one of their kids. Maybe Emma had stayed friendly with them? Tyler and... God, what was his sister's name? Allison? Abigail? Something with an A. Amy?

They took a tight corner at a good clip, and the teddy bear went sliding off the seat.

Jesus. He wasn't going to take that as some sort of weird-assed omen, was he? No.

The trip didn't take very long. Hardly surprising, given the driver had NASCAR aspirations. He asked the guy to be back in an hour and climbed out of the car, then suddenly remembered and grabbed the bear off the floorboard before heading up the sidewalk to the little white bungalow-style house with the gabled roof. It looked almost exactly as he remembered it.

Gordon had no idea what kind of reception he was in for. He didn't know how well they knew Emma or the circumstances. He hadn't even spoken to anyone on the phone before showing up. Chuck had arranged the whole thing. He'd never felt so out of his depth in all his life.

He sighed. Well, it wasn't getting any fucking warmer out here. He reached up and knocked on the front door.

A vaguely familiar face appeared at the door, which then opened, and he was pulled into a hug. "Gordon. I'm so, so sorry."

Christ, he couldn't remember this woman's name.

"Hi," he said, avoiding the issue entirely. The hug felt kind of good for a minute, and he held on until he started to choke up a little. He really didn't want to go there right now. "Thanks."

"Sure. Come on in. Coffee?"

Tell me your name, dammit!

"That would be fantastic." He followed her into the kitchen. *Angela. Addison?* He was going to have to ask, wasn't he? "So, you're good?"

"As good as can be expected, I guess. Olivia is a wreck." She pulled out a couple of mugs, then pointed to a full K-Cup rack. In another time, she'd be a lovely woman, but right now she looked exhausted.

"Mm. I can only imagine. Were you and Emma close? Did you see a lot of her?"

"We were close once, but I haven't seen much of her the last few years. I have a two-year-old, and I got busy, you know?" She teared up, her hands fluttering. "I'm sorry. I didn't know she was in crisis, Gordon. I swear to you."

Knowing the woman's name would really... *oh. April! Fuck. Thank God.* "Hey." He stepped closer to her and took her hands in his. "April. Don't. I didn't know either. We hadn't really even spoken in a couple of years."

"She seemed okay when I saw her. Olivia was always busy, happy. I told her she didn't have to leave with you today. That's right, isn't it? You have a few days?"

"Yeah, she can't leave with me today anyway. I have court this afternoon. I don't think I can get us on a plane until the weekend at least. The attorney gave me her...." He let go of April and turned his back to her, looking through the K-Cups. "I have to clean out her place."

He pulled one out and put it in the machine. Mostly just to keep his fingers busy. "It'll be a couple of days at least."

"That's totally fine. I want her to get used to you. She's... scared."

"Yeah. To be truthful, that makes two of us." He shook his head. "What can you tell me about her?" Christ, he was the world's worst uncle. All those things people say about how time goes by? Yeah. This was one mother of an object lesson.

"She's in kindergarten. She's bookish, loves her tablet. She has a stuffed kangaroo that is absolutely necessary." April handed him his coffee, then chose one for herself. "She never gives me trouble with food, she wants a dog, and she still believes in Santa."

"Okay." He accepted the coffee with a nod and took a deep sip. He had no idea what he was going to do with all of that information, but he was glad to know it. He wondered if Olivia knew anything at all about him.

"I thought it best that I keep today's visit short, so my car will be back in an hour. We should probably.... How do you think we should do this?"

"How about you come back after court? We'll order pizza. You can see the bedtime routine?"

"Oh, sure. Sounds good." Bedtime was a routine? He wasn't going to be able to deal with a routine if he had to be at the restaurant. He'd have to look into that au pair thing Chuck talked about or something. A nanny. Something. He just wasn't a bedtime-routine kind of guy.

He realized he was frowning and rubbing his forehead, and sighed. "Pizza's on me."

"You.... How can I help you guys? Seriously, what do you need?"

This would be easier if she was a bitch, some-how. He'd at least be able to keep up the arm's-length, unemotional thing. He crossed the room and sat down at her kitchen table before his knees could buckle under him.

"I don't even know what I need. I need Emma back. Olivia needs Emma back. I'm a fucking disaster, honestly. Oh—excuse my language." His hands start-ed shaking, and he put his coffee down on the table a good foot away.

"Me too." She sat with him and reached out, held his hand. "I don't know how to do this. I've never known anyone with a little one that… died."

Gordon didn't even know anyone who had a little one. Or a big one, for that matter. People with kids just weren't part of his world at all. He cupped his other hand around hers.

"Okay. We'll just figure it out as we go along." Had April always had eyes that blue? He couldn't re-member. They were almost as blue as Colby's. She sure had grown up pretty. The more he looked at her, the more he remembered about that hippie teenager with the flowy skirts and funky sunglasses.

"We will. Do you want to—"

"Mommy! Mommy, cookie?" Two little ones came in—one just toddling and one who made his chest hurt with how much she looked like Emma.

"Sure. Sure. Livvy? You remember your Uncle Gordon?"

"No." Olivia shook her head and turned away from him. "Do you have chocolate chip? Those are my favorite."

She wouldn't, of course. Gordon just watched silently as she followed April across the kitchen. She was so... small.

"Well, he's here to meet you. You just don't remember him, but he remembers you."

"You were a lot smaller. About the same age as your friend there." Gordon got up to grab the bear he'd brought for her. He looked down at the girl, not even half his height, and got down on one knee to give it to her. "I brought this guy for you."

"Oh. He's—what's his name?"

What's his name? It was a bear.

He glanced at April, who shrugged at him and gestured for him to go ahead.

"It's uh…. His name is Jack." As in Daniel's. As in God, he needed a drink.

"Jack." Olivia looked at the bear and reached out to pet its white fur. "Can I call him Snowball?" She took the bear in both hands and nodded at it. "Snowball."

"Sure. Much better."

"Thank you. He's pretty."

She had lovely manners.

"You're welcome. I'll have to meet your kangaroo later."

"Her name's Jessica. My mommy got her for me."

"I'm sure she's something special. I hear you are too." Good Lord. He had no idea where that had come from, but the girl seemed pleased and gave him a shy smile. "I bet you want your cookie."

"Uh-huh. Bye." She went to April, who was fighting tears again. "Cookie, Auntie?"

"Sure, honey. Here you go."

"Thank you!"

Gordon stood up and watched Olivia run from the room, Snowball clutched in one hand. He shook his head and went for his coffee. "That wasn't awful." He sat down and picked up his mug.

"No. That was a brilliant move, bringing the bear." She brought over a plate of cookies. "Want one?"

Too bad the bear hadn't been his brilliant move. He was going to have to thank Chuck later. "Normally I'd say no, but... thanks." He picked up a cookie and took a bite. "Mm. Good." He took another bite, trying to remember the last time he'd had a cookie. "The attorney suggested the bear. Family lawyer, guess he knows what he's talking about."

"I'm glad we have someone to help. What are you supposed to do with the apartment, the things? Did he say?"

"Just that I was the only one named in her will, and so whatever is there is.... I mean, did you want something?" He had no idea what to do. He figured he'd send a truck to Goodwill.

"No. No, I mean, she'll need her toys, of course."

"Oh, sure. I'll box all of that up for her and ship it. And anything else I think might—" He stopped himself and swallowed. This was much harder than he'd expected. "—that Olivia might want later."

"Oh God. Right. Right. I.... We'll help. Me and my husband, Dan. He's in there watching the girls."

The fact that Dan hadn't even ducked his head in to shake Gordon's hand spoke volumes. He probably didn't want any part of this train wreck. Gordon couldn't blame him.

A horn beeped twice outside.

"That'll be my ride." Gordon stood up and moved to the sink to put down his coffee mug.

"We'll see you after. We'll have pizza. Do… do you want me to come with you? I will."

"To court? No. No, that's kind of you, though. It's just a formality thing and some signatures and it's done. Thanks, April. And thanks for the coffee." He stood there awkwardly, then finally leaned over and kissed her cheek. "I'll see you after." He headed out the door.

Pizza for dinner with a five-year-old. God, he was never going to get that drink. Maybe that was just as well; he wasn't sure he'd stop once he started.

But maybe he could stop at a bar after the court hearing, just for a shot.

Chapter Eleven

COLBY HAD a truck-full of things—a little bed and bedding, curtains and toys and books. Little girl things. He went with owls and foxes on the purple curtains. That seemed like something less specific, less of a cartoon character, but still fun and gentle.

He hoped he'd done well enough. God knew, he'd done the best he could.

He parked at the back of the restaurant and knocked on the delivery door. That manager guy was supposed to be here doing paperwork or some shit, and he had Gordy's keys.

The door opened slowly, and Gordy's manager raised an eyebrow. "Mr. McBride."

"Hey, man. Gordy says you got keys for me?"

"I do. Gordon told me you'd be stopping by. You need a hand?" He stuck a stopper in the door to hold it open. "The service elevator is just behind me down the hall a bit."

"Yeah, I... I got a truckload. Literally. Lots." He'd assumed he'd have to drag it up the stairs.

"I've got a dolly. Let me grab it. I'll meet you at your truck. Give me two minutes." The manager guy disappeared down the hall.

"Cool. Thanks," Colby called after him. Busy guy. He had to wonder if Gordon had hooked up with him.

"Okay. What have you got? You tiling his kitchen or something?" The guy rolled the dolly up to the back of Colby's truck. "He just had the bathroom redone like a year ago. Wait—you did that job, didn't you?"

"Uh." Dude. Dude, what if Gordon didn't want anyone to know? Wait. Wait. What if he didn't want anyone to know? What? He was going to hide the kid in a closet? Put her in a secret shed? That would be... creepy as fuck. "You know about his sister, yeah?"

The guy looked at him. "His sister? Wait. Don't tell me that was the death in his family?"

Well, shit. "Yessir. And she's got a little one that's coming here. I'm gonna make her a space."

Brown eyes went wide for a minute, and then the guy snorted. "Well. That asshole sure keeps his cards close to his vest. Not only did he not tell me it was his sister that passed, but I didn't even know he had a niece. What is the matter with him?"

"He's a turd. That's the best explanation I can think of."

"Did he tell you—" His cell phone rang, and he pulled it out of his pocket. "Excuse me a second," he said as he paced away from the truck. "Delmara, this is Oscar."

"Oscar." *Oscar. Oscar. Oscar. Oscar the Grouch.* Oh, man. That was going to slip out. He knew it.

Colby dropped his tailgate and started unloading shit onto the dolly. He had most of it stacked up before Oscar got back.

"That guy wanted to know if we deliver. Gordon would love that. Can't you just hear him? 'Yeah. I can deliver a boot to your ass.'" Oscar reached up and got hold of the last two bags.

Oh, that was a damn fine imitation. He hooted, applauding. "Man, do that again!"

Oscar laughed. "Ha! Don't you dare tell him. I like my job." He looked at the dolly. "He's really bringing a little girl home? Is he out of his mind?"

He set the bags down and closed the tailgate, then picked them up again and led the way inside.

"What? He's supposed to just let her go to an orphanage?" Were orphanages a thing? Surely not, or you'd see them on the news or in the phone book.... Were phone books still a thing?

"What? Come on. I'm just having a hard time seeing him as a father." Oscar held the elevator door open for him, and Colby wrestled the dolly inside.

"Yeah. He sounds a little freaked." Not that Colby blamed him. This had to be the weirdest thing that had ever happened to Gordy. Seriously. Insta-Dad.

"Guess it's a good thing he's got money. He's going to need help." The elevator doors opened up on the third floor, and Oscar helped Colby roll the big cart down the hall, which was just barely wide enough. "I don't think the cart is going through this door," he said, putting the key in and unlocking Gordy's apartment. "Can you squeeze by?" Colby took the bags Oscar had carried inside and set them down in the living room.

Then he started unloading the cart, using the front room as a staging area. He'd have to empty the room first, he reckoned, then start filling it.

Once they got everything inside, Oscar shut the front door and gave Colby a look. "So…. McBride. I've known Gordon since he opened this place. But he runs off to the East Coast for a funeral and doesn't give me any details. No, instead… instead he calls the tile guy and asks him to go shopping for his niece. That's… interesting."

Well, shit marthy, how the fuck did he answer that?

"I got the tile work because me and Gordon are friends." There. That worked.

Or maybe not, because that laugh didn't sound like Oscar was buying it. "Gordon doesn't have friends, McBride. Especially not ones covered in tile dust. But it's all good. No business of mine, I guess."

Okay, so now he felt tiny, and damn, didn't that piss him off. "Or maybe you don't know dick-all about your boss that he don't want you to. Just sayin'."

"Right?" Oscar snorted. "That's pretty fucking obvious, isn't it? Wasn't trying to offend. You want a beer?" Oscar headed into Gordy's kitchen. "He usually keeps a good one up here."

"God, yes. Please." It was weird as fuck, being in Gordon's place without Gordon.

Oscar came back with two tall ones. "If he's asking you to be his errand boy, the least he can do is share his beer." He handed one off to Colby and looked at the pile of pink in the living room.

"Thanks." He sighed. "I'm going to run down and grab my toolbox. I got to put the furniture together and hang curtains."

"You got it. Which room is she going in?"

Colby knew that Gordon had started the cleaning process, right? "There's a room partially cleaned out already."

"Right, I'll find it. Hopefully it's the one without the porn and the kinky stuff." Oscar headed down the hall, turning on lights as he went.

Kinky stuff. So Oscar was likely not family. Good to know. He jogged down to the truck, grabbed his toolbox out of the... well, the toolbox. Why didn't they have two names? Why did this little box and one of them fancy-assed multi-drawered boxes and the truck boxes all have the same name?

By the time Colby got back upstairs, Oscar had stacked a couple of boxes in the hall. "Found it. Room across from the master. Also, looks like he's moved all his porn to the living room since I was here last. And the dresser is empty. Maybe the cuffs and the blind-folds are under his bed now." He laughed.

Good Lord and butter. "Nah, I took them home to polish."

He let the drawl just spread out, nice and slow.

Oscar laughed. "I like you, McBride." He took a long pull on his beer. "Come help me get rid of the mattress and box spring. We can put them right out by the dumpster."

It was a long afternoon, but not nearly as long as it would have been if Oscar hadn't hung out to help. They got the big bed gone, he put the new one togeth-er, and they moved things around until it seemed like

Gordy's niece would have some room to play. All that was left was the curtains. And the bottom half of his third beer.

"Lord have mercy. I may have to crash on the couch." Last thing he needed was to get a DWI.

"So crash. I'm on shift in... oh. Less than an hour. I'm going to have to grab my suit from the office and shower here, I guess. Your truck will be fine out back." He grinned. "And there's a wee pink bed you can squeeze into."

"Fuck you, man." They both laughed, and Colby shook his head. "The food good down there?"

"There's always a wait list. And the menu is huge." Oscar shrugged. "Let me shower and then I'll get you a seat at the bar on my tab. Or better yet, Gordon's."

"Yeah? You sure?" He'd love to see Gordon's life, at least a hint of it.

"Of course. I'm going to run grab my suit. I bet there's a clean shirt you can borrow in the armoire in the master." Oscar ducked out of the bedroom, and a few seconds later, Colby heard the front door close behind him.

For a second, he just stood there, feeling like all sorts of an imposter, and then he shook it off. This was Boulder, for fuck's sake. North Face, crunchy-granola, mountain-biking country. Totally his people.

Oscar took the fastest shower he'd ever seen, but kept the little shadow of a beard. When he came out of the bedroom, he was in a dark gray suit and a black tie, hair combed perfectly, and he looked almost nothing like the guy in the blue jeans and the grubby T-shirt who Colby was drinking beer with half an hour ago.

That guy looked like good fun. This guy wasn't mountain biking anywhere.

"They need me down there. Come on down whenever you're ready. Just take a seat at the bar, tell Liam it's on me, and I'll find you."

"Will do. I got to get these curtains hung first." And he needed to sober up. He'd be damned if he said anything to embarrass Gordon in the restaurant.

"Right on. See you downstairs. Nice work on the room. I think she'll like it." Oscar disappeared through the front door again.

He sure as shit hoped so. He was going to be eating beanie-weenies for two weeks as it was. He'd spent all Gordon had left, plus a little.

Colby grinned. Which was the perfect excuse to hang those curtains and go down and eat on the free, right?

Right.

Chapter Twelve

GORDON NEVER did get that drink.

Not the night they had pizza and he learned all about baths and bedtime stories and the little unicorn-shaped nightlight. Not the next two days either, which he'd spent in Emma's apartment boxing up anything that looked like it belonged to Olivia to send home, and sending nearly everything else to Goodwill. He decided that buying a bottle of anything and drinking it alone in her apartment all day was worse than a bad idea.

And it wasn't looking like he was going to get one tonight either. He was doing this whole nightmare sober. Score one for Uncle Gordon. With a kindergartener in the house, he guessed it was just the beginning of many sober nights to come.

Olivia sat on the couch with Snowball in her lap, watching Gordon warily as he tried to figure out how to start the conversation about their travel to Colorado in the morning.

He looked over at April, who gave him the same encouraging smile she'd been giving him for two days, and then back at Olivia.

"Tomorrow, you and I are going… to fly on an airplane."

April tried to help. "An adventure on an airplane, Olivia, how cool is that?"

"Right. An adventure."

"Are we going to get Momma?"

Shit. He looked at April for help, but she shook her head, got up, and left the room. He got it. This was hard. But what was he supposed to tell Olivia?

"No, Liv. I'm sorry." He shook his head. "We're going to have to go without her."

"Is it scary?"

"What? My apartment? No. No, it's nice."

"No. The airplane."

"I don't think so. I think it's neat. You can look out the window and see highways and mountains and all kinds of stuff." God. The last thing he needed was a freaked-out five-year-old on an airplane. He remembered Emma didn't like to fly either. And then he remembered what their father used to tell her. "Anyway, there's no reason to be scared, I'll take care of you."

That was good, right? And if that didn't work, maybe he could sneak her some whiskey.

"Okay. I want my mommy. I promise I'll be good."

That stinging in the corners of his eyes and the lump at the back of his throat were familiar to him now, and he fought it all back—again—just as he'd been doing for the last several days.

What was the matter with him? He'd built a successful business up from nothing on borrowed cash, he could wheel and deal and schmooze with the best of them, he could hire and fire and tell someone to shove it where the sun don't shine, but he didn't know how to tell this little girl that her mother wasn't coming back.

And the longer he looked at her, the more he felt his control slipping. He was losing the fight with the tears too.

He slid off the couch to his knees and took her little hands in his. "Baby, I miss your mommy too. But she was sick, none of us knew how sick, and she... uh." He swallowed hard and gave up on trying to stop the tears. "She's... we're not going to be able to see her again, Olivia. She's up in Heaven with the angels now."

Olivia frowned at him, then sighed, the sound terribly adult, horrifyingly sad. "Don't cry. I'll be good. I promise. Don't cry no more."

Shit. Shitshitshit. Pull it together, Gordon James. He dried his cheeks on his shirtsleeves and put a tight lid on all of it—the tears, the emotion, the fucking knot in the pit of his stomach. What the hell had Emma done to this girl to make her think an adult in tears was her fault? Or was that normal? How the fuck was he supposed to know?

"Hey, I'm okay." He took a deep breath, willing it to be the truth. "I was just sad for a minute is all. I know you're a good girl. It's not your fault, baby. What about you, are you okay?"

"I'm sad too. I want to go home now." She frowned at him. "I can have ice cream at your house? And library days?"

"Yes. Lots of ice cream. You like the library?" Surely Boulder had a library. Somewhere. Gordon couldn't remember the last time he read a book.

"I can read lots of books. I like Junie B. Jones the best."

"Well, okay. We'll find you some when we get home, then." He hauled himself up on the couch just as April came back into the room. Gordon glanced at her but didn't say anything. She looked like she was barely holding it together too.

"She's all packed. I guess you're coming for her early tomorrow?"

"I couldn't get a morning flight. I'll be by to get her about noon for a three o'clock flight to Denver." Then an hour drive to Boulder. They wouldn't even walk in the door until maybe seven thirty. That was bedtime, right?

God, bed sounded so good to him right about now.

Olivia rested against him, listening to them both. He was never going to be able to say anything, ever again.

"You don't mind if I tuck her in, then?"

"Oh, no. Uh. I'll get out of your hair." He turned to Olivia. "Hey, I'll see you tomorrow, okay? So we can have that adventure on the plane."

He pulled out his wallet and fished around, finding a business card. "I wanted to give you this. So you know how to reach me and… if you wanted to call her or something." He held it out to April.

"Of course I will. We're family now, right?"

Gordon didn't know how to answer that, so he just didn't. He hadn't been great at keeping in touch with his actual family. "Good night, Olivia." He carefully untangled himself from her. "I'll be back around noon tomorrow."

"Night, Gordon."

He ducked out the door as fast as he could manage. He'd forgotten to call a car, so he just started walking. He needed some food, and... hell, his phone was burning a hole in his pocket. He pulled it out and dialed Colby.

"Hey, stranger. How goes?" Colby sounded happy to hear from him, maybe? Maybe not. Oh, who the fuck knew?

"Hey. I'm coming back tomorrow." Saying that felt good. He was ready to go home; he'd had it with Boston and... everything. "I don't guess you'd be able to pick us up at the airport?"

"Sure. When?" That was the thing he liked best about Mr. Texan. No fuss. No worry. Just yes.

He'd like to get his hands on that Texan right now. Colby would say yes to that too, he'd bet. "Plane lands at six-something. I'll text you the details."

"That's fine. How's the little one? Holding up?"

"Um. No, I don't really think so. I think she has no idea what's going on. She's asked me at least twice if she can see her mom, asked when she's going home, and I think I've lost count of the 'I want my mommys.' I tried to explain it to her, but... well. I got kind of emotional, and she told me she'd be good if I stopped crying. So no, she's not... great." He sighed so heavily his shoulders sagged, and he headed for a bench on the sidewalk. "Sorry. Long day."

"Hey, I'm here. She's only little. She'll adjust. One of my sisters, she does foster kids, and she said to be patient."

"How many sisters do you have?"

"Five."

Christ. Gordon felt himself smiling a little. That was refreshing. "No wonder you're easygoing."

"Hey, when you're the baby, you're adorable or dead."

"Well, you've got that adorable thing down. It works on me too." He was definitely smiling. It was nice to talk about something else after five depressing days.

"Yeah? Good on you. I miss your face some."

"My face, huh?" Gordon snorted, grinning. "Been keeping busy? That bathroom all set?" Work. Yeah, he missed that. Normal shit. He was starting to feel like maybe he could breathe again.

"Of course. The bedroom's ready too. I ate at your restaurant. It was good."

Gordon laughed. "Are you surprised?" He was trying to picture a dusty Colby sitting at the bar drinking beer. Liam probably loved him. "Thanks for doing the room."

"You're welcome. I was glad to help. You ready to get home?"

"So ready to get back. The longer I'm here, the more I'm reminded why I left Boston. I miss the sun. It's been gray here since I got off the plane. Doesn't feel at all like spring."

Gordon got up and started walking again, seeing if he could find a cab. Hailing a cab was nearly impossible in this part of Boston, but it was worth a shot.

"I bet the humidity's a bitch too. You need to make sure you get her sunglasses."

"Good call. Hopefully I can get them in the airport. I have no idea where to get any around here." Part of him wanted to keep Colby on the phone and talk about nothing, but he was just wasting the man's time now. He'd also stumbled on a T stop, and he was going to lose service as soon as he headed underground. "Listen, I better run. I'll text you our arrival details. Go have another meal on me." He liked the idea of Colby hanging out at his bar.

"I might. Take care of you, huh?"

"I'm headed back to my hotel, and I'm going to bed. I'm so tired, I could fall asleep standing up." Or on the T. "Night, Colby."

"Night, honey." Colby sounded... sort of gentle, maybe, like he was afraid Gordon was shattered.

Gordon hesitated, part of him aching as he listened to the open air between them. Maybe Colby was right. He did feel shattered. Didn't matter, though—he had a business to get back to and a little girl to fit into his life somehow. There was no room for anything else. He didn't have the bandwidth.

He missed that man, no question. But he couldn't get his head around that tonight. With a sigh, he ended the call.

Chapter Thirteen

OKAY. OKAY. The bathroom was stocked with bath toys and pink towels from the hostess station folks.

There were clothes and toys and books in the bedroom from Oscar, a handful of hand-me-down DVDs from Marj on the waitstaff, along with the promise of more, once folks knew sizes. The guys in the kitchen had made meatballs and taco meat and buñuelos and pink cake to fill up the kitchen.

Then, this lady that owned the hotel he was working at this morning? Dude. A whole year of dance classes.

Colby sat in the cell lot at DIA, bouncing his knee, and waited, feeling pretty damn proud of himself.

The plane ought to have landed on schedule. Giving Gordy a little time to get through baggage and take the little one to the bathroom, and he figured his phone should be ringing any minute.

When close to twenty minutes went by, he found himself squinting in the direction of the terminal and debating whether to call Gordy himself. He was just about out of patience when the thing finally starting buzzing in his hand.

"Hey, there!" He went for cheery, because God knew Gordy would be wiped.

"Hey." Gordy sounded a little winded. "We're headed for the curb."

"I'll be there in two shakes. I cleaned the truck and everything."

That got a chuckle. "You cowboys love to impress the girls."

"That we do. See you in a sec." He told himself he wasn't nervous, because he was the good guy. He'd been a help. He loved little ones.

Traffic wasn't too bad getting up to arrivals on level four, and he couldn't miss Gordy—he was the one in the blue jeans with the dress shoes and the little blond-haired girl hanging on to his neck for dear life.

"Lord, Gordy and his pussy shoes. God love him." He pulled up and hopped out. "Hey, y'all."

"Hi. Um… there's a booster seat on the cart there, and… hang on. Olivia? Liv, can I put you down for a minute?"

She shook her head no. Gordy tried anyway. "I'm just going to put you on the seat here, okay? Wait." He reached over and pulled a stuffed kangaroo out of one of her bags. "Jessica. She… uh…. She needs a hug too."

Olivia loosened her grip on him enough that he was able to sit her in the passenger seat. He set the kangaroo in her lap. "Okay. Great. Okay."

"You're doing good, man," he whispered. "Hey, Miss Olivia. I'm Colby. Pleased to meet you."

Olivia eyed him over the top of her kangaroo with enormous and slightly watery hazel eyes. "Hi."

"Olivia is not a fan of landing in Denver. It was a little bumpy, you know how it gets." Gordy gave him a meaningful look. "We're very glad to be on the ground now." The man looked like hell, now that Colby got a look at him. He'd never seen Gordy look so haggard.

"Ah, I hear that. I tell you what, though, I'm tickled pink that you were brave and came out to the mountains. You're going to have some fun, I bet, once you get settled." *Poor baby doll.* "You want a Sprite? I got a bottle in here."

Olivia stared at him. "Mommy says soda rots your teeth. And you talk weird."

"Mm. I'm going to pack the truck up." Gordon obviously needed a break. He hauled a suitcase off the cart and headed for the tailgate.

"Ah, well, I can understand that. For me, sometimes that's the thing that settles my stomach." Shit, if he had a dollar for every time someone commented on his accent, he'd be a wealthy man.

"Oh. Well, maybe I could share some with Jessica, then, please?"

"Do you know how to put that booster in your truck?" Gordon picked up a pink suitcase and a little lavender backpack and put them in the back.

"You most certainly can." He pulled out a little half bottle and popped a straw in. "Have a sip, kiddo, and then I'll get your car seat in here."

"Thank you." She offered a sip to the kangaroo first and then took a sip herself. She gave him a smile. "I like it."

"That's because it's tasty. Hold up, darlin', and I'll get you settled."

He slid the car seat into the back and looped the seat belt through the little bracket doohickeys on the armrests, and she climbed right over the center console into the back and got comfy. "Thanks!"

"Look at you, chickimama! You got this down." He winked at her, and she giggled.

Gordon slid into the passenger seat. "All set. God, I can't wait to get home. Wow." He looked around under his feet. "You really did clean your truck."

"I did. Y'all hungry at all? There's supper at your house."

"Yeah. I bet Liv is too. We got lunch before the plane, but she didn't love the snack choices on the flight."

"What's for dinner, Uncle Gordon?"

"We have to ask, uh… Uncle Colby over here. He knows."

"Meatballs, baby girl. Meatballs and noodles. Unless you want pizza. You want pizza, I will order pizza."

"I like meatballs." She yawned so loudly he could hear it from the front seat.

Gordy snorted. "Assuming she makes it to dinner. It's been a long week for everyone."

"Yeah, I bet." He reached over, squeezed Gordy's arm. "You want me to run through and get you a coffee?"

A warm hand slid down his thigh in answer, and Gordy let his hand rest on Colby's knee. "That sounds great. Thanks." Gordy dropped his head back against the headrest and sighed. "Did you drink all my beer?"

"Lay that at Oscar's feet, man, not mine." That man could hold his own.

Gordon laughed. "He can give me a run for my money, that's for sure. He said you ate enough for three, though."

"I work hard, swear to God. I can burn me some calories."

"Hey, I don't see anything to complain about." Even tired, Gordy had a hell of a bedroom voice.

"Good." Colby glanced up in the rearview. "She's sacked out, man. Starbucks?"

"God, I might drool." Gordon sat up straighter and reached for the radio. "Something big with an extra shot. Or four."

"Do not turn off King George, honey." He winked and pulled off, heading for the big green circle. "Sweet?"

"God, no. Triple grande nonfat latte. Thanks." Gordon grinned and held his hands up. "And don't touch the radio, got it."

He looked as the song changed. "You can hunt something now. Triple grande nonfat latte. Lord have mercy." He pulled up and rolled down the window. "A triple grande nonfat latte and a cup of coffee, please, ma'am."

"Nine forty-four. Pull up to the next window, please."

"I got it." Gordy dug out his wallet as Colby pulled his truck up to the next window. "Here. And don't make fun of my coffee. I might just be decent company in a minute."

"I would never make fun of your coffee, sir. Not ever." Colby shot him a wink.

"Just for that I'm going to dial up some Zeppelin or something."

Colby traded the ten-dollar bill for two coffees, and they got back on the road.

"I got you a 3 Musketeers in the glove compartment."

"Right on. Now that's what I'm talking about." Gordy opened up the glove compartment. "Who needs meatballs when there's caffeine, sugar, and chocolate?" He tore the wrapper off and held it in front of Colby's nose. "Bite?"

He opened up and took a bite. Not bad. Not bad at all. He hated when he bit into a stale one.

"How was your week? Work okay?" Gordon's mouth was full, the 3 Musketeers almost gone already.

"I'm working at that one hotel, doing the whole lobby. I'll be working there for another week."

"That sounds like nice steady work. I've got a project for you the next time you have a lull. Not a rush." Gordy looked over his shoulder. "Wow, she really is toast."

"Yeah. She's pretty as anything. I assume she looks like her momma?" At Gordy's curious look, Colby shrugged. "She looks a lot like you, so she's gotta look like Momma."

"Yes. Exactly. Especially the big eyes. Emma's hair was darker, but her eyes were remarkable." Gordon took a big sip of his coffee. "And Emma looked just like Mom."

"Well, she's a sweetie. I'm glad to meet her." She'd need friends, he reckoned, as Gordy figured shit out.

"She took to you pretty quickly. Of course, I'm just meeting her too, so…."

"I'm glad she didn't hate me on sight."

Gordy laughed. "Trust me, cupcake, you make a damn good first impression."

Well, shit. Didn't take a mind reader to tell what was on that man's mind.

The traffic on 36 was a breeze at this hour, and they made it to Canyon Boulevard in no time. Gordy tipped his coffee cup up high, swallowing down the last drop. "Home. Hey, can you park around back? We can go in the service entrance. I can't make nice with the staff tonight."

"You got it. The place is booked tonight, anyway. Oscar was stoked."

"Getting to be that time of year. Oscar hasn't had a night off since I left. I'm going to have to spell him this weekend. Not quite sure how that's going to work. I'll think about it tomorrow."

"You got some time, and I'm here to help so long as you need me." He wouldn't leave a friend to cope with this, much less a lover.

"Thanks." Gordy shrugged off his seat belt as they pulled around back, and turned in his seat. "I guess I should carry her in first."

"I'll grab the bags. No big."

GORDON WASN'T sure what bothered him more, that he had no real idea what was going on in his own restaurant right now, or that Colby did. Sounded like Colby and Oscar had gotten along while he was gone, which was more than a little disconcerting.

Colby was a sight for sore eyes, though. Clean shirt, fancy boots, shiny belt buckle. That cowboy cleaned up well. And Gordon was pretty sure it wasn't just to impress Olivia.

"Stay asleep, little girl," he whispered as he unbuckled Olivia's seat belt and lifted her out of her seat. She didn't weigh anything usually, but somehow she felt heavy as lead when she was sleeping.

He didn't stop to talk to Colby; he just headed right inside, propping doors open as he went.

The apartment was dark, and he left it that way, making his way down the familiar hallway to what was going to be Olivia's room, but the room itself was so dark he had to turn on the little lamp by the door.

"Holy shit." Gordon didn't even recognize the room. He was expecting some girly bedding and maybe some curtains, and that was it. "Holy shit," he said again as he moved to the little bed against the back wall, then set Olivia down in it. He made sure he tucked her in with her kangaroo and then turned to get a good look at the room. "Wow."

It was a real little girl's room—Colby'd put up owls and other birds on the walls, there was kid-sized furniture. Hell, the built-ins were filled with toys and books.

This was his "I'm going to the mountains to pee on a tree and drink crappy beer for a week" Texan?

He just stood there, staring around the room at the little pile of stuffed things in one corner and the line of books on the shelves until he heard Colby come banging through the front door, and he remembered he hadn't turned any lights on when he'd come in. He turned the little lamp off again as he left the room and hurried back down the hallway. "Sorry, cowboy, I'm coming. I didn't want to wake her by turning on a lot of lights."

"No worries. It ain't that dark in here. Christ, I bet it's good to be home."

"Even better than I thought." Gordon took the suitcases out of Colby's hands and set them down. "C'mere."

Gordon hooked his fingers behind Colby's neck and shoved his tongue past Colby's lips, intending to kiss him breathless.

Colby blinked—just like he had the first time Gordon had kissed him—and then opened up, easy as pie, to let him in.

Gordon grinned against Colby's lips. There was a reason he'd kept the man around longer than any lover he'd ever had. Everything about Colby was easy.

He could kiss the cowboy all day long, but he decided that at some point he probably ought to actually say something. He pulled away, still smiling. "That room is incredible. That is the best thing to happen to me—the best thing to happen to that little girl—all fucking week. You didn't have to do all of that. Thank you."

"I had help. Food, dance lessons, stuff—I'll tell you when you're rested. You have friends here, honey." Colby's eyes were so fucking pretty, so warm.

Gordon was a little surprised by that. He tried to be a fair employer, he tried to give back to the community a bit, but he didn't have people he hung out with. It was far more likely that Colby was the one who had

friends. Colby was charming. He could talk to anybody. He'd probably put together quite a crew since he
moved up to Boulder—not that Gordon would know;
they weren't in each other's business that way.

Well, they hadn't been. Seemed like Colby kind
of made himself at home while Gordon was in Boston.

He gave Colby one more light kiss. "What do you
need? You hungry? You want a drink?"

"There's all sorts of food in the fridge and all. I'm
easy. You tell me what all you need."

"I don't know. A drink. Sleep. Company." *A week
in Turks and Caicos. Mmm. Beach.* "Tequila." He
kissed Colby again. "You."

"I can give you all those, honey."

Just as easy as that. Here. Take it.

Gordon felt like he'd been suffocating for a week
and finally found air. He reached out and tugged Colby's shirt out of his jeans and ran his hands up under
it, then kissed him again.

Christ, he loved that tight little belly, the way it
went hard under his fingers. Colby made the sweetest
sound, all raw need trapped in their kiss.

He pushed Colby's shirt up and off, and he let
Colby help him with that, but when Colby's fingers
reached for his fly, Gordon batted them away. "Uh-uh.
You just kick off those boots, cowboy, I'll take it from
there."

"Come to the bedroom, huh? Don't want to scare
the little one."

"She's asleep." But Colby had already stepped
back, and Gordon felt the little buzz he'd had one second ago get crushed under the weight of his new real-
ity. It didn't matter that Colby was right. He'd had to

rethink everything in the last few days; he didn't want to have to rethink this too.

He let Colby lead him down the hall to the bedroom, and he quietly closed the door, feeling that tension creep back into his shoulders. "So now we're grown-ups, huh?"

He should have had that tequila.

"Honey, I hate to break it to you, but you got a car payment, a mortgage, and all them investments. You passed young'un a long time ago."

"Funny. I worked for all of that. I wanted all of that. I didn't want someone to tell me I shouldn't fuck in my living room."

Colby's soft laughter cut off like a faucet being turned. "Let me get you a shot, man. Two shakes."

He let Colby go, not so much because he needed the shot but because he needed a minute alone to adjust his attitude. He was not dealing well with all the shit that was out of his control right now. He'd felt really confident two minutes ago, but then he'd been schooled by a cowboy who, incredibly, knew everything he didn't about five-year-old girls. And here he was pouting like one.

A soft knock sounded, and then Colby opened the door, handed him a glass and a wedge of lime. "Here you go, man. You want to get in something comfortable? I called for a couple pizzas from Cosmo's. You mind if I have a cigarette on the porch?"

"You smoke?" *Colby smoked?* Gordon swallowed down his tequila before he dropped it and stuffed the lime into his mouth so he couldn't say something stupid. He nodded, pointing to the balcony doors off the bedroom.

"Not very often, no. I let myself buy a pack once a quarter." Colby shrugged, just once. "When I need one."

"Right." He needed a sweater. It had dropped about twenty degrees in his bedroom. "Colby, I didn't exactly mean that like it sounded." He dropped the lime into his glass and set it on the dresser, then followed Colby out onto his balcony.

"You got lots on your shoulders. Lots. I should have... shit, I don't know." Colby lit up, pulled in a deep drag, and blew it out his nose. "I'm real sorry about your sister."

It was chillier outside than he'd expected, and he stuffed his hands into his pockets. "I am so angry at her, Colby. I know I'm an asshole big brother who wasn't close enough to her to see this coming, but I'm still so.... I mean, how dare she?" *Whoa, hello, tequila.* "Anyway, you were right about taking it behind closed doors. I'm just... frustrated."

"You think? Shit. I'd be losing my fucking mind. What... I mean, you don't have to say, but... what the hell happened? Was she real sick?"

"No? Maybe. I don't know. Her friend April didn't know either. Depressed, I guess. Overwhelmed for sure. Her apartment was tiny but neat. There were definitely bills.... April thinks she was out of work."

Another tequila would be good. Or one of Colby's smokes. Or maybe some answers.

"She asked April to babysit Olivia for the weekend and then didn't show up to get Liv on Sunday. She'd hanged herself." That was easier to say than it should have been. He really was pissed.

"Jesus Christ." Colby stared at him, cigarette dangling from his fingers. "Oh, honey. I'm so sorry. That sucks so hard."

"She had an iron-clad last will, Colby. She knew I'd get Olivia. The court didn't even blink at me. She knew Olivia was coming to me, but she couldn't fucking call me? Maybe ask for help? Or money? She just, what? Thought her little girl would be better off without her? Fuck her."

He reached over and plucked Colby's cigarette from his fingers. "You mind?" He didn't wait for an answer.

"I don't." Colby's hand landed on his belly and rested there, solid and warm.

God, he hated cigarettes. He liked the quick little buzz, but they tasted like crap. He tossed what was left of it on the concrete balcony floor and ground it out with his toe.

"Then again, I could have… should have, kept in better touch, huh? I don't know what the right answer is here." He covered Colby's hand with his own and tangled their fingers. "Sorry. I don't do crisis very well."

"Shit, baby. This isn't crisis. This is… I ain't got words for the raft of shit this is." Colby shocked the crap out of him by grabbing the back of his neck and kissing him, hard.

Hell, if that didn't light a fire in him. Colby had never been shy about what he wanted; he'd smile, he'd tease, but he always let Gordon make the first move.

Gordon took hold of Colby's jaw with both hands and kissed him back, herding him against the brick balcony wall.

Colby's hands were everywhere, grabbing at him, pulling him closer, like Colby intended to meld them together.

"Okay. Okay, babe." Gordon got hold of one of Colby's wrists and held it tight to his chest and then the other, which he pinned over Colby's head against the bricks. "Let's take this inside."

"Sorry."

Jesus, that was a sight, Colby stretched up for him.

"The only thing you need to apologize for is not starting this somewhere warmer. Shit, Colby. You're hotter than anything right now." He kissed Colby again, he just had to, and tightened his grip on that wrist pinned to the wall.

Colby's kiss grew teeth, digging into Gordon's bottom lip enough to make him burn.

"Inside." He'd meant that to sound more like an order and less like a growl, but he went with it. He let go of Colby's wrists but kept close contact as they made their way back to the bedroom. "Still want a piece of me, cowboy?"

"What the fuck do you think? I'm so hard a cat couldn't scratch me."

Gordon grinned. How did he not know his happy little cowboy had this in him? "I just wanted to hear you say it. Don't make me ask you twice about those boots."

"Be nice. These are the dress ones." Colby sat on the edge of the bed and yanked his boots off, one right after another.

"No wonder I've never seen them before. I usually get you dusty." Gordon kicked off his shoes— also dressy, but he wasn't going to draw attention to that—and tugged Colby back up by his belt. Colby was a little flushed, his eyes bright. "Hey, hot stuff."

"Hey. I missed you." Colby cupped his package, rolled his balls like he meant it.

Oh hell yes. Gordon grunted, and he made quick work of Colby's belt, button, and fly. "Yeah. I'll make up for it." He tugged Colby's jeans down and wrapped his fingers around Colby's shaft. Damn, that had to ache. He stroked, rubbed a hard line from the tip down to the base, not worrying about being gentle with it.

The sound Colby made was rich and hungry. It made Gordon's knees weak and his cock hammer impatiently at the fabric of his jeans. He put a hand on Colby's chest and shoved the man back a step, locking eyes with Colby as he slowly stripped.

"Pretty son of a bitch." Colby started stroking himself, gaze dragging over him, almost heavy enough to bruise.

Gordon swallowed hard. That look made every minute he'd ever spent in the gym worth it. He tossed his jeans aside, found lube and a rubber in the nightstand, and tossed them on the bed.

"All right. Let me show you how much I missed you." He stepped close, kissed the side of Colby's neck, and then set about raising a lovely mark on Colby's shoulder.

"Mmm…." Colby stretched up and out, proving how much his cowboy liked wearing his mark. *Whoa. Wait. His cowboy?* No. This was Colby. It didn't work like that.

This was the man who hadn't even been in this bedroom except to cut through it while remodeling the master bath. They met in his office a lot, his living room a few times, whatever. His nothing. This was a casual thing, had been from the start. Colby was a free spirit, and Gordon liked it that way, didn't he?

Shit, he needed to stop thinking so damn hard.

"Now that's pretty." Gordon ran his fingers over the mark.

"Aches, man. Throbs." Colby arched for him, then took his lips again, demanding that he meet Colby halfway.

Those were good words. Gordon might have said as much, but Colby nipped at his lip, and his thoughts went right to his groin. He didn't try and stop his moan and crowded Colby until Colby's knees hit the bed.

Colby bounced, eye to—well, eye—with his cock. It took a bounce and a half before Colby had him in that hot mouth, pulling at him like Colby needed nothing more.

"Colby." Gordon hissed and reached out, sliding his fingers into Colby's hair. Colby's hands felt like they were everywhere again—his thighs, his ass, his balls. Gordon watched him, eyes on that furrowed brow as Colby drew every last rational thought he had right into his cock. It didn't matter what kind of week he'd had, the man seemed determined to fix it for him. Gordon wasn't sure where that was coming from, but he couldn't think about it anymore. It was working like a fucking charm.

Colby's hair tickled his palms, making his fingers curl. He let them, until they tightened right into a fist at the nape of Colby's neck. Colby could turn a blow job into a work of art, but it wasn't what Gordon was after tonight. He tugged on Colby's hair with just enough force to make his intentions clear.

Colby let him go, staring up at him with those bright baby blues. Oh, that did it for him.

"Want you." Fuck, that came out rough, and his cock had turned to stone. He didn't just want, he wanted right now.

He bent down and claimed Colby's mouth in a hard kiss and then encouraged him to move farther up on the bed. "Move it, cowboy."

"Listen to you." Colby wriggled onto the bed, the sweet body making a golden slash across the white sheets.

"That's your doing." All that hard work had sculpted Colby in ways you couldn't imitate at the gym, and Gordon wasn't shy about looking him over as he opened and smoothed on the rubber. He slicked his fingers with lube and then crawled over Colby to kiss him again, shoving one of Colby's knees up and out as he went.

"Mmm." Colby opened for him easily, a deep moan pressing into his lips as Colby kissed him.

"That's right," Gordon whispered against Colby's lips. That was the man he was used to, easy as anything. He slipped two fingers in slowly, but he knew how this went. Colby didn't need much warning.

"Come on, now. Give me what I need." Colby arched up, bucking into his hand.

Gordon grunted and pulled his fingers away. "You know how to do it to a man, I swear to God." He shifted his weight and lined up, not holding anything back as he pushed right in.

Colby rode him, meeting every one of his thrusts head-on, slamming against him, fingers pressing into his hips hard enough to leave bruises.

Suited him just fine, and he drove in hard against Colby's ass. He reached down and gave Colby's erection a squeeze, tight enough to frustrate him and make him ache. He loved his cowboy a little crazy.

"Fucker." Oh, that was a needy little snarl.

A grin tugged at the corner of his lips. "Yeah?" He let up on the pressure so Colby's cock could slide right through his fingers. "Better?"

"Yeah...." Colby went heavy-lidded, lips damp and parted.

Christ, it sure as hell was. Gordon ducked his head and kept up the steady, solid rhythm. He'd started gulping in air, and he could feel the sweat run down his back and over his forehead into his eyes.

His head spun the barest bit, the altitude laughing at him as he drove into that tight heat.

"Come on, I feel you," Gordon managed to grunt. He looked up at Colby's face again. "Give it up for me, gorgeous."

"Fuck yes." Colby's ass gripped him like a fist, the pressure threatening to make him scream.

He might have, though he was pretty sure whatever he did was something more strangled and desperate. His vision went dark, and a freight train rolled past his ears as he started to come, his blood rushing to places far away from rational thought. He had to hope that Colby was okay because he sure couldn't figure it out for himself; he was too busy trying not to pass out.

"Breathe, honey. Breathe." Colby stroked his back, long, slow pets that tried to bring him back to earth.

Gordon nodded and took in a couple of deep breaths, his chest heaving with the effort. He swiped at his face but couldn't tell the difference between sweat and tears, so he just focused on Colby's voice, blinking and willing his eyes to focus.

He didn't think Colby said anything, but the nonsense patter soothed his soul. When his vision finally did clear, he leaned down and kissed away the worried look on Colby's face. His breath was evening out finally too. "You okay?"

"Good as gold." Colby stretched, making Gordon groan, his dick so sensitive it ached.

"Christ. Hang on." He hissed as he tugged himself free and rolled over onto his back before his arms gave out. "Yeah, me too." Mostly. He felt a little raw, mentally, and completely exhausted. He struggled to sit up, figuring he'd better go clean up before he gave in to sleep.

"Stay. I'll toss you a wet rag and get you some water, huh? That'll help."

Oh, that was perfect. He sighed and settled right back down in the pillows. "You're good to me, cowboy."

"I hope so." Colby patted his calf, nodded to him. "Two shakes."

He'd be lucky to make it one.

Chapter Fourteen

COLBY MADE himself a meatball sub, texted Oscar to tell him that Gordon was home, then plugged in his phone and turned the TV on, hunting something to watch that wasn't loud.

I figured. Saw your truck out back but Cosmos tried to deliver some pizzas and said no one answered the door. I'm sure you and Gordon were just taking a little nap, right? Kitchen staff sure appreciated the veggie supreme. How's the boss?

Tired damn near to death. Little one's cute as a bug in a rug

Fuck-a-doodle-goddamn-doo. He'd plumb forgot those pizzas.

can't wait to meet her

Oscar had to be damn tired himself. He'd been running two restaurants alone for nearly a week without a day or a night off. Not that he'd complained at all, that Colby had heard.

"Mommy?"

Colby looked up and squinted down the dark hall.

"Mooooooommy!"

gotta go

"Hey, baby doll. You're at your Uncle Gordon's house now, remember?" He stood at the door, making sure she could see him. "You've been sleeping."

"Came on the airplane." She rubbed her eyes and yawned. "When's dinner?"

"Do you want meatballs? I made me a meatball sammich." He whispered, "Your uncle is too pooped to pop, so I'm letting him sleep."

"Yes, please. Uncle Gordon fell asleep on the plane. He was tired. I watched *Moana*. Do you live here too?"

"Nope. I'm just hanging for a while. Come on, Little Bit. Let's find you some food. How's that *Moana* show? That big guy, he was something, huh? All them tattoos?" Good thing he'd never met a stranger, huh? Poor baby girl, losing her momma like that. It wasn't right that… well, any of it. Being that desperate, being that sad for the momma, and being left for Olivia. Being guilty for Gordy.

"He's funny. Moana is so pretty. She has the best hair. Do you know Ariel? She's my favorite." Olivia pulled out a kitchen stool that was taller than she was and climbed the rungs until she was sitting in it.

"I do. I think that was the first movie I ever saw in the movie theater." That, then *The Lion King*.

"You saw it in the movie theater?" Her eyes opened wide. "Mommy says that was a long time ago." She sat her kangaroo on the breakfast bar and started singing.

"Eons, Little Bit, I swear to God. How many meatballs? Two?"

"Okay." She looked at Colby and gave him a big smile. She really did look like Gordy. "Is there sauce?"

"Yep. You like the red sauce? You want bread?" He poured her a cup of milk and handed that over.

"Yes, please." She picked the milk right up and drank most of it in a couple of sips. "Do you have kids my age?"

"I don't, but I have nieces and nephews back home in Texas. My niece, Carrie Dawn? She's going to be six on Saturday."

"That's a pretty name. I'm going to be six in July! I want a friend from Texas. I like how you talk. It's friendly." Colby cut up her meatballs for her and set them on the counter, and she dug right in. There was something anyway; Gordon got a good eater.

"You mind if I grab my sandwich and join you?"

"Nope. Do you know where Snowball is?"

"No, but if you tell me what kind of critter Snowball is, I'll go hunt him for you."

"He's a bear. He's white." She stuck her hands out to show him how big. "Uncle Gordon gave him to me."

"I'm on it, kiddo. You sit tight, okay?" Bear. White. Fairly good-sized. He'd bet Gordon's carry-on.

Sure enough, the fluffy friend was the first thing that popped out at Colby when he unzipped the leather bag. Right underneath it was a beat-up Red Sox cap. The thing had seen better days, the brim had a worn spot on one edge, and the blue had nearly faded to gray with the sun. Next to the cap was a little velvet jewelry box and a small stack of what looked like family pictures.

He pulled out the bear and closed the rest away. He could hear Momma's voice in his head, clear as day. "Snooping never did no good to a soul. You mind your own biscuits and stir your own goddamn gravy."

Still, it looked like Gordy had a sentimental streak, and that was interesting.

"That's him!" Olivia bounced in her seat when he came back with the bear in one hand and his sandwich in the other. She snuggled the bear right up and pushed her plate toward Colby. "Can I have another one, please?"

"Yes, ma'am! You like those, huh?" He grinned at her and warmed up another meatball. "What's your favorite food, Little Bit?"

"Macaroni and cheese. And… strawberries. Also waffles."

"I do love me some mac and cheese. You like it baked in the oven or out of a box?"

"Both. Mommy makes it in the oven with bread crumbs on top." She turned her great big eyes on him. "Do you make it in the oven?"

"I can, yes, ma'am." In theory. Momma'd have a recipe he could use.

"We could have some tomorrow maybe." Olivia smiled at him and dug into her third meatball. "Can you take me to the library too?"

"I bet it's open of a Saturday. If your uncle says it's cool, I would be tickled pink." Colby'd bet his bottom dollar that Gordon would love an hour or two to look at the restaurant.

She wrinkled her nose at him. "Tickled pink is good?"

He tilted his head. "Yes, ma'am. Don't they say that where you're from?"

"Nope. But I like pink!" She patted her tummy. "Sorry. I'm full."

"You did good. So, I don't reckon you're ready to head back to bed, huh?"

She shook her head.

"I tell you what. Why don't you grab your jammies and all. I'll find *The Little Mermaid*, and we'll sit on the sofa and watch."

She grinned and hopped off her stool. Her little suitcase was still in the middle of the living room, where he'd left everything since Gordy had barely let him get in the door with it.

While Colby searched the on-demand channels, Olivia dug through her suitcase and changed into a Little Mermaid nightgown.

"Can I bring my friends?" she asked, holding up the fluffy bear and her little kangaroo.

"Of course you can. Now, this is Mr. Snowball, and this is…?" Lord help him, he was tired. Good thing he didn't have to pay too close of attention.

"Jessica. She's my best friend." She climbed up on the sofa next to Colby. "Did you find it?"

"I am a little magical. I most totally did." He looked the well-loved kangaroo over, then shook her paw, keeping his face serious. "I like her."

"She likes you too." Olivia leaned into him and rested her head on his arm. "Are you really magical?"

"Just a little bit. All cowboys are."

Chapter Fifteen

IT WAS kind of early. Gordon figured he must still be on Boston time, but he felt pretty good anyway. He was home—the glorious Colorado sun was streaming into his bedroom, and he could hear the supply trucks out back unloading fresh vegetables and meats for the restaurant. All he needed was some strong, hot coffee and he'd be fine. Maybe he'd even work out later.

He stretched and rolled over, surprised to find himself in bed alone, and more surprised that he felt disappointed by that. Colby must have had to work this morning. What day of the week was it? Saturday? Did Colby work on Saturdays?

He hit the head and then found some sweatpants and pulled them on, grateful that Olivia was quiet. If Colby was working, Gordon wasn't getting a workout in, that was for sure, but if she was still asleep, he could maybe get some coffee in him before he had to figure out what to feed her for breakfast—and then figure out everything else.

He'd only taken a few steps down the hall toward the kitchen when he heard it. It had been a long, long while since he'd had anyone stay the night, but he was pretty sure that had to be Colby he heard in the living room. That heavy, rhythmic sound sure wasn't coming from a five-year-old girl.

He crept into the front room, eyes going wide as he saw Colby holding Olivia on his chest.

He watched them for a while, both of them completely out, and it occurred to him that he'd never seen Colby quite in this light before. That cowboy even slept easy. Couch? No problem. Little knee biter? Didn't seem to faze him one bit.

The two of them couldn't be more different, but honestly? In light of the events of the last week, thank goodness for that.

He debated. Risk waking Olivia so he could wake the cowboy? Or leave them both be?

He shrugged and walked past them, deciding to make that coffee.

Colby's eyes flew open, searching for and finding him straightaway without waking Olivia up.

"I was trying not to wake you," Gordon whispered. He leaned over Colby and gave him a quick kiss.

"Hey, honey. She got up in the middle of the night, snarfed down three meatballs, and we watched *The Little Mermaid*."

Gordon shook his head. "And you let me sleep. Here." Gordon gingerly lifted her weight off Colby's chest. "Come on out of there."

He let Colby roll out from under her and then set Olivia down again and covered her with a blanket off the back of the couch. "Was about to make coffee."

"You are my hero, man. Pour me a double."

Colby stretched up tall, back popping as he twisted.

"You got it." Gordon looked Colby over until his fingers started to twitch and then forced himself to move away. Sleep-rumpled was a damn good look on that cowboy. "Coffee. And something to eat. I'm starved."

"I bet. You didn't get your supper. You want bacon and eggs? I know how to do that."

"Sit, cowboy. You may find this difficult to believe, but I actually own a restaurant." Colby had to be beat, and it wasn't very often he got to show off his cooking skills anymore. The least he could do was make breakfast. He started with setting up the coffee.

"You own it, sure…." Colby's eyes twinkled, but at least he sat down, chin on his hands.

Gordon pulled some eggs and a package of bacon out of the fridge. "Next time you're in my office, I'll have to let you look up higher than my beltline so you can see my diploma from Escoffier."

"Escoffy-who? You got one of them there fancy papers?" Colby's eyebrows were gyrating madly.

Oh, he was going to beat Colby's ass.

Somewhere behind a closed door so Olivia couldn't see. Good grief.

"That's all right. You're much better-looking on your knees." He grinned and waved some scallions and a package of mushrooms at Colby. "You want veggies? Or do you rednecks just suck the egg right out of the shell?"

"You know full well what I suck, honey," Colby murmured, so quiet.

Christ. Really? If Liv walked in here right now, she'd get an eyeful. "Watch yourself, Mr. Let's Take This in the Bedroom." Gordon pulled a frying pan out of a cabinet and set it on the stove. "Veggies it is."

"Sounds great." Colby took the coffee he offered with a smile. "Oh, that's the good stuff. So you got into the restaurant business from the kitchen side?"

"Well, no. But there are some required kitchen practicals even for the management majors." Gordon chopped up the mushrooms and scallions and threw them in the pan. "You have to be able to get by doing anything your restaurant needs. I took bartending too."

"That's cool. I learned tile from my dad and uncle."

So Colby's family was as handy as he was. He knew people who learned the restaurant business from their families. "Nothing wrong with a hands-on education. It's probably the only way with a craft like yours. I'm crap with that stuff. I don't have the patience."

"I talked about going to art school, but that's a lot of money for something no one cares about you having, you know?"

That was telling. He'd never felt the need to ask Colby why he left Texas. The reasons seemed pretty obvious to him, and that little fact was just one more to add to the list. "They'd care if you were an artist. What medium?"

"I'm…. Well, good morning, Little Bit! How's my mermaid?" Colby opened his arms, and Olivia went right to them.

Saved by the bell. But Gordon was curious now; he'd get it out of Colby eventually.

"Good morning." Gordon watched her snuggle right into Colby's hip. "Morning, Uncle Gordon."

"Hey, Liv. Did you keep Uncle Colby up all night? Are you hungry? Do you like eggs?"

"We watched *Little Mermaid*. Eggs are good."

He'd been just about to serve some up, so he put some on a plate for her first, along with a piece of toast. "For you." He set out another plate with a cowboy-size portion, a few slices of bacon, and two slices of toast. "And these are for your uncle." He leaned across the counter and grinned at Colby. "That bacon is perfect."

"It most certainly is. Thank you for breakfast, sir. I appreciate it." Colby grinned at him, and this time it was pure happiness.

"Least I can do." He grabbed the pot and refilled their coffee mugs, then served some breakfast up for himself. "What's your schedule look like today? Are you working?"

"No, sir. I thought, if it was okay with you, I'd take Miss Liv to the library, and then I promised her mac and cheese. I wasn't sure if you wanted to come with and show off her new town, or if you needed to go spend a few minutes in the restaurant."

"Well, you two did some talking last night, huh? If you really don't mind, I'm anxious to get down there and touch base with Oscar. I'd really appreciate it." Anxious might be a little too subtle a word. It was driving him mad, not seeing how things were going firsthand. Never mind that he'd checked in with his manager at least twice a day while he was gone.

"I think we will have a ball. We'll go get the ingredients for mac and cheese in the oven from the King Soopers." Colby shot him a wink.

Gordon laughed. "Knock yourselves out." He reached out and laid a hand on Colby's. "Thank you."

"You're welcome, honey. I know you've been worried."

Gordon picked up Olivia's empty plate. "Are you looking forward to your day with Uncle Colby?"

"Yep! I'm tickled pink!"

Gordon laughed. "Oh, she's got you now, cowboy."

"That she does. We are going to have a bit of an explore and a shop." Colby fist-bumped with Olivia.

It was good that Olivia had hit it off with Colby, right? She hadn't taken to him the same way at all, but that didn't matter. Right? As long as she was smiling finally. Everybody loved a cowboy.

"You want to get her dressed and stuff? I'll clean up in here." There were meatball dishes in the sink too.

"I can do it, Uncle Gordon. I can. I need help with my hairs, is all."

"Okay, sweetest. One of us can help you with that when you're dressed. Let me know if you need help brushing teeth, okay?"

"Okay!" Olivia disappeared down the hall, dragging her little suitcase behind her.

The air felt a little heavy after Liv left the room. Gordon cleared his throat and turned around to load the dishwasher. "Meatballs were good?"

"Yeah. There's still a ton. Sorry about the dishes."

Gordon looked over his shoulder at Colby. Meatballs and dishes weren't what they should be talking about, and they felt like code words for something. He dried his hands off and turned around again to look into those blue eyes. "Hey. Are you okay?"

"I am. How are you doing? It's cool with you if I take her to the library? I mean, I'm not trying to step on anyone's toes…."

"It's fine. It's good, in fact. I'm useless right now. I haven't been able to give anything the focus I should. Including her. It'll be good to get downstairs and get my head back in the game. Feel more like me. You really don't mind?"

"I don't at all. She's a good girl." Colby grinned, lips quirking in a way that made Gordon ache to kiss them. "Seriously, I have lots of little ones that I'm Uncle Colby to. One more is just fine in my book. I would have made a great daddy, I think."

"I bet you would." Gordon had to stop himself from saying "Have at it." Olivia was lovely, and Colby was right; she was a good girl. But never once, in all of Gordon's life, had he wanted children. There was no title in the world he was less suited for than "Daddy." His own had been less than a shining example, for one thing, but more than that, he knew himself, and he had to be honest. His love was his work. He didn't have time for things like family.

He decided not to think about what that might have meant for Emma. "I better get dressed."

"Yeah. I'm going to get my jeans on. I brought a couple of T-shirts and stuff, just in case you needed me."

Gordon moved around so the counter wasn't between them. "Thank you." He slid a hand around behind Colby's neck and kissed him. "I don't deserve this, but she does."

"You're my friend, Gordon. You need a hand. You'd help me if I needed it." There was no doubt in Colby's voice.

"I would." Gordon put some space between them before his prick got any more ideas, and he winked at Colby. "If you begged sweetly enough."

Chapter Sixteen

"OH…. UNCLE Colby, can we stay for another story time?"

That little girl was having a ball, but they needed to get a move on and get some water in Olivia. The elevation and dry needed a little adjusting to.

"Nope, but if you're decent, we'll check out a couple books and stop for a drink and a snack."

Colby wasn't above bribing children. He figured it taught them how to horse-trade in the future. Everyone needed to learn that.

"Okay." She moped for about one second, and then she smiled and bounced up next to him. "Can I take home the one about the Frog and the Toad? And the picture book about the planets?"

"Totally. Hey! I remember this book!" Dude, that sort of rocked, in a Jesus-you're-old way. "I loved this one."

"I can read it to you. They're best friends. And they're so silly!" She handed Colby the books so he could check them out and slipped her hand in his.

"I will let you. What's your favorite book on earth?"

"*Where the Wild Things Are.*" She tilted her head. "Or *Harold and the Purple Crayon.* No. *Where the Wild Things Are.*"

"Is that one scary?" He carried the books under his arm and held her hand in the other. Momma had sent him directions for mac and cheese and dump cake, so they ought to be loaded for bear.

"No, it's about a boy that talks back to his mom and then becomes King of the Wild Things, but really it's all a dream, because your room can't really turn into a forest." She looked at him. "And he has a boat."

"Yeah? I used to have a boat. I liked it a lot." Once upon a time.

"Did you have a sailboat? Mommy says Grandpa used to have a sailboat on Cape Cod, and he used to make Grandma seasick."

"It was a motorboat. I used to go fishing with it all the time." He'd loved that old boat with a passion. He'd caught bass and bream and catfish on Lake Tawakoni for a good chunk of his life.

"Is that hard? Catching fish?"

"Sometimes. Sometimes it's not. We can go sometime, if your Uncle Gordon wants to. Drive up into the mountains and catch trout."

Liv waited while he bought her a bottle of water. She wrinkled her nose at him. "Uncle Gordon knows how to fish? He doesn't look like he likes to play outside."

"No? I bet between us, we can get him to go camping, maybe. Sleep in a tent?" Lord, that would crack him up.

She nodded. "I've never slept in a tent, but it sounds like fun." She took a big sip of her water and tugged him toward the library doors. "Can we go make mac and cheese? I'll help."

"Yes, ma'am. You mind if we stop at the store for the stuff to make it?"

"Nope." As soon as they stepped outside, Liv tilted her face up to the sun. "Sun is nice in Colorado. It was yucky in Boston."

"Yucky how?" *Boston. Lord.* His sister was going to give him no end of shit about him babysitting this poor lost little Yankee baby.

"Like, gray. When Uncle Gordon and I went to get on the plane, it was raining and cold, and we drived all the way to the airport like that. Yucky." She shrugged. "Summer is nice, though. My birthday is in the summer."

"Oh? Mine is near Christmas." He hoped Gordy knew that. Summer was damn close.

"Uncle Gordon said Mommy is up with the angels and she can see me better in Colorado because we're high up in the mountains. You think that's true, Uncle Colby?"

He unlocked the truck door, then knelt down beside her. "Little Bit, I have no doubt at all. She's watching over you, and there ain't nowhere on earth closer to God than the Rocky Mountains. You're in good hands now. Momma watching over you, me and your Uncle Gordon down here to do the same."

Liv nodded and then threw her arms around his neck. "I wonder if Mommy knew about magic cowboys?"

"I don't know, Little Bit, but I bet she knows now." He held her a second, because a girl needed a momma and Liv's was gone. "Come on, chica. Store and then mac and cheese."

"Okay!" Liv gave him a peck on the cheek and climbed right up into his truck. "Were you a good girl, Jessica?" she asked, scooping up her kangaroo and settling into her car seat.

He got her buckled and went around to get them moving. Noodles, cheese, and milk—he had this.

Chapter Seventeen

GORDON WALKED through the back of house and said hello to his prep folks, who smiled while they chatted for a bit and seemed glad to have him back. By all reports, Oscar had been stellar in his absence, but even the prep guys were joking about when he planned to give his manager a vacation.

It was work enough to manage one restaurant. That alone was a fifty-hour-a-week gig, and maybe more in the warmer weather when they got crazy busy and they opened up the patios. But Oscar had been sitting on both restaurants and hosting in the evenings. Gordon wouldn't want that job for one night, let alone a week.

The first thing he was going to do was punch in a bonus for Oscar. Then he was going to find some tickets to something and call in a favor at Frasca so Oscar could take his girlfriend out. Gordon would bet she hadn't loved his work hours this week, but she did love Italian food.

He headed for his office, the walk down the familiar back hall lifting his spirits a bit. Stepping back into his office was like fresh air. This was good; he'd get caught up, get his head back on straight, start moving forward again.

Gordon had asked Oscar to stop by when he got in but also told him to take his time. Colby had Olivia occupied, and Gordon had the whole afternoon.

Which was a good thing, because the pile of mail on his desk was a little intimidating. He'd shuffled through almost half when he heard Oscar's voice, booming in the hallway.

"Is it true? Is he home?"

Gordon grinned, not looking up from the pile of paper. "Nope. It's a big lie. Get back to work."

"Uh-huh. You're lucky I didn't call in sick for a month." Oscar plopped down across from him. "Good to see you, boss."

"I am. God, you look like I feel." Oscar was a handsome devil, that was for sure. But even handsome suffered from a lack of sleep. "Everyone I've talked to says they didn't miss anything but my winning personality. I really can't thank you enough."

"You're welcome. Glad I could help."

"You'll have to meet Olivia soon." There was an idea. "Hey, your girlfriend is a teacher, right? Would she know a nanny, do you think?"

"I'll ask her, sure. She's here? You okay being downstairs?"

"Oh. Well, yeah. I've got someone watching her."

"Colby?" At his nod, Oscar chuckled. "I tell you, boss. That man cracks me up. Simple, but decent."

"Hm. More than decent." More than simple too. Gordon laughed. "You two cleaned me out of beer while I was away. I don't even want to know how you two got on. All I know is Colby knew more about the bookings for Friday night than I did. But I'll tell you what, he is good with Olivia. He's got like a hundred sisters or something, so I guess he just gets kids. You saw the room, right?"

"I did. I helped him unload. I didn't feel right, just letting a stranger in your house without someone else there."

"That was nice of you. I appreciate the help. I'm sure he did too." Oscar still thought Colby was a stranger? Or did he just think Colby was a stranger at the time? Surely he knew better now. Gordon really wished he'd been a fly on the wall while they were polishing off his beer. "He did my master bath last year; he's trustworthy." And completely seducible. Such an easy cowboy.

"I figured that out. That bathroom he fixed looks fine."

"Right? He does good work. Anything dire that I missed, other than this pile of mail? Anyone quit?" He grinned.

"Everyone was on their best behavior. I swear. It was unnatural."

Gordon nodded. He was more gratified than surprised. He hired good people and treated them with respect. "Great. You make me a short list of anyone I need to be sure to thank in their next paycheck. Now let's talk about your schedule. You need me to pick up your shift tonight?"

Oscar tilted his head. "You don't need to be home? I mean, everything's cool?"

"Pretty sure I can talk McBride into hanging out tonight, yeah." He'd bribe Colby with dinner from the restaurant and a six-pack of the good stuff. Or a blow job. Whatever worked. "I'll give him a call. You should stop up and meet Liv on your way out."

"Absolutely. I'd love to." Oscar stood, held out one hand to shake. "I am sorry about your sister, man. Seriously."

Gordon nodded and took his hand, giving it a shake and an extra squeeze. "Thank you. And thanks for having my back."

He waited for the door to close behind Oscar and then speed-dialed Colby from the phone on his desk. He hated to spring this on the guy, but Oscar really looked like he needed a break. Though, if he were honest, taking the shift was really as much about him as it was about Oscar.

"Yo." He heard music playing, heard Olivia laughing.

"Hey there, sweet cheeks, how was the library?"

"We had story time and checked out books. We are learning how to two-step while the dump cake cooks. You get some work done?"

Gordon grinned and shook his head. Only cowboy in the world who you could call sugar puff or sweet cheeks or gumdrop and the man didn't even blink at you. He did it just to see if he got a reaction.

"Yes, I'm working through a pile of mail as tall as Olivia right now." Two-stepping was cute. Colby really would have made a good dad. "Listen, I had a chat with Oscar. His ass is dragging; can you hang on to Olivia tonight so I can take his shift? You'll see what I mean when you see him. He's going to come up and meet Olivia in a bit."

There was a second's quiet, then a "Sure. Sure, I can do that. I'm making mac and cheese for supper, but it won't be done for a while, and I don't reckon you'll be needing it with professionals cooking for you."

See? He knew Colby would get it. "Hey, that's great. Thanks. You want me to send up a tuna steak or something? It's one of Chef's specials tonight." He'd send someone up with a six-pack for sure.

"Nah. The mac and cheese is good. Or I hope it will be."

"Uncle Colby! We're dancing!"

"I know, Little Bit. Two shakes, huh? Then we'll try another dance."

"Save me a bite. I'll have it after closing. And thanks again. I'll check in with you later if it's not insane." Who was he kidding? He knew it was going to be insane. They were booked solid.

"Good deal. You want to talk to Liv?"

"Oh. Sure." Not that he had any idea how to talk to a five-year-old on the phone.

"Honey, it's your Uncle Gordy. He's got to work tonight, so you and me are going to hang out. You want to tell him hi?"

"Okay. Hello, Uncle Gordy."

Good grief, she called him "Gordy" too. "Hey, Liv. Have you been having a good day?"

"Yep! I read a book to Uncle Colby, and now we're dancing!"

"Is Uncle Colby a good dancer?" Somehow, Gordon knew he was. He smiled, picturing Colby two-stepping smoothly in his living room.

"Yep!"

"You be good for him tonight."

"Okay."

"Great. Well, you enjoy your mac and cheese."

"I will, bye!"

The phone changed hands, and then he heard Colby's husky laughter. "Don't work too hard, man. I'll talk at you later."

"I'll see you for a few around five. I'll have to change for work tonight." Back into his suit. Like normal. "Thanks again."

"Sure. I got to go, buddy. I promised the lady another dance."

"Enjoy." He smiled and hung up. Olivia was obviously in good hands, and Colby seemed like he was enjoying her company. Gordon looked at the remaining pile of mail on his desk and decided to take a break and head over to Gaia to check on his people over there. He pushed back from his desk and grabbed his keys, thinking that pretty soon he could change out his hardtop for the soft one on his Jeep.

THEY'D MANAGED to get the cake out of the oven and the mac and cheese in the oven without a catastrophe.

A tear or two, yeah. A catastrophe, no.

God, Colby wished he knew more about this. So he did what everyone did when faced with a situation like this. He texted his momma.

Still babysitting. Do 5 year olds nap? Is 430 too late for a nap? What about baths? I don't want to get arrested for seeing a naked little girl or for her drowning in the tub

where is her uncle?

working

It took a bit before Momma texted back, which he got a little, because who went back to work and left their sister's girl with a guy that had never been allowed in the bedroom before yesterday?

Whoa. That was convoluted.

if you put her down now she won't go to sleep after dinner. Time for a nap was right after lunch. Try a movie if you need her occupied. Bath before bed will help her sleep, and it's not like that man left you a choice. Very warm water, read her a book, lights out.

k. Love you Momma. Thanks.

Love you baby boy. Call if you need me.

Will do.

"So, Little Bit. What should we do? You want to watch a movie?"

"*Little Mermaid* again!" Liv scurried over and hopped up on the couch.

There was a knock at the door and Oscar popped his head in. "Just me, Colby. Boss said I should come meet his niece."

"Oh, hey, Oscar. Miss Liv, this is a guy your Uncle Gordy works with. This is Mr. Oscar."

"Hello, Mr. Oscar." She smiled at him. This little girl was about as brave with strangers as he'd ever seen.

"Well, hello, Miss Olivia. Aren't you a pretty one?" Oscar glanced at Colby. "Wow, she looks like Gordon."

"She does, doesn't she? She's a smart one and a good dancer." He thought she was something else—decent and patient as all get-out.

"Do you like *Little Mermaid*, Mr. Oscar?"

"I can't say I've ever seen it, personally, but my girlfriend probably has. She's a teacher."

"Does she teach kindergarten? I'm in kindergarten."

"No, she teaches third grade." He looked at Colby. "Boss needs to register her for school ASAP."

"I'll tell him."

"Can you come, Uncle Colby, on my first day at the new school?"

"Yes, ma'am." He could swing that with his jobs, surely. "I will be there with bells on."

Colby was relieved to find he was magic again today, and put *Little Mermaid* on, not really caring what it cost Gordy.

"So... did you talk to Gordon?"

"About an hour and a half ago, I guess, yeah." Why? What was it now? Colby was good at cowboying up, but he was reaching the end of what he knew how to do. He was happy to help, but... *okay. Stop it. Stop it right now.* Gordon was a friend who needed a hand. He found a smile for Oscar, hoping he didn't look worried. "Has he run away from home?"

"Sort of. Did he tell you he told me to take the night off? He also told me he could talk you into babysitting. Are you sure you're cool?"

"We are right as rain. We made macaroni and dump cake. We're going to watch *The Little Mermaid*, then have supper and take a bath."

"Are there bubbles? Oh, Uncle Colby, can I have a bubble bath?"

"I don't know if your Uncle Gordy has bubbles, baby girl…."

"Oh, look. It's a party." Gordon walked right in. "Just going to put this in the kitchen. Ice cream to go with the little girl's cake and beer for the big boy. Everyone getting along?"

"I was just saying to Colby that Miss Olivia looks like you."

"He said that too. I don't see it as much. She looks like my sister and my mom for sure." Gordon came back from the kitchen and headed over to Olivia. "I didn't think Emma and I looked that much alike. Guess I'm wrong. Hey, little girl." Gordon kissed her on the head.

"You're blocking the TV, Uncle Gordy."

"Sorry about that." He moved out of the way. "Just gonna get changed. Don't let me interrupt."

Colby stood there for a second, then nodded once. *Okay, then.*

"Big boy, huh?" Oscar said.

"Apparently so." He shot Oscar a tight smile. "At least he ain't calling me the little woman yet. I'd hate to have to feed him his own Rocky Mountain oysters."

Oscar winced. "You know, I'm totally into watching *The Little Mermaid* if you want to…." He nudged his chin toward the hall.

The temptation was huge, but this was more than a friend of Gordon's; this was a manager, someone who could make troubles for Gordy, and vice versa.

"You know what would truly help me out? Can you run to the drugstore and get me some bubble bath and baby shampoo? Also, some little kid's toothpaste. She wasn't impressed with your boss's super-minty whitening stuff. I got a twenty, and I'd appreciate it."

"You know you don't have to do this for him, right?"

"I'm not doing this for him." He was doing this because it was what a man did. He stepped up and helped out. "She's had a lot of change in a week. Right now, I'm steady and new and all."

Oscar gave him a sharp nod. "Right. Keep your twenty. I'm on it." Oscar tapped him on the back and headed right for the door. "Boss has my cell if you think of anything else."

Gordon was making his way back down the hall. "Gotta hit the dry cleaner tomorrow. I need shirts."

"Good luck." Oscar disappeared through the door.

"Thanks." He told himself, no temper. There was a five-year-old girl watching him right now. A five-year-old girl who had lost her momma to suicide a week ago.

"Oscar take off?" Gordy was fixing the cuff links on his perfectly pressed shirt. He laid his suit jacket over the back of a chair while he fussed with them. "He looked tired, right?"

"He's going to run to the drugstore for me. I'm sure he wants to spend some time with his girlfriend." He did his damnedest not to think, because the thoughts that were down there, bubbling under the surface, weren't very nice. In fact, they were down-right toothy.

"Kaitlin. I had to think about it earlier, but that's her name. It was driving me crazy." Gordy tucked in his shirt. "I'm calling in a favor over at Frasca for them as a thank-you. You think Oscar would be into theater tickets? I'm sure she would, right?"

"Doesn't everyone like the movies? I'm sure that would work." Colby didn't know anyone that was all "I hate the movie theater." Even his Granny, who was in her sixties, went to the movies to see things with her church group.

"I meant live theater, cowboy." Gordy hooked his fingers around Colby's bicep, backed him up a few steps behind the couch, and kissed him. "Hi."

"Hey, you." A thousand things wanted to be said, but none of them came out. He guessed that meant they weren't to say. "How's it going?"

"Okay. Better. This helps." This time Gordon's kiss was a little deeper and a little hungrier. "Stay tonight, I'll thank you properly."

"I'll hold you to that." Christ on a pink sparkly crutch, Gordy ran as hot and cold as an old faucet. Least the man didn't leak or gurgle in the middle of the night, right?

"Good." Gordon stepped away again. "It smells great in here. You guys have been busy. Enjoy your mac and cheese. I guessed about the beer, but you liked my other stuff so...." He shrugged on his jacket and then stopped a minute, eyes on his niece, then took in a deep breath and let it out slow. "Okay," he said, like he'd just found courage. He bent over and kissed Olivia on the cheek. "Be good. Sleep well."

"Night, Uncle Gordy."

"Night, Liv."

Gordy fussed over his jacket, straightening the sleeves. "I'll see you later, baby cakes." He bumped shoulders with Colby and headed for the door.

"Why did he call you that?"

He hoped it wasn't because the man thought poorly of him. "He's teasing with me. You know how that works?"

"Mommy used to call me a monkey."

"Well, see. That's what that is. He's just playing." Colby sat down beside her. "What part of the show are we on? Has she talked to the seagull yet?"

"Yep!" Liv pulled her feet up on the couch and leaned on him. "The king is about to get mad when that shell opens up."

Chapter Eighteen

CHAIRS WERE up on the tables, waitstaff had all cashed out, and Liam had just polished the bar. Gordon reached out and turned the lock on the front door. "That's it, Liam."

Liam nodded. "Was a hell of a good night."

"Yeah, your tip jar looked happy."

"Very happy." Liam set a shot of tequila on the bar, and Gordon just picked it up and followed it with the slice of lime Liam had set out for him, both on a clean bar towel so Gordon didn't smudge the polish.

"Thanks. You good?"

"Just wrapping up, G. I'll let myself out the back."

"Right on." Gordon headed back past his office to the elevator. He was tired, but it was the right kind of tired. That accomplishment high. The "I kicked ass and made a buttload of cash" kind of feeling. Not like the floor was constantly shifting under his feet.

He fixed his hair and straightened his jacket. He was going upstairs to company, and he figured Colby deserved him dashing.

He didn't know how to tell the guy thank you, not really. Colby had just… taken care of things. The beer had just been a gesture, after all. He figured if words failed him, he'd find another way. Something he was much better at.

And then he'd ask the cowboy for advice, because Olivia was all over Colby, and Gordon had barely gotten more than yes or no answers out of her for a week. He was mostly off on Sundays, and Monday his restaurants were closed, so maybe he'd come up with something for the morning. Maybe he'd make breakfast again. He was good at that.

God. Part of him was afraid to go upstairs. That was ridiculous. It was his home, and he loved it. But it was Olivia's home now too, and it didn't feel the same anymore.

Colby hadn't exactly returned Gordon's little gesture of affection earlier either. He didn't balk or anything. He just… wasn't quite his usual willing self. Maybe it was because Olivia was right there? That was probably it. Gordon had felt that way too.

The tequila was kicking in; that would help with all of this, right?

He got off the elevator and only let himself hesitate for a second before heading into his apartment.

The place smelled really good. Colby was stretched out on the sofa, wearing nothing but a pair of his pajama pants, asleep with a dog-eared copy of *Lonesome Dove* in his hand.

The cowboy looked delicious, stretched out on Gordon's leather couch. Gordon shrugged off his jacket and loosened his tie. Colby's voice was in the back of his head, reminding him not to traumatize the five-year-old, but maybe if he made this quick….

He knelt next to the couch and licked at one of Colby's nipples, figuring he could wake the cowboy up nicely at least.

"Oh…." Colby arched, eyes opening, one hand landing on his head. "Well, hey, honey."

"Hey." Gordon leaned across him and gave the other one a little nip. "You look great on my couch."

"You look pretty fucking good yourself. Good night?"

"Yeah. Really good. The place was packed, there was a two-hour wait at one point, and no major issues. The bar was busy, and Liam went home a very happy man." Colby tasted almost as good as he looked. Gordon drew a wet line from his sternum to his beltline with a hungry tongue.

He decided to gauge Colby's level of interest with a mundane question. "Mac and cheese was a success?"

"Uh—uh-huh. Fine." A hard ridge tented the thin cotton, proving that Colby was right with him.

"Good." Oh yeah, that came out just like he wanted. Rough and low. He didn't waste time, and slid his hand under the hips of Colby's pajamas. Trying to get Colby off without Olivia making an appearance added a heightened level of naughtiness to the moment, and he grinned. "Lift up, cowboy." He was careful to make it a request and not an order. No small task given the sudden state of his own prick.

"Oh hell yeah." Colby arched, those stunning abs rippling for him. A wet spot began to form, turning the blue cotton dark.

"Attaboy." Gordon slipped the pajama pants right down to Colby's knees. "You're gorgeous, you know that?" He finished the slow march his tongue had been making around Colby's belly button and straight down into his curls. He paid attention to Colby's breathing, listening, focusing, wanting everything just how Colby wanted it. "You take my breath away."

"Sweet Jesus, I want you." The words were pure need, making the air vibrate.

Christ—those words and the way Colby looked right now—it made Gordon ache in places he didn't know he could. He fought the urge to flip Colby over right there and just take what he wanted.

But no, not this time.

It had gotten fucking hot in here. Gordon reached up, loosened a few more buttons on his shirt and tossed his tie. He didn't touch Colby's cock at all with his hands yet, only his tongue, which he drew lower, bathing the base before running it along Colby's full length and around the dark head. "You like that?"

"Please. Please, honey." Colby grabbed the base of his cock, offering it up to him.

"Jesus. Colby." Gordon wrapped his hand lightly around Colby's fingers and let the man's name hang out there for just another second before he opened and took that lovely hard cock right down his throat.

Colby sobbed once, fist pushed in that lovely mouth, muffling the sound. He hummed, slapping Colby's shaft with his tongue hard enough his lover had to feel it.

Gordon slipped his hand under Colby's balls and rolled them firmly in his fingers. He started working Colby over, the pair of them hotly focused on the same goal. Gordon didn't do this often; it was usually something he preferred to hold in reserve, but tonight he wanted to gift all of his attention to Colby. He tried to offer it freely the same way Colby offered everything to him. He wanted what Colby wanted.

He felt the touch to his head, featherlight, like Colby couldn't bear not touching him. Every time he went down, Colby's cock throbbed, Colby begging for him, body and soul.

Fuck, if it had been him, he'd have been bucking his hips off the couch by now. Colby was too damn polite for his own good. Gordon released Colby and reached over to shove Colby's pants down farther, until Colby got the hint and kicked them off completely. Then he slid his hand farther back, grinning smugly as Colby opened right up for him.

"Goddammit, Colby. Look at you." Gordon spit on his finger and pressed it against the cowboy's ass, then licked and bit the inside of Colby's thigh.

"Fuck—" Colby arched in a hard, tight bow, heels pushing deep into the leather of the couch, before bearing down and taking his touch in.

"That's so pretty. Do it again." He nipped Colby's thigh once more, and sure enough, he was treated to that sweet arch again.

"Gonna have to remember that one." But for now he figured he'd gotten Colby just crazy enough to get selfish. He shifted higher on his knees, took the base of Colby's cock tightly in his free hand, and drew him into his mouth again. He growled a little around

Colby's length and hooked the finger inside that sweet ass just so.

Colby bucked for a wild couple of seconds, a choked-out warning filling the air right before Colby stiffened and shot for him, filling his mouth with seed.

Feeling pretty smug, Gordon enjoyed every salty, bitter drop his lover had for him and took his time about letting him go. Then he set about finding every bit of sensitive skin he could from Colby's hips all the way up to his shoulders, kissing, nibbling, babying Colby back down.

Next to that hot, wild-eyed moment Colby had last night on his balcony, this was maybe the most beautiful the cowboy had ever seemed to him. A little breathless, a little glassy-eyed, skin flushed across his chest and shoulders. He wasn't sure where Colby was at the moment, so he offered a kiss without taking it, hovering his lips over Colby's.

He got another of those smiles that he wasn't sure he understood, but that he wanted more of, and Colby drew him down into a long, lazy kiss. He let his hands roam over Colby's warm abs and shoulders and just enjoyed the moment. He hoped that smile meant that Colby understood him, because he still wasn't sure he could find words for everything the cowboy had been for him in the last week in general, and the last twenty-four hours in particular.

"Good to see you, sir." Colby grinned against his lips, lines beside his eyes wrinkling up.

"You too. I've been looking forward to this all night." He was smiling back, which was kind of an amazing feeling. Gordon kissed him again and stood. "Want a drink?" He reached down and scooped up

Colby's pajama pants and dropped them on his lover's chest.

Lover. That was what they called people who actually spent the whole night together sometimes and maybe had a little more happening between them than quickies over a desk. Right?

"I do. There's leftovers if you want. The dump cake is good with beer, I understand." Colby slipped the pants on, then came right to him, working the rest of his buttons open, one at a time.

"Perfect. Dump cake and beer it is." He let Colby fuss, enjoying the touch. "Kitchen's that way."

"Uh-huh." Colby opened his shirt up to the waist. "Go get something comfy on. I'll get the beer."

He kissed Colby quickly. "Don't skimp on the cake."

He grabbed his tie off the floor and his jacket off the chair, then went to change and tossed his entire rumpled suit in the bag for the dry cleaners. He washed up, found his pair of red flannel PJ bottoms, and pulled those on before heading back out to the living room.

Colby had two bottles and two bowls on the coffee table, long legs stretched out under. "There. You look more comfortable already."

"I wrinkled my suit for you. I don't do that for just anybody." He sat on the couch, pretty much as close as he could get without sitting in Colby's lap.

"I appreciate it. Hell, that was worth a lot more than appreciation." Colby handed him a beer.

"That was my appreciation of you, cowboy." He took a big swig of his beer. "Oh, that's good."

"Yeah?" Colby snagged his beer, took a long swallow. "Not bad. Not bad at all."

He reached for one of the bowls. "I don't know that I have ever had dump cake." He poked at it with his spoon and then took a bite. "I'm not usually a sweets guy, but this is pretty good." It was good, until he swallowed it down with another sip of his beer, and then he set the bowl back on the table. "Oh, I think you were misled on that pairing, though."

"You don't love pineapple, cherries, and beer?" Colby's laugh was pure evil.

Gordon laughed right along with him. "There's a sucker born every minute, huh?" He leaned back on the couch, beer in one hand, and rested the other on Colby's thigh. "You staying?"

"You want me to? I was sorta hoping you wouldn't throw my ass out."

"Not throwing that ass out, no. I want you to stay. Careful, though. Two nights in a row—I might be possessed. I'm not real familiar with the guy that wants his lover to spend the night."

"Duly noted." Colby snorted. "FYI? My clothes are in the dryer. Someone makes a mess in the tub."

"Oh, boy. I'll add a wetsuit to my shopping list. You're totally off the hook now, by the way. I'm basically off for two days, and hopefully I can find a nanny fast. I'm sure you want your life back."

Staying the night, clothes in his dryer… he wasn't going to examine why that made him feel both happy and panicked. Nope. Not at all. Not tonight, anyway.

"I didn't mind helping. She's a good girl. I guess you'll get her enrolled in school soon and such?" Colby sounded so… interested?

"Yep. First thing Monday. I set that up while I was still in Boston. Harmon, the attorney, helped me out. But did you know kindergarten is optional here? And also, school lets out the end of May, so she doesn't have much of the school year left. Harmon said I don't even have to enroll her, but I figure she needs some structure. Friends and stuff. Routine? April told me that's good for kids."

That was probably way more information than Colby had been asking for.

"Sure." Colby offered him a half smile, a shrug. "I promised her I would come her first day. I hope you don't mind. She's hard to turn down."

"Oh. Uh, no. I guess that's fine. It'll be Tuesday. We're just going in Monday to sign some paperwork and so she can see the classroom." Then again he'd be showing up with his lover to drop off his niece? God, everything was complicated and changing so fucking fast.

"By Tuesday I'll be the guy that likes *The Little Mermaid*, honey. Don't stress it." This time Colby's laugh sounded almost brittle. "It was a great night downstairs, huh?"

Wait. Don't stress what? "What are we talking about now?"

"The restaurant? I was asking about your night?"

"Oh, that's it? Yeah, it was a good night. Busy, fun." But that question felt like a distraction now. "Listen, I'm glad the two of you are getting along, you know." He was. He wished his relationship with Olivia had started off on a more positive note too, but he wasn't at his best, and Colby just had that personality.

"I know. I could just tell that I have to watch that. Making promises and all. I guess I miss my nieces and nephews more than I thought. There's lots of us back home."

Oh. "Yeah? Tell me. Just not safe for you there?"

"Nope. It's good here. I got my mountains, and I'm starting to get a name, so it's all good." For a second, there was this look—this lost, lonely expression that made Gordon's soul hurt a little.

He found Colby's hand and gave it a squeeze. He'd never met a kinder man than Colby and couldn't imagine anyone who knew Colby would drive that cowboy away, but he knew better than to pry just because he was curious. He'd removed himself from his family in Boston pretty thoroughly, and those emotions were raw right now for him too.

"It's all good." He repeated the phrase with the same irony he'd heard in his cowboy's voice. "You can borrow my niece anytime, you know. She already loves you, you're already Uncle Colby, and she... needs people to keep their promises. I'm pretty sure you're still going to be the same sweet cowboy who taught her to two-step come Tuesday."

He leaned over and kissed Colby. "And then there's this," he said, grinning and gesturing from his shoulders to his knees. "I mean, I can't compete with the Rockies, but talk about all good."

"I can't argue with you there, honey. You're fine to me, I swear to God."

Gordon laughed. Maybe the most relaxed and happy laugh he'd had in days. "You're damn good for a man's ego, sugar lips."

"Lord have mercy. Sugar lips? I'm gonna pinch you."

"Ha! I've been trying to find one you'd object to! It's about time. The next one was going to be love muffin." Something about the way Colby said "Lord have mercy"—the drawl, the little hint of a smile, just warmed him right up. It was worth risking a pinch; he'd do it again.

"You're a butthead." Colby pushed into his arms, soft laugh teasing him.

Huh. That was nice. He waited for Colby to settle on his chest and just held him. "How many times did you watch that movie with the mermaid?"

"Three. And a half. I just went ahead and bought it for her."

"Good Lord. You are a patient man, McBride. I couldn't even watch that Hawaiian whatever movie she was watching on the plane. I fell asleep." Three times. He wasn't even sure he could parent for six hours in a row.

"She was pretty easy. Two books from the library. She likes to cook." Colby shook his head. "She let me wash her hair. That was weird."

"Damn, you really would make a good dad." A bath, taught her to dance—"Hey, when are you going to teach me how to two-step?"

"Whenever you want me to. I love to dance." Look at that happy smile.

"Could be fun." Fun? Really? Did he just say that? "I don't dance. At all." Must be the beer. Or Colby. Could you get high on cowboy?

"No? Never? I don't go to the clubs or nothing, but I like to move around the floor."

"Just not something I ever got into. Plus it's kind of hard to dance to Zeppelin and ELP." Those were great to make out to, though. "I'll let you teach me sometime. It's something to do. I recommend steel-toed boots, though." He laughed. He'd be such a di-saster on a dance floor.

"We'll both just be barefooted. Makes it easi-er." Colby grinned. "You know you have the musical tastes of an old dude, right?"

Gordon laughed. "I am an old dude, you asshole." He couldn't quite reach to slap Colby on the ass, so he poked Colby in the ribs instead.

"You're not that old. You're not 1970s-music old."

"Oh my God no, I'm not that old." He pretended to look shocked. "I'd be a fossil if I were into seven-ties music." *Houses of the Holy* was released in like 1973, right? He decided he'd just keep that detail to himself. "I just had an appreciation for my father's vi-nyl collection."

"I can understand that. I have listened to a fair amount of Kenny Rogers and Dolly Parton."

"'The Gambler' and… '9 to 5.'" Gordon nodded. "That's about all that made it to Boston." He snorted. Colby wasn't likely to be impressed. "You ready to turn in, cowboy?"

"I am, yeah. I feel like I worked my tush off today, and I bet you do too." Colby hauled himself up and then reached for Gordon.

He took Colby's hand and groaned as he stood up. "Thanks for giving an old man a hand up, sonny."

"You're welcome, Gramps."

"Little shit." Gordon kept hold of Colby's hand as they headed into the bedroom. "What's your plan to-morrow? Head for the mountains? Go home and sleep all day? Watch *Die Hard* and scrub the mermaids from your brain?"

"I hadn't made a plan, man. I wasn't sure what you needed."

Had he asked Colby to wait around for him? He didn't think so. "I'm not sure either. I have to work in my office for a couple of hours at some point. Finish with the mail and make sure the orders are in for the week. I figured Liv could come hang out with me. But most of the day I'm free."

"You want to go out to breakfast?" Colby cupped his ass, squeezed him, nice and easy.

He returned the attention, dragging his thumb across Colby's nipple. "We could do that. We could hit Motherlode. Olivia would probably dig their french toast."

"Works for me." Colby hummed, the sound utterly satisfied.

He leaned in and kissed Colby, just a light taste, and then tugged Colby right into bed. He did feel like he'd worked his ass off, because he had, and it felt great. He was feeling pretty damn satisfied himself. He let Colby snuggle right in and hugged an arm around those strong shoulders. "Mmm. Sleepy."

"Yeah. Rest, honey."

Rest. He could do that.

COLBY WOKE to the smell of food cooking, the sound of Olivia chattering, and Gordon's low voice answering her.

Had he overslept? He'd been pretty sure he'd invited Gordon out.

Of course, if Little Bit was hungry, she might not have been able to wait.

He rolled out of bed and got himself dressed and presentable for both little and big people waiting on him in the front room.

"What is that?" Olivia was full of questions, as usual.

"This?" he heard Gordy answer. "This is an avocado. You've never seen an avocado?"

"It's ugly."

"Very. And delicious."

Colby turned the corner into the kitchen to find Olivia up on one of the high stools and Gordy at the cutting board slicing the avocado they were talking about with a knife.

"I don't believe you."

"Try it." Gordy held out a slice on the flat side of the knife for her.

She stared at it dubiously but reached out for it. "It's squishy."

"It is squishy. And delicious. Try it. Oh, hey. Good morning, Uncle Colby." Gordy gave him a smile. "You were right. Olivia does like to cook. She's been helping me with breakfast."

Olivia turned around to look at him. "Morning, Uncle Colby! That is an av… av…?" She looked at Gordy.

"Avocado. That you are about to try a bite of."

"He wants me to eat it."

"You should totally eat half and let me have half. I love avocados."

"Yeah?" Liv pulled off half.

"Good. I'm making you an avocado and tomato salsa for your Mexican omelet."

Liv popped the avocado in her mouth and chewed, watching Colby closely.

Colby hummed, making a show of how good it was.

Liv nodded, then smiled. "It's good! Squishy, but good!"

"Told you." Gordy went back to dicing up the avocado. "You okay with cilantro, Colby?"

"I am. There coffee made?" He needed a cup of joe.

"Oh, yeah. Hang on. Just black, right?" Gordy wiped his hands off on a towel that was hanging over one shoulder and reached for a mug.

"Uncle Gordy made me a mole-in-a-hole for breakfast. It was yummy."

"Mole in a hole?" What the fuck was that?

"Rabbit in a hole? Monk in a hole?" Gordy offered. Colby just shook his head. "Bread, cut a hole in the middle, crack an egg in the hole...?"

Liv nodded. "So cool."

"Oh, eggs in a basket. My mom makes those for me. I haven't had that in a long time." He loved how the same foods had different names, depending on where you were from.

"You Texans have a different word for everything." Gordy winked at him. "Cheddar or pepper jack?"

"Pepper jack, please." He sipped his coffee, moving to sit next to Liv. "What all are y'all doing today?"

"Uncle Gordy said I can color in his office."

"While Uncle Gordon sifts through the rest of the mail." Gordy poured an egg mixture into an omelet pan, and it sizzled nicely. "And then I thought maybe a hike. It's a nice day."

A hike? He'd love to see Gordy hike in his shiny shoes.

"Yeah? It's going to be stunning today. Lots of sun." Was this a "go away" or a "you're welcome to come"? He knew that Gordy wasn't wanting him at the Little Bit's school, so maybe Gordon thought he needed to back the fuck off.

"Are you hiking with us, Uncle Colby?"

"Liv." Gordy glanced at him and then added all the veggies to a bowl with some lime juice. "You probably have things you need to get done, huh?"

Okay, he didn't know what to do. *Dammit. Dammit.* "Yeah. I have to… uh… do laundry."

"Well…." Gordy reached for the pepper jack. "If it's just laundry, you could… I mean, I have to work for a couple of hours this morning. We won't be going until after lunch. But listen, I get it if you need a break."

"Sounds like way more fun than laundry, doesn't it?" *Okay. Okay, right.* Lord help him, this was awkward and weird. "You mind if I tag along, Little Bit?"

"Nope! Uncle Gordy says you know the mountains waaaaaay better than he does."

Gordy snorted and grinned. "One Mexican omelet, pepper jack cheese, avocado and tomato salsa." He put a plate down in front of Colby, then added two slices of avocado and some cilantro to the top. He stuck a smaller plate with more avocado and some strawberries on it in front of Olivia. "I did say that."

"Are you not eating, honey? I'll share." Of course he knew the mountains better. He loved it up there.

"I'm eating. Only have one omelet pan." Gordy started the whole process over again for himself. "So, hiking. Good. You do your thing while I work, and then.... Yeah. That works, right?" He pulled the ched-dar out of the fridge.

"Absolutely." He took a bite, his eyes on Gordy's ass. Damn, that was fine.

"I'm done!" Liv shoved her plate across the counter and hopped off her stool. "Can I go play? There's stuff in my room!"

"There is stuff. You can thank the cowboy for that."

"He's my magic cowboy. I love him, Uncle Gordy, so much."

Well now, didn't that feel good? Colby couldn't stop grinning.

"I'm sure he's very happy about that. Go play, Liv. I'll come get you when I'm headed to the office." Gordy slid his omelet onto his plate and set the pan back on the stove pretty hard, the metal ringing against the burner grate. "Sorry." He sighed. "More coffee?"

"No, sir. I'm good." Christ, he felt like he was walking on eggshells all the time. "Thanks for the breakfast. It's good."

Gordy refilled his mug and slid his plate around to take Olivia's seat next to Colby. "I'm glad you like it." He picked up his fork and dug in.

"You okay, man?" He reckoned he'd just try and figure out where Gordy's complicated head was.

"Sure. Hungry." He took a bite and chewed for a minute. "You want to do your laundry here, or do you have stuff at home too?"

"If you're cool, I'll just do it here. I can watch Little Bit if you wanted...."

"I'd like to take her with me," Gordy said, maybe a little too quickly. "She wanted to see my office. I used to like hanging out in my dad's office with him when I was a kid."

"Sure. I can totally head off too, man. I'm not trying to be a stalker." But it probably didn't look that way, did it? Christ, Gordy probably thought he was a... what was the term for male "single white female"? Single Texas gay-male?

Gordy pushed back from the counter and stood up. "I need a shower. You've got your eye on her, right? Magic cowboy?"

He stepped right around Colby and headed back toward the bedroom.

Whoa. Right. He tossed the rest of the food and put his plate in the dishwasher, then waited until he heard the shower and packed his backpack up and put it by the door. Then he peeked in on Liv, smiling down at her, watching her play.

He missed home and kin so bad he couldn't hardly bear it, but this wasn't his family, and it wasn't going to take the place of what all he'd lost.

It wasn't fair to this little girl to pretend that Gordon was going to want him here either.

He waited until he heard the water cut off, and then he knocked on the bathroom door once. "She's playing. I'm outta here, man."

Then he grabbed his shit and slipped out the door.

Tomorrow he had work to do, so he'd best get his skinny ass to the laundromat.

Chapter Nineteen

GORDON HADN'T quite understood whether Colby meant he was off and he'd be back after lunch, or he was off and fuck you. But a couple of unanswered texts and a long, beautiful hike later, the cowboy had made his point pretty damn clear.

Olivia had done really well on the hike. Colby would have been proud of her. The altitude was no joke on the mountain trails and Gordon didn't know them that well, so they'd done some wandering, and it took them longer to get back to his Jeep than he'd anticipated.

He'd texted April a picture of Olivia sitting on a boulder with the wide-open sky behind her, figuring she'd appreciate it, and he'd gotten back a smiley face and a request for a FaceTime call with her later.

Thank God for that, because he'd had a hard time explaining to Olivia why Colby wasn't on the hike with them, so the call with April was a welcome distraction.

Her bath had been one long pout, though, and by that point, Gordon was ready to do some pouting of his own. With that bottle of Jameson sitting on his kitchen counter.

"Come on out of the tub, Liv. You're all pruny."

"I need Uncle Colby to come wash my hair!" She glared at him from the sea of bath toys. "He does it right."

"I washed your hair, Olivia." He held out the towel to make his point. "Come on out."

"Is he going to read me a story at least? So I can sleep?"

"No, Liv, he… has to work tomorrow. I'll read to you, okay?" *Please just get out of the damn tub.* He offered her his hand this time. "Up you go."

"He promised he'd come with me to my first day of my new school. Can I call him and tell him good night? Please?" Her eyes filled with tears.

Oh for fuck's sake. "Yes, baby, you can call him and tell him good night, but your first day isn't until Tuesday. He'll be there, okay? Uncle Colby's not going to break a promise to you."

That he could at least say with confidence. Colby would keep a promise he made to Olivia whether Gordon was on his shit list or not.

"Don't cry, sweetheart. Come on out and let me give you a hug." He was careful to keep his impatience out of his voice, but he was so ready to reach in and haul her out of there. How did parents not lose their fucking minds?

She went to him, sniffling softly. "I love Uncle Colby. He puts me to bed here."

Yeah, he guessed Colby had been the one constant for her in this apartment so far. It ought to be him, but…. God. And she'd even said she loved Colby. Fuck. He couldn't compete with that.

"Give me a chance, huh?" He wrapped the towel around her and gave her a hug, surprised at how the contact made his chest ache. This was too goddamn hard. How was he supposed to do this?

He let Liv go and toweled her off, then helped her into her nightgown. "Where's your toothbrush?"

He missed his sister. Having her gone made him miss his parents all over again too. Even his dad. He needed to figure out this parenting thing fast. He just wished he could want it in the way Colby wanted it. That would make all of this so much easier.

He had some thinking to do, that was for sure. Even he missed Colby right now, and that idea deserved some of his time. He hadn't meant to run the cowboy off earlier. He was just feeling… well, kind of the way he felt right now. Insecure. Incompetent. Things he wasn't used to feeling. Things that didn't sit well with him at all.

Colby had come in like he knew what he was doing, and to be honest, that wasn't how their relationship tended to work. He didn't think Colby was stupid or anything, just young, a little footloose and fancy-free.

With the promise of a phone call hanging over his head, he was able to get Olivia's teeth brushed, her hair tamed, and her backside in bed, but not without disappointing her one more time when he didn't know how to braid her hair. He'd managed to get her to settle for pigtails, but not without being reminded that Uncle Colby braided horses' tails.

"Just a quick good night, okay?" he said, his finger hovering over the Call button on his phone.

"Okay!" She beamed at him, bouncing hard enough to knock her bears off the bed.

The phone rang twice before Colby answered, the sound of a pool hall unmistakable. "Whatcha need?"

It wasn't warm, but Gordon sighed, relieved. He'd been half worried Colby wouldn't answer at all. "Hey, Uncle Colby. Olivia would like to say good night." He handed her the phone.

"Hi, Uncle Colby. Where are you?"

"Hey, Little Bit! I have to work tomorrow, so I had to come back and go to the laundromat. I sure miss you. Are you ready for bed?"

"Yes. But Uncle Gordy doesn't wash my hair right, and he can't braid! Are you coming tomorrow?"

Gordon shook his head. "I'll learn," he told her, not really expecting to be heard. He'd try to learn. God, his self-esteem was suddenly being measured by the opinion of a five-year-old. He needed that drink.

"I doubt it, honey. You got your Uncle Gordy now. You don't need this old cowboy. You're in the best hands ever."

"No. I do! You have to come over tomorrow. Promise?"

Gordon stepped closer, wishing he'd just left the room instead of putting his phone on speaker. "Liv—"

"Uncle Gordy! Please let Uncle Colby come see me? Please? Just for a minute? You don't have to see him if you don't like him. You can wait in the bedroom."

He stared at her. "Wait. I never said.... Colby, I never said that. I didn't even.... Olivia, he's welcome. It's up to him." Shit. Shit, how had he even given her that idea? And now Colby was—shit.

"All right, y'all." There was an odd mixture of sharp and gentle in those words. "No one needs to wait anywhere. I'll come by after I get off work, but I'll have to set a time with your Uncle Gordy, okay? You can't be all fussing and stuff either. You got to lay your head down like a good girl. Fair deal?"

"I promise. I promise I will be good all day." Her little face was so serious, so damn like his sister that it hurt.

"All right, Little Bit. I love you. You get some sleep."

"Love you too!"

Dammit. "I'll, uh… let me get her tucked in and I'll call you back."

"Sure. No problem."

The line went dead, and Olivia handed him a book.

He'd read it. Twice. Then he'd tucked her in, tucked in Jessica and Snowball, tucked in this long stuffed shark and two dolls, and got her a glass of water. Then he'd kissed her cheek and headed straight for the whiskey.

Now he was on drink number two and was staring at his phone like it was out to get him. He hadn't been looking forward to this conversation before Olivia had taken it upon her five-year-old self to make sure Colby knew just how badly their evening had gone.

Maybe he could just keep it to business, make a plan for tomorrow and then be done. Maybe he could. But he didn't really want to. "Oh fuck it." He made the call.

"Hey, there." It was way quieter on Colby's end of the phone line now.

"Hi." *Okay, Gordon, talk. You called him.* "So… tomorrow."

Awkward didn't begin to describe how he was starting this conversation. He took a sip of his whiskey. "I'm off, so whenever you come by is fine. Maybe you want to stay for dinner? Tuck her in after?"

"Look, are you pissed at me? I'm not real good at this whole reading signals shit, obviously, so you'll just have to be straight up with me."

"No. Not… no. It's me. I'm not good at… well, anything, apparently. Fuck. I'm sorry." Colby shouldn't have to read him; he should just speak his mind. And he would, if he understood what his mind was up to. He sipped his whiskey again. "Nothing is a more honest mirror than a five-year-old, huh?"

"I swear by all I hold holy, I wasn't trying to step on your toes. I just wanted to help y'all, and yeah, she's something else."

"I know. You're not stepping on my toes. I couldn't have done this without you this far. I don't think I—" *Whoa, hold on.* What was he about to say? He cleared his throat. "She misses you."

That wasn't all, was it? He got up off the couch and paced across the living room. "I need… I need your help."

"Okay. What do you need?"

God, it would be easier if Colby told him to fuck off a little.

He needed Colby there, in his apartment, wearing those pajama pants he had on the other night. He needed the happy tile guy who just happened to have mad skills with little girls. He needed to stop making these conversations so hard and overthinking everything. He should tell Colby all of that, but he didn't want to. "I don't know. Let's talk tomorrow night, okay? Maybe I'll have... figured it out by then."

Maybe he'd man up and say it this time. *Coward.*

"What are you making for supper?"

Gordon laughed. "I don't even know what I'm wearing to bed yet."

"Well, you let me know. About the supper, not your pjs. I'll bring beer." Colby chuckled. "And wear the red pants. I like them on you."

"You've seen me in them exactly once." But they happened to be Gordon's favorite too. "If you stay tomorrow night, we can go to Liv's school together in the morning. I mean, together like at the same time. You'll want to bring your own truck, right? So you can head straight to work. So not really together. Wow, this is good whiskey." He put the glass down and walked away.

"You need to breathe, Gordon. Seriously. We'll talk tomorrow night, and you can decide what you need me to do, and I can decide whether I can give it to you."

"Sounds fair. Sounds good, even." Finally, something from Colby that he could push back against. "Maybe I'll bring dinner up from the restaurant. You like fish?"

"I've had a lot of fried fish, and I like it. I'll try it."

There was no way he was serving Colby fried fish. A nice swordfish or tuna steak maybe. "Good. Beer goes great with fish. You gonna come straight here from the hotel job or stop at your place first?"

Was it wrong of him to want Colby to show up as is? God, he loved that working-man thing. Dusty and musky and mmm. Yep. Colby.

"I'll probably come straight over, if you don't mind."

"Nope. Perfect." He smiled, he just couldn't help it. "Looking forward to it. Sleep well, cowboy."

"You too, man. Rest your brain."

Gordon snorted. "Night," he said, and didn't wait for a reply before hanging up—they'd be at it all night. He dumped the rest of that second glass of whiskey in the sink and went to find his red PJs.

Chapter Twenty

"COLBY, YOU'RE zipping through this job." Miss Terri leaned on the front desk and grinned. "I might think you wanted out of here."

"I got a dinner date, and I will have a late start tomorrow. I'm going to accompany a little girl to her first day of a new school."

"Are you now? That's exciting." He got a bright grin that proved he could run late tomorrow with no snarls. "Not your little girl, obviously. Your date's? It's late in the year for a first day of school."

"He's the guy I told you about, lady, remember? The one whose sister died?"

"Oh, yes, I remember. And you're taking his niece to school with him. That's sweet. Adorable. You two are pretty serious, then. Good for you—and good for that little girl too." She reached out and gave his shoulder a pat. "Don't you worry, you take your time in the morning. You're ahead of schedule anyway."

"Thank you, ma'am." Serious? He didn't think so. He wanted to be, but he didn't know if he wanted to be because Gordy did it for him or because he was lonesome. He wasn't sure Gordy wanted to be serious with him, at all.

"He's a lucky man, Mr. McBride." Miss Terri pushed away from the desk. "You make sure he knows that. Doesn't hurt to make a man work for it a little." She smiled. "You know what I'm saying?"

"God no." He was a bit of a horndog, after all. He winked at Miss Terri, though, playing hard.

She put on a little show right back, sighing and batting her eyes, barely hiding a grin. "Shame. Grass is much greener in this pasture." She laughed.

"Lord save you. I'm going to clean up a little and then head out. I'll see you around ten-ish?"

"See you then, Colby. Be good."

"I promise." Actually, he thought he might be a little mean. He needed to stop the games, though. He didn't like them.

He stopped to pick up a six-pack on his way to Gordy's and parked his truck right next to Gordy's Jeep. He checked his phone as he was headed inside, and he was glad he did. There was a text from Gordy warning him that Liv's visit to the school had been a little stressful.

Oh man, that sucked for her. Still, once she made friends, right?

He clomped up the steps, then knocked on Gordy's door.

After a minute Gordy answered, in a pair of dress slacks and a crisply ironed shirt with a couple of buttons open at the top. "Hey. Come on in."

Olivia was nowhere in sight, and the apartment was quiet. Gordy must have read the look on his face. "She's in her room, watching cartoons on her tablet. She's tired."

"Poor baby. It was harsh, huh?" That broke his heart.

"It didn't seem to be what she was expecting. I wish I could have prepared her better, but I don't know what her old school was like. Honestly, I thought the classroom was cute, and the teacher was friendly. She just wouldn't let go of my hand." Gordy sighed. "She told me on the way home that she's not going tomorrow."

"Oh, dude." He went to Gordy and hugged him, because what else would he do.

Gordy pulled him in with a sigh. "We've been talking a little about it, and the teacher suggested we start her on a half day. I think I'm making progress, but I guess we'll find out tomorrow." Gordy pressed his face to Colby's neck, and Colby heard him breathe in. "God, you smell good."

"Tile dust and sweat." He liked hearing that, though. A lot. "Thanks for the invite. It's good to see you."

Gordy released him a little to kiss him. Not too heavy, but not exactly light either. "Good to see you too. I guess you want to shower?" Gordy's hands were roaming, but there was a little girl who needed a pep talk, and dinner....

"I reckon I ought." He was probably messing up Gordy's floor.

Gordy let him go with a grin. "Shame."

"Yeah. Yeah, man, I—"

A little ball of energy came hurtling toward him. "Uncle Colby! You came!"

He caught her up, swung her around. "I did, Little Bit. How's you today?"

She gave him a kiss on his cheek. "Uncle Gordy made me go to that school today." Oh, the look she shot Gordy was pure five-year-old evil eye.

"Yeah? I can't wait to see it. Did you get to meet your teacher?"

"Yes. Her name is… Mrs.… uh…." She glanced at Gordy.

"Collins."

"Mrs. Collins." Liv followed that with a nod like she'd remembered that all along.

"She was nice, wasn't she?" Gordy prompted.

"I guess. She was pretty too."

"Yeah? Rock on. Are you excited? I am. I can't wait to meet her and see your classroom." He knew it was damn near impossible to be evil in the face of happy enthusiasm. He used it on clients to get them to change their minds all the time.

He thought he could feel Gordy holding his breath.

Liv's eyes lit up. "You're still going to take me?"

"Well, sure. Me and your Uncle Gordy will be there with bells on. Have you decided what you're going to wear yet?" And if Gordon got weird, Colby would just shove one boot up his ass.

"No! I should wear a dress, huh?" She wiggled to be let down. "Will you do my hair?"

"You should wear what makes you happy and that you can have fun at recess in, silly girl." He grinned at

Gordy, super relieved. "And yes, ma'am. Your official hairdresser is on the job."

"I have a butterfly barrette that Uncle Gordon bought me in the airport! Maybe the blue dress with the flowers?" She took off down the hall toward her room.

Gordy snorted. "Shit. You really are a magic cowboy." Colby winced a little, but Gordy seemed more amused than ornery. "I get it. It's like a good cop, bad cop thing, right? I'm all 'go to bed, go to school, take a bath, eat your veggies,' and you're all cheerleader and hairdresser." He laughed. It was maybe a little tight, but it was a laugh.

"Rah, rah, shish boom bah. Go team!" Colby shrugged, because it was what it was. "I come from a big family. Lots of little ones."

He'd been watching how this worked for a long time.

Gordy shook his head. "All I got today was tears and arguing. I'm trying, and I get that this is a sink-or-swim kind of thing, but I feel like someone put the starting line down pretty damn deep in the pool."

"My daddy says that means she trusts you won't walk out on her." Gordy raised one eyebrow, and Colby shrugged and pressed on. "I guess when my sister was getting a divorce, that's what the headshrinker said. That the reason they're bad is because they can be and you'll still love them."

"Really?" Gordy wandered off toward the kitchen with a thoughtful look. "Huh."

"I'm like Santa Claus right now. You're her home."

Gordy turned right around again and came back to him, gave him a kiss and an odd smile Colby wasn't sure he'd seen before. He couldn't quite get a read on it. "Thank you, Uncle Colby." Gordy winked. "Go clean up. Dinner in twenty."

"I'm on it."

He waved at Liv as he walked by. "Gonna get showered, Little Bit."

"'Kay!"

It was good to see her smiling, and he headed into the bathroom with his own grin. Colby took a little bit of a longish shower, enjoying the heat, and then he put on the pair of old jeans and a clean T-shirt, plus a little smell-good.

The apartment smelled amazing, and he took a long sniff as he left the master bedroom. Liv wasn't in her room, but he noted the clothing she'd laid out on her bed.

"Okay, now sprinkle some of that right on top. You can use your fingers."

"Like that?"

"Little more." Gordon's voice was pretty damn patient.

"Good?"

"Yep. Perfect. How's the table? Did you put out the salt and pepper?"

"Yes, Uncle Gordy. You asked me that already."

Gordon laughed. "Sorry. Sorry."

"Man, something smells like heaven." Oh, that was so damn cute. "What are we having?"

"Fish!" Liv piped up from the dining room.

"I can't take credit. Chef made the fish and sent it up. But I made the sides. I didn't know what you'd like to try—there's grilled salmon and seared tuna steaks."

Gordon scooped up the platter of fish in one hand and two beers in the other. "Come on and sit."

"Wow. I feel spoiled." He felt warm and happy too, and he hadn't had his beer yet.

"Good." Gordy nodded to Liv. "Olivia?"

Liv pulled out Colby's chair for him. Not an easy thing to do as it was bigger than she was. Gordon set beer in front of him. "Help yourself. There's asparagus and garlic mashed potatoes too."

"Y'all! It's like it's my birthday!" Lord have mercy, now that was fine. He took a nice dollop of mashed potatoes and some asparagus. "Tell me about the fish."

"Sure. Chef did a nice simple grill on the salmon; there's a little salt and pepper and some lemon on it, and that's it. And this one is the tuna steak. He did a quick pan sear on it, and the inside is very rare and cool. The tuna is more mild than the salmon, but there's enough you should try both. Oh! Liv, let me get you your chicken."

Gordy disappeared into the kitchen again.

"Do you like fishies?" Liv asked, and he nodded.

"I think so, yeah. I'm looking forward to trying these." They both looked fancy and good. "How about you?"

"No. Smells bad."

"Here you go, girlie." Gordy set a plate of plain cut-up chicken in front of Liv and started serving her potatoes and veggies. "Decide which one you're trying first, Colby? Don't wait, just dig in."

"Sounds like the tuna isn't as bright, so I'll try it first." It was the closest he could come to a reason. The salmon just flat-out sounded better.

"Works for me. I'll start with the salmon." Gordy served him up some of the tuna, and Colby reached for his fork. "Work was cool about coming in late tomorrow?"

"No problem. I worked my heinie off today. Seriously, I got some tile laid." And it looked fine—all browns and deep reds and a pale blue.

"No doubt. As your occasional employer, I can tell you your work ethic is unheard of. You should raise your rates, Colby; you're worth it. Especially when it comes to things that take some real skill, not just bathroom tile."

"I'm trying to make a name still, you know? It's hard to be the new guy, but I'm starting to get repeat clients." He loved his job, which was probably stupid, but he did. He got to make art, work with his hands, get dirty. The good stuff.

"Why don't you let me help? I know nearly every restaurant owner in town. I'm a Chamber member.... You should give me some of your business cards."

"Do you like the fish, Uncle Colby?"

"I do. It's not what I expected, but I do." He took another bite. Yeah. It was good. Nowhere near as good as Gordy offering to pass out cards, but tasty. "Thanks, man. I have a box in my truck. I'd appreciate that a lot. Referrals are important."

"I wouldn't have hired you so quickly myself except that Nancy Howell said you did a really good job of the bathrooms in her house, and I trust her because I know she runs a solid business. Always good to have a personal reference in this town." Gordy grinned. "And I can give a pretty personal reference."

His cheeks started to burn. "Be good, Uncle Gordy."

Gordy laughed, seeming pretty pleased with himself. "Hey. How is your chicken, Liv?"

"Yummy. Can I have more potatoes?"

"Yes, you may." Gordy hopped up out of his chair to help. While he was up, he put some of the salmon on Colby's plate. "This is fantastic."

He wasn't sure why Gordon was so happy, but he liked it. A lot. "Smells pretty good, thanks."

"Sometime over the summer, when the restaurant does a special, I'll make sure you try some swordfish. It's hard to come by here without a special order, but I grew up on fish, ocean fish, living near Boston and going to the Cape in the summer. It might be the only thing I really miss about the East Coast."

"Boston is where I'm from!" She looked at Colby, frowning deep, want lines carved into her forehead. "Did you go to Boston?"

"I haven't been, no." He froze a little, not wanting to ramp her up.

"Uh. Hey, girlie, are you done eating? You look full. I think I see an asparagus sticking out right... here!" Gordy poked her in the belly.

"That's not asparagus!"

"It's not?" He grinned at her and poked her again. "Is it chicken?"

"No, Uncle Gordy." She rolled her eyes.

"Why don't you take your plate to the kitchen, and then maybe your cowboy will get you all set for bed."

"Okay!" Liv slid off her chair and carefully took her plate into the kitchen.

Gordy picked up his beer and took a long sip.

Colby finished his salmon and his mashed potatoes, gaze fastened on Gordon's throat.

"Well, she didn't freak, so maybe I'm learning," Gordy said as he put the empty bottle down on the table. "Sorry if I cut your meal a little short there."

"No. No, you did great. That was damn yummy. Thank you, honey. I appreciate it." He stole the last bite of fish.

"Glad you liked it. It was pretty good, huh? Liv won't go hungry anyway." Gordy winked. He got up and picked up Colby's plate. "I got this. You keep that promise."

"It was delicious. Thank you." He finished his drink, and then went to see his girl.

"Hey, Little Bit, you 'bout ready?"

"I'm ready." She ran right to him to be picked up.

He grabbed her and hugged her close. "Oh, I do love you, Little Bit."

"Will you braid my hair?"

"Of course. Have you brushed your teeth?"

"Yep, see?" She opened her mouth and breathed fruity toothpaste breath in his face.

"Very nice." *Oh gag. Hooray.* "Go grab me your brush."

She let him put her down, and she hurried off toward her room. By the time he arrived, she had a brush, a couple of barrettes, and a pink elastic. She held them all out to him as he walked in the door. "You have to teach Uncle Gordy to braid. He can't do it."

"He'll figure it out, I bet. Okay, let's do this." Colby sat with her on one leg. He brushed her hair out, trying not to tug even a little bit.

"I'm going to wear that blue dress with the flowers on it, and I have shorts I can wear under so I can still do the monkey bars. And Uncle Gordy bought me that backpack in Boston." She pointed to a little pink-and-lavender backpack leaning against her bookcase and went on, with hardly a breath in between. "I told him I didn't like it, but really I do. And Mrs. Collins said I can bring Jessica, but she has to stay in my cubby sometimes. Ow. Uncle Colby, there's a knot there!"

"Sorry!" He eased up, working the knot with his fingers. "I like the backpack. Your teacher sounds like a nice lady. I'm looking forward to meeting her. You like the monkey bars? I loved the merry-go-round best."

"Uh-huh. I can climb all the way across. That's how come Mom used to call me a monkey." Colby held his breath a second, wondering where she was going to go next, but she just picked right up where she'd left off. "If I stay the whole day, there's SunButter and jelly sandwiches for lunch, and Mrs. Collins says there's apples for snack."

"What's SunButter, Little Bit?"

"It's like peanut butter only it has sunflower seeds."

"Neat. I'll have to try it. I like peanut butter sandwiches a lot." He separated her hair out, braided one side, and fastened it off.

Liv yawned and then started to hum something he didn't think he recognized. It was pretty, though. He already knew she could carry a tune after three or four times through *The Little Mermaid* movie.

The second braid went easy, and he nodded. "All braided. You want a story?"

"Okay," she said, yawning again. He didn't think she'd make it through, but he took the book she handed him all the same.

He tucked her in and started reading, keeping one eye on her, and sure enough, she was sound asleep by the time he was five pages in. He kissed her forehead and turned off the lamp. Lord have mercy.

As he left her room, he closed the door behind him. Gordy's music was playing, quieter than usual, but playing all the same, and he found Gordy sitting on the couch, reading and sipping a glass of red wine.

"She's out like a light." Suddenly he wasn't sure what to do, whether he should sit close or in one of the chairs.

"That was fast. I guess the emotion of the day wore her out." Gordy was watching him, but he was no help at all. Was this a test or some shit? "You want some wine?"

"You mind if I have another beer?" Wine was weird, and he never felt like he knew how to drink it.

"Sure, of course. You want me to grab it? Or you can help yourself…."

"I'll get it, honey. You look comfy." And fine. Damn fine.

He pulled a bottle from Gordy's fridge, not sure what they were in for exactly. Gordy had been in a good mood over dinner, but he was damn hard to read just now.

"There's leftover dump cake," Gordy called from the living room. "I hear it goes great with beer."

"Shut up." That made him laugh, and he'd be damned if that didn't make him feel better. He came to rest next to Gordy, his thigh pressing against Gordy's.

"Dinner was good?"

"It was delicious. Thank you. The mashed potatoes were my favorite part." The mashed potatoes, the company.

"It was nice, right? Just… hanging out together?" He felt Gordy glance over at him for a second.

He shifted a little on one hip, meeting Gordon's gaze. "I like you, man. Genuinely. I mean, if nothing else, I'm your friend." And he thought it was more.

"If nothing else?" Gordy sighed and shifted too, so he was facing Colby on the couch. "That. That thing you do? That's why I bailed and took a shower the other morning, Colby. That right there. Tell me something, why did you walk out? What was that about?"

That thing he did? He did a thing? What did that mean? He told himself to calm the fuck down, to breathe. Gordy had asked him a question; surely he could just answer it. It wasn't like he'd been evil or nothing. "You seemed so damn mad at me, and I didn't want to step on your toes."

"I wasn't mad at you. I was frustrated, but it wasn't about you. Well, I wasn't mad until you…. I mean, I invited you on a hike with us, didn't I? I thought maybe it'd be fun, but then all of a sudden you were doing your thing—walking that line. Like it didn't matter that much, it was cool, you were happy to head out if I didn't want you around."

"I don't want to be that guy that hangs around bothering people." He wasn't happy to head out, but it was better than pushing himself where he didn't want to be. "I've never"—*loved*—"been with someone like you. The rules are different."

He felt like he was stupid and young and naive, and fuck, he didn't like feeling that way.

Gordy reached for Colby's hand and pulled it into his lap. "Okay. That's… fine. Me neither. And I'm not used to wanting more. But I've started to see you differently than I used to, and I don't know why, but that's… raising my expectations. Of you, and of myself."

"This is hard, huh? To want to say the right thing because it feels so damn important?" Because this could be fucked up so easy.

Gordy nodded. "It feels important because it is important. Even more important because of that little girl sleeping at the end of the hall."

Colby watched Gordy lift his wineglass, take a sip, and set it back down. It was so deliberate. So Gordy.

"You're not just a friend, Colby. But you're… easygoing. Free-spirited. I feel like it's asking a lot for you to step in where I need you to be."

"It is, but I'm willing to man up." Free-spirited? Him? He liked that. He was just getting to the place in his life that he felt like he knew he could afford groceries. Where he wasn't stressing paying his phone bill. He didn't feel like that was all that free-spirited. Maybe… shit, maybe that was what poor and scared to death looked like from the outside.

"I'm not just talking about Olivia." Gordy leaned forward and kissed him lightly. "I've… got something on my mind. Tell me what you want, Colby."

"I want to be with you. I want us both to be happy. Is that stupid?"

"No. That's what I want too. It's not stupid at all. It's just not that simple. Or… maybe it is that simple; it's just not that easy? It scares me a little to think about everything I want because I've never wanted any of it before. Ever."

He didn't even want to think about Gordy being scared, because the son of a bitch was so damn put together. Still, it was what it was, and he could stubborn through it. "Well, we don't have to think about everything all at once. We'll just eat it like an elephant."

Gordy laughed, soft and low, and nodded. "All right, cowboy. That's how we'll do it. But it's still going to move faster than you think, because tomorrow morning we're taking Olivia to school. Presumably together? That will make an impression."

"Does that make you scared?" So far, most folks here on the front range seemed pretty decent, especially in Boulder, but Gordy had restaurants.

"If you mean being outed? No. I don't think most people know for sure, but it's not a big secret. I just don't really date, so they haven't seen me with men." Gordy shrugged and licked his lips. "But if you mean showing up as a couple, being a couple? Especially at Olivia's school? Yeah, it's a little intimidating. People are going to have expectations of both of us. And I'm not usually the show-up-with-a-date kind of guy."

"I don't want to be in anyone's face, but... I don't wanna be like a backdoor whore either, you know?" Been there. Done that. The T-shirt didn't fit.

"No." Gordy shook his head, and his voice grew a little louder, a little more intense. "No, that's just it, Colby. I want you to be in everyone's face. I want you to be in my face and making a fucking nuisance of yourself. I want you to know... I need you to believe you matter. Because you do." Gordy was looking at him hard. "Because I love you."

All the air in the room sucked out in a rush, and he searched Gordon's eyes, needing to know the man wasn't fucking with him, wasn't just saying words. "I never thought I'd hear that in my whole life."

Gordon's gaze didn't leave his, and the hands holding Colby's were rock steady. "I honestly never thought I'd say them. But please trust me when I tell you I'm not using those words lightly."

"Then I reckon you and me need to figure this shit out, 'cause loving each other—well, that's special."

Gordon smiled at him, relaxing a little. "I really hope I'm hearing that right." Gordy leaned in and gave him another soft kiss. "Not a road I've traveled before, so I'm going to need you with me on this one. You know what I mean?"

"Yeah." He could do that, now that he knew it wasn't unwelcome. Christ, why wasn't there a handbook? *Coming Out Cowboy* or *Handbook for Homo Hombres*? Something.

"Okay. Good." Gordy reached for his wine and took a sip. He sighed as he set it down. "If I can run a business, I can figure this out, right?" He shifted on the couch, looking relaxed.

"I got to be less complicated than that, honey."

"Oh, I don't know about that. Texan, cowboy, gay, frustrated artist? That's a lot of layers. I guess we'll see." Gordy winked at him. "I can't tally you up on my adding machine."

He pinched Gordy's thigh, then tilted his head. "Can I try a sip of your wine?"

The question probably seemed weird as hell to Gordy, but if he couldn't try things here, where could he?

"Ow! Yeah, of course. You sure?" Gordy picked it up and handed the glass to him. "It's a Malbec. This one is from Argentina, as most of the good ones are. Chile produces a good grape as well, but I prefer Argentina. Historically speaking the vineyards are older and the grape more pure."

"That's cool." It smelled a little like the cough medicine Momma used to give him when he was a kid, so he took a careful sip. It tasted a little odd, but not nasty, sorta… fuzzy.

"You like it?" Gordy was watching him. "Wine isn't everyone's taste. Take Oscar. He's a beer drinker, and he has very specific taste in his brews. Doesn't care at all for wine."

"I don't know. It tastes like…." Like it wanted to be something else, except that didn't make any sense, so he wouldn't say it. "It's a little weird, kinda heavier than beer, I guess."

Gordy nodded. "It's fermented over time, so it's got a little acidic bite, right? Not like grape juice, which is sweet because the juice is extracted as soon as it's picked. Try another sip. The other thing about wine is that they don't all taste alike, you know? Some of them are stronger and bolder, some of them smoother. Maybe you'd like to sit with me and Liam sometime and sample a few."

Gordy was just explaining, even if it was a little technical, but he wasn't talking down at all, or bragging. He just sounded like he was sharing something he cared about. Just conversation.

"I totally would do that with y'all. Liam's a hoot." He took another sip, this one a little bigger, and he ended up leaning into Gordon's body as they talked. "What's your favorite?"

"You're drinking it. I buy it by the case."

"Cool." Was that expensive? Beer could be, but it tended to come in multiples. He'd have to look it up. "My folks don't drink, so I had to sneak my beer and stuff."

"How long ago did you leave Texas?" Gordy reached over and lifted the glass from his fingers, took a sip, and handed it right back.

He surprised himself by taking another sip. It was heady, so different. "Four years ago at New Year's. I tried New Mexico, then California, before I came here."

He hadn't tried them long, God knew—there wasn't work to speak of in New Mexico, and California liked to kill him with how pricey it was—but he'd tried.

"Hm. Any particular reason you left at New Year's?"

His cheeks got hot as hell, and he looked into the wineglass like there was a better answer than the truth in there. "Uh. I got caught with a man around Christmas. The man was married and a preacher and…. My folks and sisters and all, they—Christ, this is embarrassing. They were getting shit, though, at home. Lots. So I left." Everyone thought his people had thrown him out, which was dumb as hell because his folks loved him, gay or not, but he knew life was easier for them now.

"Wow." Gordy took the wineglass but didn't give it back right away this time. "Of all the things you could have told me…. That's…." He sat up a bit and looped an arm over Colby's shoulders. "Was it the gay thing, or the preacher thing, or the married thing?"

"He told his congregation I drugged him and molested him. County sheriff is a deacon there." Of course he hadn't, and the sheriff sure as shit wouldn't have hesitated to arrest his sorry ass if it had been true, but he hadn't been pitching when the cleaning crew had opened the sanctuary doors, had he?

"Mother. Fucker." Gordy looked at Colby sharply. "Because what, a twenty-four-year-old kid is gonna…. He's a piece of shit, huh?" He handed the glass back to Colby.

"I have called him that, and worse, but that's why I left. I like it here, though, a lot."

"Well, I can't say I'm unhappy about that." Colby closed his eyes, and Gordy kissed his temple. "But your family. I know you love them. I'm sorry."

"They love me too. We all went to the beach at Christmas, remember? This is my place now." He had a name now, a reputation. Hell, he had a bank account.

"Is that where you went? Sorry, I didn't really…." Gordy snorted. "Sorry."

"Dork. You were so damn busy you didn't notice I was gone, and I know it." Him? He had been dead. No one wanted to renovate at the holidays.

Gordy just laughed. "I'll notice this Christmas, I promise."

"I bet you will." Colby would guarantee that baby girl sleeping in the other room would assure it.

"Thanks for sharing all of that with me. You could have asked me to mind my own business. I'd have respected that."

"I ain't proud of it, but I was just needing a touch, you know? I wanted someone not me."

"Hey, I'm no one to judge. I just realized the other day that we've been… whatever we were before tonight, for over a year, even if we weren't sleeping together yet. Before you, though, I was either a one-night stand man, or I'd move on pretty quick. Hell, our first… well. That was amazing, but it wasn't one of my more gentlemanly moments either."

"Can I kiss you?" He knew they were talking, but talking was better with a little connection.

"Any time, cowboy." Gordy smiled at him.

He leaned forward, holding Gordon's gaze the whole time, caught in bright green. He wondered if it was going to be different, now that they knew they were in love.

Their lips pressed together, Gordy meeting him halfway with his usual strength and confidence, a little hungry, a little heat. That was just Gordy. That suited him down to the bone. After all, it was Gordy that he wanted. Not Gordon Lite.

He blinked when Gordy pulled away, but it was only long enough to take the wineglass out of Colby's hand and set it out of the way on the coffee table. "I'll take some more of that," Gordy told him, pressing Colby back into the couch, pinning him with his kiss.

Oh damn. He did love this, the way the hunger just showed up in a rush. He even liked forcing it to slow down, letting himself need.

Gordy's hands were starting to roam, slipping up under his T-shirt, hot palms sliding over his skin. "I'm getting ideas, cowboy, you with me?"

"Uh-huh. I am." His entire body responded, not just his cock.

His nipples went hard and tingled under Gordon's fingers, and Gordy laughed softly and then whispered darkly in his ear, "Come on, lover, let's go to bed."

"I would love to." Goddamn, he couldn't stop smiling. "Fuck, I feel like…. Yesterday I was scared I wasn't going to get to love on you again, and today? A whole new world."

Gordy helped him up off the couch with one steady arm. "You want the truth? I was worried. I didn't think there was any way you'd want this. And I'm not going to lie, Colby. I think we both have work to do. But I'm so ready to get my hands dirty."

Gordy steered him around the coffee table, laying kisses on his neck as they went.

Okay, so that sounded perverse and wonderful and more than a little wicked. He followed like they were dancing, two-stepping nice and easy to the music in their heads.

Gordon growled and bumped Colby with his chest. "Cute. Get your ass in the bedroom, twinkle toes."

"Bossy bossy. One day I'll teach you how to two-step, if you're nice."

"I already told you I'd like to learn." Gordy's voice was rough, and he was hustling Colby along, down the dark hallway toward his bedroom. "Some time when you haven't turned my prick to granite."

"Honey, if we're dancing and you're not hard?" He nipped Gordy's earlobe. "I'm doing something wrong."

That earned him a groan, one Colby could feel vibrate in Gordy's chest.

Gordy worked the buttons of his dress shirt open and let it slide off his shoulders as he crowded Colby into the bedroom. He spun Colby and pressed him back against the door, closed it, and turned the lock.

Gordon wasn't the only one with a diamond-hard prick. Hell, he ached, his balls so tight they'd squeak, and when Gordy pressed one leg between his thighs, giving him the pressure he needed, he did a little squeaking of his own.

"That's the stuff, cowboy. Let's get this shirt off." Colby raised his arms up, and Gordy slid the soft T-shirt over his head, tangling the fabric in Colby's fingers and pinning them to the door. He claimed Colby's mouth in a hard kiss and bit at Colby's lip.

"Hungry motherfucker. You make me need." He stretched up tall, his abs pulling tight. Gordy's eyes dropped to his belly, so he flexed again, showing off.

"Goddammit, look at you. You make me crazy." Gordy tossed the T-shirt in favor of running his fingers over Colby's belly, then went to work on his jeans. "Off." Gordon sounded a little winded.

He managed to open Gordon's slacks, his jeans, and grab ahold of both their cocks as soon as he fished them out.

Gordon gasped, and his hands landed flat against the wall on either side of Colby's shoulders. "Fuck, Colby. Yes."

This he knew Gordon liked. There was something about his hands that suited his lover down to the ground. He stroked them together, base to tip, using his thumb to drag over the sensitive tip of first his cock, then Gordon's.

He soaked in Gordon's sounds, another harsh gasp followed by a needy moan and "More."

Colby knew it was all Gordon could do not to buck right through his fingers, and he squeezed a little tighter, pulled a little faster.

Gordon reached down and started to roll Colby's nipples in warm fingers, first one and then the other. "Close," he breathed, lips right next to Colby's ear.

"Jesus. Little more, please. Just a little." He set to jacking them like he meant it.

Gordon nodded, but the son of a bitch gave Colby's nipple a pinch and a twist as incentive.

His eyes went wide, that sting making him go up on tiptoe, rock them both harder together.

"So easy." Gordon groaned, pressed Colby's shoulders back against the door and kissed him again, stealing his air.

Like that was news. He wanted Gordon more than his next breath.

Gordy lingered over that kiss a while, pulling back enough for each of them to get air now and then, but when he ended it, Colby could tell Gordy was about out of patience. He dropped a hand between them and started to curl his fingers around Colby's, but pulled them away quickly with a moan and pressed them into Colby's abs instead.

He fixed Colby with a stare, green eyes flashing. "Please, baby."

"Anything you want." Christ, that touch was like a brand, his own hand trying to start a friction fire on their pricks.

"Just need you to catch up, cowboy. Let me help." Gordy took hold of Colby's wrist, forcing him to go still. Then he dropped right to his knees and took Colby's cock into his mouth, that searing hand on Colby's abs staying right where it was.

His eyes were fixin' to pop out of his head. "Oh fuck. Fuck, honey."

Those were all the words he had in the world.

Gordy hummed at him, but he didn't let up. Seemed like the man was trying to suck Colby's brains right out his cock, and hell if it might not work.

"Gonna. I—please, Gordon!" He thought the goal was together, and he was hitting the edge of his control.

Gordon let him go and rocked back on his heels before standing up. "About time." He was grinning as he gently moved Colby's fingers back in place, giving them a squeeze. "I got ahead of you," he whispered. "Breathe. We're good now."

"Breathe. Right. Christ, love." He slammed their lips together, pushing them both toward the bed as his shaking hand worked them furiously.

"Okay, I'm going." Gordy moved backward smoothly, half moaning and half laughing into the kiss. "Jesus, babe."

"Need you." Gordon made him dizzy with it, made him reckless.

That ended Gordon's playing pretty damn quick. Gordy got a little grabby, and then next thing he knew, Colby was falling into bed and Gordy was dragging his jeans the rest of the way off.

Together they got themselves butt naked, and Colby climbed up Gordon's body so they could fit together, get to rocking against each other like they meant it.

"Yeah." Gordon pulled Colby down by the back of his neck for a kiss and rolled his hips. The room filled with their sounds, grunts and groans, heavy breath and filthy words.

Better than that were the endearments, the whispered, furious promises that burned him to the ground.

"Colby. Please, baby, I'm… fuck!" Gordon's fingers dug into his hips hard enough to bruise. "Please."

He threw his head back, throat working as he groaned, low and deep, spunk spraying from him.

Gordy sure was right there with him. He grunted and bucked, hot liquid mixing with Colby's and leaving them both sticky and spent.

Gordon's eyes were on him. "Jesus. That was fun," he said with a sigh and a low laugh. "You're a crazy cowboy."

"No. Magic. Remember?"

"Mm. How could I forget? Magic hands for sure." Gordy was gliding warm hands lightly over his skin. "And beautiful."

He knew better, but he'd take it.

"I'm too old to be rubbing off like a horny dog." Gordy stretched and groaned.

"Uh-huh. Poor old horny dog man."

"You're a little shit, mister." Gordon rolled him onto his back and kissed him. "Come on. I made that shower big enough for two for a reason. We need to be presentable in the morning."

"Yes, sir. We got a little girl to get to school." He kissed Gordon right on the nose. "Let's do this."

Chapter Twenty-One

"MORE COFFEE?" Gordon poured himself a second cup and hovered the pot over Colby's mug.

He'd made Olivia blueberry waffles, and she was munching away happily. Despite all the drama of the day before, she didn't seem nervous for her first day of school at all, now. Colby sat right next to her, eating his bacon, which seemed to be the way with breakfast for them, while Gordon hung out on the other side of the island where he could easily serve up more eggs or another waffle.

He'd struggled over what to wear, which was exactly as ridiculous as Colby told him it was, but that didn't change the fact that he wanted to look… right. Like a guy who gave a shit. Like a guy who had things under control. Like a guy who knew damn well he was going to be remembered. Even more ridiculous was that he'd settled on his usual casual wardrobe anyway—jeans and a button-down oxford—and he had a sports jacket in case the morning was chilly.

Colby seemed more relaxed. But Gordon knew there were a handful of ways to play this, and he needed to pick just the right one.

He blinked at Colby. "Sorry. Did you say yes?"

"Yes, please. You want I should cook some eggs for you? I will."

"Thanks, I'm good." Gordon filled his mug and set the pot back on the warmer. "How are your waffles, Liv?"

She nodded. "Mmm" was all she said because her mouth was full. Emma had taught her girl some manners, that was for sure.

"Good." He pulled out his phone and checked the time—again—and then stuck it back in his pocket. "You riding with me or taking your truck?"

"I'll ride with you. Parking is a challenge at best at a school, huh?"

"I would think." He could handle this. He had to handle this. He'd asked Colby to step up; he wasn't going to do anything less himself.

He sipped his coffee, watching Colby and Olivia chat. The two of them were adorable together. Colby really was pretty remarkable. It didn't get much worse than what happened to him—and then his family's reputation, their safety—that was a lot to put on the shoulders of a kid who just wanted….

Who just wanted to be loved. And a man who never believed he'd hear anyone say it.

Yep. He needed to play this right for sure. It was a hell of a lot more than just the first day of kindergarten.

"You guys ready?"

"I am. I am so ready to meet your teacher." Colby grinned at Liv. "Mrs. Copenhaver? Mrs. Copper?"

"Uncle Colby! She's Mrs. Collins."

"Yeah, Uncle Colby. Get it together." Gordy winked and gave Colby a pat on the ass on his way by. "Get your backpack, Olivia."

Olivia took off down the hall.

"You good?" Gordon asked, in that voice his mom used to use when she didn't want him to overhear. He leaned in and gave Colby a quick kiss.

"I am. She's in a good mood." Colby wasn't looking like he was in a bad mood either.

"Yes. Thank you for that."

"Okay!" Olivia arrived with the backpack on her shoulders.

Gordon looked at her. "You need your jacket, sweets."

"I don't want to wear it."

"Olivia, get your jacket, please."

"Uncle Gordy!"

He stared at her, trying out his best stern-dad look. He wanted to cheer when she turned around and marched back toward her room. It fucking worked. Wow.

"Nicely done," Colby murmured, finishing his coffee. "I do love the coffee in this joint."

"Only the best for love-interests. Speaking of which, I'll have to try that look out on you sometime."

"What look, honey?" Colby smiled at him, the expression warm, happy.

Gordon winked at him. "You know, the one that just made Olivia do exactly what I wanted."

Olivia reappeared in her jacket this time. "Ready!"

Gordon grabbed his keys and his wallet and opened the door. "Out you go!"

Olivia was skipping and singing, a totally different little girl from yesterday. Was that normal? Gordon shook his head and leaned close to Colby's ear. "I'm going to get whiplash trying to keep up with her, I swear to God."

"Always felt like that with my sisters. They changed fast as the weather."

"Come on, you guys!" Olivia called back to them.

"Right behind you, sweetie." Gordon grinned and hustled Colby out the door.

When they got downstairs, Colby helped Olivia into her car seat and buckled her in.

"Should be a pretty quick trip," he said, backing the Jeep out of the parking lot.

"Do you think they'll like me, Uncle Colby?"

"What's not to like, Little Bit? You're going to fit right in."

The simple way that Colby reassured her seemed to come so naturally to him. Gordon would have come up with some dissertation on being new, or being brave or something—or worse, just said "Yes," and that wouldn't have been reassuring at all. No wonder she was such a basket case yesterday. He probably should have just taken her out for ice cream.

Lesson learned. Or learning. Constantly.

He smiled over at Colby and put his hand on Colby's knee, liking the cowboy in his Jeep. "You look good over there in my passenger seat."

"You got a nice Jeep, honey. Cushy."

"You like it? Thanks. It's fun to drive. I have a soft top I'll put on in a couple of weeks. We could take her out with the top down." He knew he sounded like he was seventeen, and he was okay with that.

"It's going to be perfect weather for it. Miss Liv hasn't ever been camping, can you believe it?"

"Oh. Well… that's not so unusual." He'd been camping maybe twice in his life. Unless you counted that skinny-dipping thing in college, but that wasn't really camping, that was more like passing out in the woods.

"Maybe, but we're up in the most beautiful place on earth. We should wallow in it."

"I'm up for some wallowing." The parking lot at Whittier Elementary was a nightmare. Cars and kids and school busses… and more kids. "Good Lord."

Gordon managed to weave his way through the chaos and lucked into parking as a woman in an eco-friendly something-or-other pulled out of her space.

"Right on."

"You ready for this, Little Bit?" Colby asked, and he looked in the rearview, seeing the hint of tears.

"What if they want to know about Mommy?"

Gordy shot Colby a quick look—part "I got this" and part "stop me if I say anything stupid"—and slid out of the front seat. He opened the back door and unlocked Olivia's seat belt.

"Well, you only have to tell your friends what you want them to know. If you don't want to say she's… uh." Oh God, that started out so well, and now that fucking lump in his throat and ache in his chest was back. Just like that. He swallowed and concentrated on Liv.

"If you don't want to say she's gone, sweetie, then you can just say that you're living with your Uncle Gordon. Right? That's the truth."

Thank God for the cowboy. Part of him wondered what she told kids if they asked about her father. Whoever he was.

"Your mom would be so proud of how brave you're going to be today."

Colby nodded, that hat brim bobbing. "Your Uncle Gordy is right on. You tell them you got folks that love you. That's what's important."

"Okay." Liv got up on her knees in the car seat and wrapped her arms around Gordon's neck. He hugged her back, giving her a tight squeeze. "I do love you, kiddo."

"I love you too, Uncle Gordy." Olivia's tone was all teenager. That statement could so easily have been followed by "Duh." She wiggled to be let down, but he hung on just another second, not ready to let go. "Uncle Gordon! Don't forget my backpack!"

"Right." He set her down and pulled the backpack out of the back seat, then waited for Colby to join them. "It's way too early for me to start drinking, isn't it?"

"Totally." Colby reached down and took Olivia's hand. "Lead on, MacDuff."

"It's Olivia."

Gordon laughed. There was no way he was going to keep up with this one. "Five going on fifteen."

They made their way up the sidewalk and into the school, Olivia leading the way like she owned the place.

"It's not...? I think it's this way, Liv."

"No, it's over here."

Gordon shrugged and followed her. "Oh, look. You're right." He looked at Colby. "She's right."

"It's her school, Uncle Gordy." Colby shot him a shit-eating grin.

"You ain't kiddin'."

Mrs. Collins met them at the classroom door. "Good morning, Olivia. You look so pretty."

"Thank you." Olivia beamed at her.

"Good morning, Mr. James. And...?" She looked at Colby curiously.

"Oh." Gordon heard his cue loud and clear. It was probably good that Olivia had him so distracted, because he didn't have time to rethink anything. "This is my boyfriend, Colby McBride. Colby, this is Mrs. Collins."

"Pleased to meet you, ma'am." Colby held out his hand, easy as anything, and shook. "I imagine I'll be picking Miss Olivia up in the afternoons a lot. I work early, and Gordon has a restaurant."

He hadn't asked, and Colby hadn't offered officially either. Colby had just taken that on. Gordon let it be for now, the gesture leaving him as winded as ever by Colby's generous spirit.

"Make sure to put Mr. McBride on the approved pickup list, okay? You can do it online on the school portal."

Gordon nodded. "Will do. Thanks."

"Okay, Olivia. Say goodbye to your uncle and Mr. McBride and let's get you inside."

"He's Uncle Colby," Olivia corrected her teacher.

"Oh. Got it." She smiled.

Olivia hugged Colby first. "Bye."

"Bye, Little Bit. Have a great day. I love you."

She let him go and then hugged Gordon tight.

"You be good, listen to Mrs. Collins. Have fun."

"I will. Bye." She kissed his cheek and disappeared into the classroom.

"We'll try for a full day. I'll call your cell if I think she needs a break." Mrs. Collins gave a little wave. "Have a great day."

"Thanks." He watched the door close. "Well, she's off."

"You did good, Uncle Gordy." Colby's eyes were twinkling, and Gordon was tempted to swat that tight little cowboy butt. Probably not the place, but the temptation….

"Why, thank you, Uncle Colby. Do I get a cookie?" Gordon winked at him and then started back toward his Jeep.

"If I didn't have to work, man, I'd show you cookie." The words were soft, heated.

Gordon knew better than to look at Colby. His self-control was challenged as it was just imagining those blue eyes going dark. "Well. That ought to give us both something to think about today." He started up the Jeep and changed the subject before Colby could reply. "I guess I'll go to the office and put your name on the approved pickup list, huh?"

"I just know how most afternoons you'll be hip-deep in the restaurant and I'll be off. Just like I should have been at work two hours ago."

"You're right, I will be." Wednesday to Saturday he pretty much lived at his restaurants. "But are you sure you want to do that? I mean, I planned to hire someone…."

"Can we give it a couple days? See what's what? You're gonna have to figure something for the summertime one way or the other, but maybe a day school where she can make friends instead?" Colby shrugged. "I don't know what's right, but we get on just fine."

"Yeah. I'm good with that. Liv will be happy to have you around for sure. We're closed on Mondays, and Tuesdays are light, so there's that. And Kaitlin sent me an email—Oscar's girlfriend? She sent a couple of links to summer programs."

This conversation was so surreal. Two weeks ago his life was so… simple. And now he had a kid and a boyfriend and was talking about summer camp? Part of him, a really big part, was trying not to hyperventilate. But Colby seemed pretty well adjusted, considering, and the fact was, panic was a luxury he didn't have the time or the energy for.

"Good deal." Colby rolled his shoulders, the seams of his Western shirt creaking. "Who knows? Maybe I'll teach her how to lay tile."

"She'd be learning from the best." Gordon turned into the lot at Delmara and pulled around back to park next to Colby's truck. "Thanks for working this out. I know it meant a lot to Olivia."

And to him, but the level at which he was starting to depend on Colby was getting a little uncomfortable, so he didn't say it.

"She's just looking for her normal." Colby sighed softly. "Man, I don't want to go, but I gotta. You mind if I run up and change real quick?"

"Yeah, I hear you, but work is work. Go right on up." Gordon handed him his keys. "Just drop those by my office on your way out. Oh, and work late or head home or whatever you need to do later; I've got Liv today." It was only Tuesday, he could swing it.

"Sure man. Thanks." Colby grabbed a T-shirt out of a laundry basket in the back seat of his cab, then jogged up the stairs to his place.

His boyfriend was living out of a fucking laundry basket in the back seat of a truck. Gordon let that thought sink in as he made his way to his office. That was going to take more thinking than he had the bandwidth for this afternoon, but he was starting to realize just how much he'd turned Colby's life on its ear.

Fuck. No pressure there at all, was there?

About five minutes later, he heard a quick knock on his office door, Colby standing there in his trashed-out work clothes and boots. "Here's your keys, honey. Give me a call, let me know how Liv's first day was?"

"Will do. But hey." Gordon hopped up from his desk to meet Colby, tugging him into a kiss by his T-shirt collar. "I wasn't saying don't come by if you want to. I was just saying take care of you if you need to. I can get away early to get the little girl. Door's always open for you."

He got a smile, warm and bright as the sun. "Well, I appreciate it, honey. I surely do."

"Good." He let go of Colby's collar and took his keys. "Work hard. Think of me often." He winked.

"I can do that. Y'all… y'all want to go out and get pizza tonight? Celebrate her first day?"

That's how it's done, cowboy. Gordon smiled. "If we can have ice cream too, I'm in."

Dinner out. Lord. He could handle that, right?

"Hell, we can go to BJ's and get one of those Pizookie deals. Chocolate chip cookie hot from the oven with ice cream. Uhn."

"Well, that's three days at the gym right there, but I guess Liv is worth it." He gave Colby that pat on the ass he'd wanted to earlier. "Do not let me be the reason you lose your job. Text me when you leave work."

"Will do." Colby headed out, whistling something he didn't recognize.

Was this a date? Gordon didn't date. He was probably twenty-five the last time he went on a date, and that was a decade ago. The whole relationship thing he could handle. Mostly. Maybe. But dates?

"Oscar's going to eat this up with a spoon."

Chapter Twenty-Two

"Is THIS where you live, Uncle Colby?"

"Uh-huh. I just have to get some clothes for the weekend and stuff. You want to come in for a second, Little Bit?"

She looked at the ancient travel trailer with doubt. "It's old."

"Yes, ma'am, but it ain't scary inside. Not a bit. Come see." He didn't imagine she'd been in a lot of travel trailers in Boston. His little place might be ancient and basically a tin can with a door, but it was clean enough that if his momma showed, he could open the door to her. "There's a dining table that folds up and a chair that turns into a bed."

Olivia climbed the step up into the trailer and looked around. She walked to one end and then the other, and then sat in a chair and swung her feet. "It's little. How come your house has wheels?"

"So that I can move it if I need to." He packed a little weekend bag with pajama bottoms, T-shirts, and a pair of jeans.

"Where you gonna move it? Closer to Uncle Gordon?" She got up on her knees on the chair and peered into his bag.

"Do you like my shirts? Will they work for our weekend?"

"I think so. I like the blue. It matches your eyes. And the green matches mine!"

"There you go. You want my cartoon DVDs to take home?"

"Oooh. Okay! What'ya got?" She bounced and smiled at him.

It had been a couple of weeks, and Liv was settling in darn well at school. She definitely had Gordy's drive, and she was friendly as anything. Mrs. Collins said that she hadn't made any close friends yet, but she was hanging out a little with everybody, and Colby figured that was just fine.

He thought he was settling in with Gordon pretty damn well too. He'd spent every evening but Monday at Gordy's place, and the one evening they'd put Liv down together and he'd left to let them both have some space? Liv'd woken up convinced her Uncle Colby was dead, and he'd had to drive back across town. That had been the last night he'd slept out here.

He'd been trying to work out when they could go up overnight to the mountains—he missed them some. But Gordy's schedule was crazy on the weekends, and he had to work on Mondays. He'd figure it—just had to keep his eyes open.

Olivia stuffed a bunch of DVDs in his bag. "I took the ones I wanted, okay? I liked the bunny ones." She hopped down off the chair. "Can we go home now?"

"We can. You want to see if we can sneak in and give Uncle Gordy a kiss before the restaurant opens? We'll have to be super quick."

"Yes, I want to. Can we have dinner there?"

"I don't think so. It's Friday, and Fridays and Saturdays are whoa busy, remember? I thought maybe we could order pizza tonight and plan tomorrow and Sunday's supper together. Tomorrow's library day."

"I don't want pizza. Please, can we eat downstairs? I'll be good. Please?" She jumped out of his trailer and waited for him, green eyes looking just like Gordy's in the fading light.

"Honey, we don't have a reservation, and your Uncle Gordy will be nuts. I'm sorry." He hated refusing her, but it was what it was.

She crossed her arms and huffed at him, eyes flashing, and then turned and stomped over to his truck. "I still don't want pizza."

"Okay. We don't have to have pizza. What sounds good to you?" He opened the truck door for her to hop up.

She climbed in and let him do up her buckles. "Um. Spaghetti? And sauce. And broccoli. And bread. Why is Uncle Gordy nuts? He'd be happy to see me! We could eat there."

"I mean nuts in that busy way. Do you know what reservations are?"

She crossed her arms again. "No."

"Ah. Okay, when you got a fancy restaurant like Gordy's, everybody wants in. Like everyone. So, you have to call, like days in advance, and ask for a table on Friday night." He gave her the big, impressed eyes.

"Days?" She gave him wide eyes right back.

"I know, right? Days! So, your Uncle Gordy is going to be dealing with all these folks that have waited days to get in. All those tables are reserved for people. If you want to eat at the restaurant, we should ask and then go on a day that's quieter. Maybe then we could meet people, see neat things." *Come on, Little Bit. I'm trying hard to make this easy.* Not that she cared, he knew, but he could try.

She eyed him for a bit, and he got the feeling that her five-year-old mind was onto him, but she nodded finally and relaxed into her seat. "Okay."

Then she got him. "Promise?"

"Yes." He hadn't said anything that would get him in trouble. He hoped.

The drive back into town was long on a Friday night, the traffic pretty heavy. He probably should have thought of that before he brought Liv out to his place, but he needed to pick up stuff. He'd remember next time and just do his damn laundry at Gordy's instead.

Olivia was good and hungry by the time they'd made it back to the restaurant, and the place was hopping, but she wasn't warming up to his suggestion that Gordy would be too busy to give her a kiss good night, and she was fixin' to pitch a fit in the parking lot.

"It's just a kiss! Everybody has time for a kiss."

"Okay, let me text him, all right? Maybe he can meet us for half a second." He shot Gordy a text.

she needs a kiss. pls.

He waited for a response and it didn't take that long, maybe a minute, but with Liv steaming up the sidewalk, it seemed like forever.

office in 5

"Okay, we're going to Uncle Gordy's office. One kiss and no fussing, deal?"

"Okay." The twerp was smiling, since she got her way, and skipped ahead of him through the back entrance.

He might have to string her up by her toenails. Lord, if he had a dime for every time his momma had threatened that....

Gordon's office was empty when they got there, and Liv went straight over to what she called "her corner" and plopped down in a little red beanbag chair. Gordy had given her the bottom shelf of a bookcase to fill up, and she had a couple of stuffed friends that lived over there as well.

He went to sit in the window and let the late afternoon sun soak into him.

They waited a heck of a lot more than five minutes, but Gordy did show. He came busting through his office door, cut his eyes at Colby, and then seemed to find a smile for Olivia.

"Hey, sweetie. You comfy?"

She ran right over to him. "Uncle Gordy!"

Gordon scooped her up in his arms. "Whoa, pumpkin, you okay?"

"I wanted to eat in your restaurant tonight, but Uncle Colby says no."

"Oh." Gordon looked over at Colby again, hugging Olivia against his shoulder. "Well, he's right, pumpkin. I don't have a single seat for you tonight. Not one."

"'Cause of the restervations? 'Cause you're famous?"

Colby stared Gordon down, daring him to argue.

Gordon raised an eyebrow at him but played along. "Well, uh… I don't think I'm famous, but yes, because of the reservations." He set her down and smiled at her. "Your Uncle Colby looks awfully hungry. Haven't you fed him yet?"

"No. He was going to take me to pizza, but I didn't want pizza." She pouted mightily. "I don't like him today."

Gordon snorted. "No? Why not?"

"He lives in a weird little house with wheels. That's not why, though. I like that. I'm just grumpy today."

She must get that from Gordon's side of the family.

"His house sounds pretty cool to me. Don't you be grumpy at your Uncle Colby. He busts his behind for you, am I right?" He leaned down to her level. "Now, give me that kiss, sweetie, because I have to get back to work or those people with reservations are going to be mad."

"Love you!" She kissed him with a smack. "We'll save some dinner for you."

"Love you too, Liv. You two take very good care of me." Gordy straightened up his jacket and tie and ran his fingers through his hair, giving it a once-over in the mirror by the door. He gave Colby a wave and a wink before heading back to work. "Love you, Uncle Colby. Text me if you need something special from the bar later."

"You rock, honey." He waited until Gordy was gone, then tilted his head. "You want supper?"

Olivia smiled at him sweetly and slipped her hand into his. "Yes, please. Can we still have spaghetti?"

"Sure, Little Bit. You want to make it together or order out?" Either way, he could have himself a beer.

"Either one is okay. What do you want to do?"

Well, all right, then. Score one for Uncle Gordy.

"Let's order something." He leaned in like he was sharing a secret. "That way? No dishes!"

"More time for bunny cartoons!" She hurried up the steps to the apartment. "Ask for garlic bread too?"

"I can do that. I think I want their lasagna and a salad."

"Can I have your tomatoes? I love the little tomatoes."

He laughed, like he didn't know that. He hadn't gotten to eat a single tomato since Gordy had brought Liv home. "I guess you can, yes."

Colby used his very own key to get in the door. Every time he used it now, he had a good chuckle at what a thing it had been to get Gordon to give it to him in the first place. He'd had about enough of grabbing Gordon's keys out of his desk every time he brought Liv home. All it took was driving off to work just once with them in his truck to get his point across.

Well, darn. He'd just been in such a hurry. How forgetful of him.

Lord, he could be a shit. "Go put your stuff away, Little Bit. You got papers to be signed?"

"I have a story I have to read out loud and you have to sign that I read it." She stopped and pulled a page out of her backpack and set it on the coffee table, then headed down the hall to her room.

He grabbed a beer from the fridge, ordering supper on his phone. God, he loved technology. Loved it.

Spaghetti. Lasagna. Salad. Garlic bread. Oh, a pizza for later to share with Mr. Restaurant. He loved feeding Gordy pizza.

Olivia joined him in the kitchen, grabbed a plastic cup off the counter, and filled it with water from the door of the fridge. "Friday night means tomorrow you'll still be here when I wake up," she commented after a huge gulp of water.

Colby watched her as she took another sip. The thing about Liv was she didn't miss a thing. And something along those lines was pretty much never just chit-chat.

"Friday night means tomorrow is our day together. And library day. And grocery day." He hoped Liv understood he liked spending time with her.

She nodded and leaned on him. "I love library day. But Uncle Gordon has to work the whole day. He never takes me to the library."

"Saturdays are busy for him." He wasn't sure what to say. It wasn't going to change.

"Yeah. He works all the time." She shrugged. "I like our Saturdays. I'm going to take out three books tomorrow."

She just thought that because he worked while she was at school and Gordon worked while she wasn't. Poor baby girl.

"Wow. Three? You're going to be reading for days."

Liv went and plopped on the couch, and she read her homework out loud to Colby while they waited for the food to be delivered. He was signing her paper just as the food arrived.

Olivia got the door, and Colby grabbed the food, and they ate on the floor in the living room, watching one of Colby's Bugs Bunny DVDs and giggling their heads off.

"The boy bunny is dressing up like a girl! He has boobies on!"

"He's trying to trick Elmer, honey." He wasn't ready to go into transgender, which he didn't think this was, or cross-dressing, which he was pretty sure this might be, but not in a good way.

"Well, that's silly." Liv rolled her eyes. "He's pretending he's a girl to get Elmer to like him?"

"Kinda. You remember before Bugs rides up on the fat horse? Elmer was fixin' to kill him. Now Elmer thinks he's a pretty girl, not a rabbit." Why was this so hard? He didn't remember stressing the details when he was a little boy.

Olivia nodded. "I get it. Because Elmer likes girls."

"Right." It was right, right? Lord. This whole raising up little people to be big was tough.

"Uncle Gordon likes boys. So that wouldn't work on him."

"Nope. Bugs'd have to dress up like a cowboy to get him." The tighter Wranglers, the better.

"Like a magic cowboy?" She leaned on him.

"Uh-huh. Like a magic cowboy." He grinned, letting himself relax a little. A little food, a little Bugs, and a kiss from Gordy seemed to be today's cure-all.

"I like magic cowboys too." Liv climbed up and kissed his cheek. "Oh no! The bunny lost her—uh, his—hat! And her hair!"

"Oops! I hate when that happens!"

Liv looked at him and started giggling again, flopping over in his lap.

After the DVD ended, they took off for a bath and bedtime. It was an early night because Olivia could barely keep her eyes open in the tub. A nearly full week at school had worn her butt out, and they didn't even get to the bedtime story.

He tucked her in, kissed her forehead. "Love you, Bit."

Then he went to pick up and shower, put on clothes that were soft and comfy, and settle in on the sofa and rest his bones.

He was in the middle of another Bugs Bunny episode and at the tail end of his one and only beer for the evening when his phone chirped at him.

Evening any better? Gordy. Taking a second to say hey.

She's just tired. Sound asleep already. Busy night?

Slammed. Even Oscar's tie is twisted.

Damn. He'd pay to see that.

Don't work too hard. He was happy up here, watching TV and dozing.

Too late. Don't wait up. Love u.

Love u.

Okay. That. That right there. That was why he was here and happy and planning to do the library and grocery shopping tomorrow instead of heading up into the mountains.

Lord have mercy, he was hooked through the balls.

Chapter Twenty-Three

THERE WERE days when Gordon wished he had the pickup shift for Olivia instead of drop-off. Colby was up and out early every morning; the cowboy had quiet feet and didn't even wake him most of the time. He was on his own for the morning shift, getting the girl up, dressed, fed, and out the door on time. The school said next year she'd have a bus, but it was too late in the year to get her into the rotation now, so off they'd go in the Jeep, down to that nightmare circus that passed for a parking lot at school.

This morning he'd forgotten his travel mug, so caffeine didn't happen until he got home. That made the parking lot something closer to the seventh circle of hell.

And it was only Monday.

And—if little Ginny's mommy didn't stop asking for a playdate-slash-wine date... ugh. Maybe when she asked tomorrow, he'd start talking about falsettos or Barbra Streisand and see if she got the hint.

But he'd managed to get a shower and pour a second cup of coffee into his travel mug before he headed out to run some errands, and it was a perfect spring morning.

Shades on, top down, Red Sox cap keeping the glare out—life was good.

He got a haircut, picked up his case of wine, dropped off his dry cleaning, and stopped by the hardware store for a couple of boxes of those weird lightbulbs that fit in the sconces behind the bar. He kept his appointment with the architect he'd been talking to about the dining room redesign, signed off on a draft budget, and got a couple of drawings to show Colby.

He really hoped Colby was into the job. He couldn't imagine anyone else doing it. He'd show his lover the plans tonight.

He was just thinking about lunch when his phone rang, and he frowned at the number.

"Hello?"

"Hello, Mr. James. This is Mrs. Albright, the school nurse at Whittier Elementary. Don't panic, Olivia's okay."

Don't panic? "Is she sick?"

"No, Mr. James, I'm afraid it's a little bit more serious than that. Olivia was climbing on the monkey bars on the playground at lunch, and she fell and landed a little funny. I think it's possible she's broken her wrist."

"Broken?" *What the hell?* It was a broken wrist. Why was his heart pounding?

"Yes, sir. I think you should—"

"I'll be right there." He hung up the phone and texted Colby.

Liv broke wrist, picking her up. Meet me at ER?

He didn't wait for a reply; he just jumped in his Jeep and took off for the school.

By the time he pulled up in front, Colby's text of *Community or Foothills* was in.

Community

Onmywayin10

tks

Okay. Cool.

Gordon took a deep breath, but he still headed into the school at a good clip. He was shown to the nurse's office by a security guard.

"Uncle Gordy! I falled!" Christ, she could squeal. "I falled down!"

"I heard, pumpkin. Let me see your arm." Not that there was much to see—it was all wrapped up in ice.

"It's swollen bad enough that I just can't tell what's going on in there. I decided better safe than sorry." The nurse sounded very calm, but then she would be, wouldn't she? Liv wasn't her daughter— niece. Whatever.

"Absolutely. Come on, do you want me to carry you?"

"Where's Uncle Colby?"

"He's on his way. He's going to meet us at the hospital." He picked Olivia up, and she dropped her head on his shoulder. He looked at the nurse. "Do I need to sign her out or something?"

"With security at the front desk."

"Right. Thank you, Mrs.… uh—"

"Albright."

"Mrs. Albright. Thanks."

Gordon was pretty sure he remembered to stop and sign Olivia out, but the next thing he really knew, they were halfway to the hospital. Olivia was very quiet in the back seat. All he heard was little sniffles and sighs. "We're almost there, sweetie."

"It hurts. Are you mad at me?"

"Mad at you? No, baby. I'm worried about you." A lot. A lot more than he thought was really reasonable for a broken wrist.

"I falled on the playground. Did you ever do that?"

"Oh, man." Had he ever. "Yes. In fact, I did exactly what you did, only I fell on my shoulder and I broke my collarbone. It hurt. Does your arm hurt badly, sweetie?"

He might have cut that last light a little close. Oh well, let him get pulled over. He'd ask for a fucking escort.

"Uncle Colby says I'm just like you. Guess he's right. Marisa's birthday party is Saturday. I can still go, right?"

She was just like him sometimes, although falling off the monkey bars didn't seem like something to emulate.

"You can still go. Promise." It wasn't a pool party, was it? He'd have to ask for a waterproof cast. Maybe he should anyway—baths and stuff.

"Okay. We're here." He parked in the ER lot, not as close as he'd like. God, there were a bunch of cars; he hoped it wasn't ridiculously busy.

"Are they going to give me a shot? I don't want a shot."

Oh. Shit. Would they? Christ, he had no idea. A shot of what? Tetanus maybe? "I don't think so, Liv. But I can't promise."

He scooped her right out of the back seat and carried her in through the sliding doors with Olivia cradling her arm against him. It did look pretty swollen, but it wasn't really purple or anything. Much.

He set her down carefully at the check-in desk, and his phone buzzed.

Lost a tire.

What? What the actual fuck?

"Can I help you?"

r u serious??

"Sir?"

"Oh. Sorry, yes. My niece fell off the monkey bars and hurt her wrist. The nurse said she thought maybe it was broken."

The woman behind the counter handed him a clipboard. "Fill these out, please."

He blinked at the paperwork. "All of that?"

"Yes, sir."

"Okay...." Christ.

No. I'm joking.

The picture of Colby's truck half-in and half-out of a ditch, boxes of tile spilled out, tire shredded, showed up next.

"What's that? Where's Uncle Colby? It hurts, Uncle Gordy!"

"Holy shit." He hugged Olivia to his leg and stared at the picture. That wasn't "lost a tire." That was lost a tire, maybe an axle, and likely a full day's pay worth of tile. Or more. "Fuck."

"You said a cuss. You have to put two dollars in the jar for our bacation."

"What?"

"Uncle Colby says we can have a bacation this summer to somewhere fun. He puts a dollar in the jar when he says a cuss, and he says if I find money in his shirt pocket, it can go in the jar too."

"Sure, sure."

r u ok?

Wait. He didn't have time for a summer vacation. Summer was tourist season. Summer was when he was renovating the back of the dining room, while he had all the outdoor patios open. Colby couldn't go making vacation promises without checking with him first.

"Why don't you go sit down and fill that out, sir."

Fuck. He snatched the clipboard off the counter, took Olivia's good hand in his, and took a seat, only just then noticing how busy the place was. Shit.

"Are they going to fix my hand? Is it going to fall off? Am I going to play on the monkey bars again?"

Okay. Get a grip, James.

"Baby, I have broken my collarbone, my arm, my right foot, and I had surgery on my knee. I'm still running around like crazy. You're going to be just fine. I know it hurts, though. I'm sorry. But they'll fix you right up." If he ever got the fucking paperwork done.

Gordon picked up the pen, watching his phone out of one eye for a reply from Colby. He wasn't dead, right? You can't text pictures if you're dead.

Pissed off. Fine. Jackass ran me off road. They're towing my truck. Cop says he'll drop me at hospital.

Okay. He could deal with Colby in person soon. Fine. Good. He texted back *love u* and left everything else for later.

An eternity went by while Gordon filled out the paperwork and the ice Mrs. Albright had given Olivia melted down to a bag of warm water. Finally he stood up, set the clipboard back on the counter, and dropped his insurance card and his driver's license on top.

"Can she get seen? She's just swelling up out here."

"Are you the father?"

"I'm her legal guardian. I want this little girl seen."

"She's in the queue, sir. We'll just need your paperwork."

"My what?"

"Proof of guardianship. Power of attorney?"

His… shit. The lawyer did give him something. Power of attorney, right. Where the hell was it?

"What if I don't have it with me?"

"We can call one of her parents and—"

"Look. I want you to get her in there with someone. Now."

"I have to have permission to—"

"She's got a possibly broken wrist! She's five! Call the goddamn school and ask them!"

"Let me get my supervisor."

Gordon snorted and shook his head. Supervisor. He pulled out his phone and dialed the attorney in Boston. It was still business hours out there. Barely.

"Lancer, Harmon, and Yates."

"Yes, this is Gordon James calling for Chuck. Is he available? This is an honest emergency."

"Uh. One moment, please."

Not five minutes later, Chuck had faxed the letter to the hospital and emailed a copy to Gordon as well. But Olivia still hadn't been seen, and he was starting to get worried about Colby.

And the supervisor turned out to be a security guard.

He groaned. "Oh, for fuck's sake—"

"What's going on?" Colby's voice cut through the chaos. "Why isn't she in the back yet? Are y'all crazy? She's only a baby girl!" Colby picked Liv up with a wince and whispered something in her ear.

Almost immediately, Olivia started screaming. "It *hurts*! Help me! It hurts so bad!"

"Olivia Rylan James!" Gordon barked. "That's enough." He looked at Colby. "And you take a deep breath, cowboy."

Colby winked at him through Liv's hair, and Olivia started wailing again. "Please, y'all? Cain't you help her out?"

That drawl suddenly was ten times stronger.

"Her guardian—"

"Uncle. I'm her fucking uncle."

"Her uncle didn't tell me she was in so much pain." The woman glared at Gordon and waved Colby and Olivia through a set of swinging doors.

"You have got to be kidding me," Gordon whispered under his breath, following them. Colby hadn't shown an ID; he hadn't been asked for a fucking letter, nothing. He just turned on the Texas and that fucking irresistible smile.

Gordon had to grin, though, watching that woman get played.

Colby set Olivia down and looked at her. "You 'member that thing I told you, girl? About the squeaky wheel and the grease? That's what that story's about."

"You have no idea what I went through before…." He looked at Colby. "Never mind. Come here." He grabbed Colby's collar and pulled him into a hug. "You're okay, you're sure?"

"Sore. Gonna have some bruises. No worries. Sorry it took me so damn long to get here."

"Shut up." Gordon let him go reluctantly, and he didn't get a chance to say anything else because there were doctors and X-rays and things happening.

Colby stood there, quiet and still, watching everything that was going on, making sure to stay out of the way. Gordy was busy with Olivia, but he was keeping an eye on his cowboy too. He made sure to find a time or two to give Colby's shoulder a squeeze.

As it turned out, the wrist was sprained, not broken. Olivia would have to spend a couple of weeks in a bright pink removable brace and she should be good as new. They got sent away with a bottle of children's pain reliever.

"I'm thinking leftovers or takeout for dinner."

"Takeout sounds good. I don't suppose I can bum a ride?"

What?

Okay, that was either a joke or Colby was in shock. Or both. He knew Colby had to have a lot on his mind.

"Sorry, you're all dirty. You can Uber it." Gordon grinned at him and caught Colby's eyes. He wanted to kiss that cowboy, but… public sidewalk, ER full of people, Olivia.

Kindergarten teachers he could handle. The whole of Boulder? That was another story.

"Do you need anything from your tra… uh, your place? Paperwork on the truck or anything? We could head out there first before the traffic gets bad."

"Nope, I had all the insurance shit in a folder where I could get to it."

"You cussed!"

Without a pause, Colby pulled out his wallet, then handed Liv a dollar. "I have to make a claim, but the police report has to show before I can really deal with it."

"You're a step ahead of me." Gordon opened his wallet, flashed a five-dollar bill in front of Colby's eyes with a smirk, and handed it to Olivia. "I didn't have my legal letter… guardianship, uh… power of attorney thing with me. I had to call the lawyer in Boston. Get on in folks."

He lifted Olivia into the Jeep and buckled her in.

"Oh, man. Maybe you need a business card with it on there? Is that even a thing?"

"Uncle Colby! I have dollars for our bacation!"

"Rock on, Little Bit. You're getting there."

He felt his back stiffen at the mention of the damn vacation. Not today. That one could wait.

"I have it in my phone, now. He emailed it to me." He glanced over at Colby. "I'll forward it to you, so you… you know. I don't think I have your email. Remind me at home."

"Sure. I'll text it to you."

Olivia crashed on the ride home, which was probably good for her, but who knew what that meant for the rest of the evening. Gordon scooped her up, leaving everything, including the wine, in the back of his

Jeep for now. Colby wasn't going to be up for a discussion about the restaurant for a few days at least, anyway.

Liv stayed asleep as Gordon set her down in her bed. He tucked her in with Jessica and made his way back out to the living room.

Colby was standing at the window, face to the sun, eyes closed. There was this hint of... not fragility, just a hum of tension, like a high wire.

There was a lot to say—he wanted to help. He would help. But for now, he just wanted Colby to know he was there.

Gordon moved up behind him and wrapped his arms around Colby's waist, pulled him in close, and just waited to find out what the man needed from him.

"Hey. How's she doing? How're you?"

"She's asleep. Tell me what you're thinking."

"I'm thinking that—" Colby sighed softly, then tightened his lips for a second. "I'm thinking that it's got to be five o'clock somewhere."

"Mhm." Gordon kissed him behind the ear and breathed in some of that hardworking Colby scent. He just couldn't get enough of it. "Choose your poison. Tequila, whiskey, beer...? Just don't ask me for anything fancy. I'm a lousy bartender."

"There ain't a thing fancy about me, honey. I'm a beer man. I'm hoping it won't be long to patch up my truck." Colby leaned back a little harder, and Gordon could feel the way Colby trembled against him.

He let the beer wait and tightened his hold on his cowboy. "Here's what we're gonna do. You'll let your boss know you'll be a little late in the morning. We'll drop off Liv and then go get you a rental. Then we'll swing by the shop and see what the deal is with the repair, transfer the load from your truck, and figure out what needs replacing. Then you'll go to work, and I'll place the order for you."

This he was good at. Logistics. Solving problems. And he even had time tomorrow. Thank God this all happened on a Monday.

Colby blinked at him. "I was still stalled at Liv was at the ER."

Yeah, but who had gotten Olivia in the room with a doctor?

"Liv's got a sprained wrist. It's not even her right hand, and she's fast asleep. She'll milk it for whatever she can at breakfast." He was a little more worried than that all sounded, but he needed to help Colby process.

He had a bad feeling about Colby's truck too. That was a heavy load that followed him into that ditch. If the front axle went, the truck was toast.

"So. A beer?"

"Yes, please. I'm going to get my boots off."

He watched Colby walk back toward the bedroom, the whole look of his lover just a little off.

Gordon stared at the empty hallway for a bit after Colby disappeared into the bedroom, trying to hit on just what was making Colby's shoulders sag. He sighed and got two beers from the fridge and a couple of slices of cold leftover pizza.

Colby wasn't that complicated, really, was he? Gordon sat on the couch and took a bite of the pizza.

It seemed like it took forever, but Colby came back, sat down close, and reached for his beer. "I sure got me some bruises, honey. Tomorrow's gonna suck."

Gordon raised an eyebrow. Colby hadn't made it sound like it was that bad at the hospital, or Gordon would have made sure he got looked at too. "Maybe you should give your body a rest tomorrow."

"Maybe, yeah. We'll see how it goes. I gotta make some calls."

"Can I see? Show me the worst of it."

Colby opened his shirt, exposing a slashed circle of raw bruises from the seat belt and the steering wheel. They weren't black-and-blue yet, but it was coming. Damn.

Gordon winced. Hopefully none of that went deeper than skin and muscle. "Jesus, babe. You can't work like that. Not tomorrow. Maybe not all week." He shifted around so he could search those blue eyes. "Listen. I'm a very independent guy, and there's nothing I hate more than someone stepping in where I don't want them. I get that you probably just want me to nod and let you handle this. But I can help if you let me. I can make a couple of calls and find someone to cover that job for you."

"You're a good man." Colby smiled for him, and he could see the strain there, the pain, now that he knew what he was looking at. "Let me think on it. Right now I'm a little rattled."

Okay. He knew exactly what that meant, even as polite as it was. Colby wasn't ready for help, and that was fine. For now. Gordon sat back on the couch again with his beer and rested a hand on Colby's knee. "Take all the time you need, cowboy. But I let one too many members of my family down. I'm not letting you fall, you got me?"

"Thank you. My daddy says never to make a decision when you're messed up. Take a breath. Stop. Then figure your shit out."

"Sounds like a smart guy." He leaned into Colby gently. "What would your mom be doing right now? Because I think you need to put some ice on those ribs."

"My momma would be hunting some son of a bitch with her shotgun for hurting her baby. She's fierce."

"Ha!" Gordon laughed, but interestingly, he was thinking something similar. Like, what exactly Colby meant when he said he'd been run off the road. "I really need to meet these people. I'm getting you ice," he said as he stood up. "You ready for another cold one?"

"Not yet, thank you. I'd love for you to meet them. They want to come up and take the travel trailer and spend a couple weeks in the mountains."

"Hey, that sounds great." Gordon filled up a gallon baggie with ice and wrapped it in a dishtowel. "I bet Liv would get a kick out of that too. Maybe they could take Olivia with them for a week or so." He wiggled his eyebrows at Colby and handed him the bag of ice.

"Oh, Lord. Momma would be all over that. Liv and I are planning a vacation to the zoo in Denver. I thought we could go one Monday this summer. See the bears."

"A vacation to the zoo?" *Hang on.* "Is that what the dollars she is collecting are for?" He sat next to Colby carefully and then helped him arrange the bag of ice.

"Yep." Colby hissed, then panted a second. "I thought that would be easy, low-key, but let her feel like she could plan it and all, you know? My sister says little stuff like that is good to teach them math."

Gordon chuckled. "Sounds great." *Good grief. A vacation to the zoo.* He should have known better. "Cold? Or hurts?"

"It's better. Don't take it away, huh? The ice?" Colby reached for him, held his hand. "Thought you'd like it. An easy fun day."

"Sure. I love bears." He tangled his fingers with Colby's. "Been a while since I've been over to Denver too."

"I used to go a lot. There's two-stepping at Charlie's on Colfax."

"Hm. Can't say I've ever been. I'm sure you're shocked. I used to drop into R&R once in a while, or I'd see who I could pick up at the Wrangler." Sundays were hopping at the Wrangler, and when Monday was your only full day off? He went where the men were.

"One day I'll teach you to two-step. You wait and see."

"I want to learn. I do. You're a little too beat-up right now, though. You want to tell me what happened?"

"I was coming out of the hotel, trying to get to y'all, and I cut this guy off. It was totally an accident, but he sure as shit didn't think so. He was honking, tailgating, then pulled in front of me. Finally I went to pull off, and he ran me off the road." Colby shook his head. "I mean, I get that he was pissed, but for fuck's sake."

Obviously not an accident. Colby was lucky he didn't get hurt worse. No wonder he was shook up. "What was he driving? You gave the police a description?"

"Blue GMC Sierra. Gave them a license plate number. You think my truck's gonna be okay?"

This seemed like a good moment to treat Colby exactly like the five-year-old sleeping in her bedroom. "Don't worry, babe. I'm sure they'll fix it right up for you."

What was he supposed to say? No, I think your truck is totaled? Because that would be news Colby might not be able to handle tonight. And maybe Gordon was wrong. He wasn't there; he only saw the picture, right?

"I hope so, honey. That front axle didn't look real happy." Colby lifted his hand and kissed his knuckles. "You need help carrying stuff in from the car?"

"Sure, you want to go get that case of wine out of the back for me?" Gordon snorted. "You are not moving from this couch, cowboy. Thank you."

Yeah, that front axle was toast. Fuck.

All due respect to Colby's dad, but there weren't any decisions to be made right now that could really wait until morning. If it were up to Gordon—*and it's not up to you*, he reminded himself—but if it were, he'd have made some calls and set up a replacement for Colby by now.

Colby wasn't going to be able to move in the morning without pain. There was no way he was going to be able to work this week. He wondered how much longer Colby was going to wait it out.

"Don't worry on me, honey. It's just a little bruise." Colby smiled at him. "So, one helluva Monday, huh?"

"Yeah? Take a deep breath."

"Pardon?"

"If it's just a little bruise, sit up for me and take a nice, deep breath." He'd had about enough of this bull. Whatever it was—pride, money, reputation, fucking insurance, whatever—Gordon would sort it out for him. There had to be a way to do it that wouldn't bruise Colby's ego right along with his ribs.

Colby sighed a little bit, but the stubborn bastard sat up and took a deep breath, color draining out of his face, leaving him ashy. Colby winked at him, eased himself back into the cushions. "I got kicked by a horse once. Broke three ribs, and I went to work the next day 'cause I wasn't supposed to be fucking around in the barns. I'm a cowboy. I got this."

"All right, asshole. You're tough as nails, right? I got it." Gordon got up. "I'm going to get that wine."

"I ain't never gonna figure this out, am I? I mean, for real."

"Colby, you've got it figured out. You're working your ass off, you like what you do, and you're very good at it. Too good. You're building something from absolutely nothing, and guess what? I've been there. It just takes time. And help."

Colby had incredible potential. If he needed to figure anything out, it was that he wasn't thinking big enough.

"I'm not a stellar example here for how to ask for help, I know. And yet, you have stepped in and picked up slack for me every day for weeks. Imagine where Olivia and I would be right now without you? You've got that figured out too."

Gordon sat down on the coffee table opposite Colby. "Today was… is… one shit day. Let me help you get back on your feet."

"Honey?" Colby took his hands. "I mean not pissing you off. I don't have the foggiest idea what to do next, and I'll sure take your help, because God knows I need it, but I'm damn tired of landing on your shit list for being... me."

Oh, for crying out loud.

"Okay." Gordon just shrugged. "So... I need to figure out how to stop making you feel that way by being me."

Christ. They were so good in bed together, so good at sharing a beer and just hanging out, great with Olivia... but they couldn't have a fucking conversation about anything more complicated than the weather without tying each other in knots.

Colby shot him one of those grins—part evil, part laughter, part wicked joy. "Well, we are speaking two different languages every time we're not fucking. Also, I probably owe the swear jar a ten." Colby held on to him. "I'm slow on some things, I know I am, but I'm not stupid. I just don't know what to do next, and I can't afford a doctor, so that's not on the table, you get me? You told me we were an us, right? That means we help each other."

"Only a fool would think you were stupid, cowboy, and I think maybe that's your secret weapon." Gordon picked up one of Colby's hands and kissed his knuckles. "We are an us. I love you. That means everything, including a new truck and a fucking doctor if it turns out you need one, is on the table. Because I can afford to take care of my family. Are we speaking the same language right now?"

"I think so. I love you too, you pain in the ass. A lot." Colby leaned back into the cushions again. "It's been a shitty day, all around. You, though? You I like."

That wine in his Jeep? He was about ready to drink the whole case.

"I am a pain in the ass. I can be a lot of other unpleasant things too, so I appreciate that you like me." Gordon grinned and got to his feet again. "You need a shower. I'm going to rescue that wine and some other stuff you might be interested in, and then I'm going to wake up that little girl and feed her something or she'll have us up all night."

"If it's okay with you, I'm gonna just sit right here a few minutes, maybe close my eyes."

"Of course. I'm going to kiss you first, though." He did, gently, and took his time. "You want some help stretching out?"

"Please." The single word seemed to be full of meaning, so he helped Colby down, find a comfortable spot.

"You want more ice? Hang on." Gordon didn't wait for an answer, just got him a new bag of ice, some water, and four ibuprofen, and then covered him with the couch blanket. "Rest up," he said after one more kiss. "I promise I won't let Liv jump on you."

"Thanks, honey. I just need a second to regroup." Before he could even scoff, Colby was asleep.

Gordon would bet Colby was out for the night. And that little shit still intended to go to work tomorrow, didn't he?

Chapter Twenty-Four

COLBY HURT from his ears to his toes, bad enough that he wanted to just curl up in the bathtub and drink himself sober. He couldn't, though. He had to go with Gordon, get Little Bit to school and see about his damn truck.

So that was what he did. By the time he got the bad news that the fucking truck was totaled, his wet saw was trashed, and he was out a shitload in supplies, he was fixin' to lose his fucking mind.

He cleaned out the glove compartment, made sure to get everything, including the car chargers.

If he was lucky, he'd just fall over dead.

"I got your plates." Gordon had gone pretty quiet after getting a good look at the damage to the truck. He'd been right there with an extra set of hands, helping out where Colby needed him, but it was good to finally hear Gordy say something.

"Thanks." *Okay, cowboy. You just do this like eating an elephant. One bite, then the next thing.*

Gordy stepped close as they headed for his Jeep. He spoke slow and quiet. "How about we grab a sandwich, and then, if you're up for it, we could go find you a new truck?"

"I think a sandwich would be good. What time do you have to be at the restaurant? Maybe I need to rent something until the insurance company does its thing?" He looked at all the crap from the truck that was in the Jeep. Jesus. What a mess.

"Oscar's going to cover. I'm all yours. Well, until it's time to pick up Olivia, anyway, and then it's anyone's guess. Depends on how her day went, right? You want to get a rental, we can do that."

"I think I'll have to. The market will be better in Denver, I bet." He felt a little like he was wrapped in cotton wool. "Jesus, my head feels gigantic."

"Yeah? Think maybe you have a concussion? I should have thought about that last night. Let me see your eyes."

"Christ, I doubt it. I'm hardheaded as anything." He turned carefully and let Gordy look at him. It seemed important to Gordon, this whole taking-care thing, so he went with it.

Gordy studied his eyes for a second. "Nope. Those eyes are pretty, though. Maybe it's whiplash. That can give you that whole heavy-head feeling too. Dr. James prescribes a beer with that sandwich. You need anything else here before we get moving?"

"Nope. It is what it is. She was a good truck, but it's over." He'd start calling the insurance company again to find out what his payoff was. They could fuss with the asshole's insurance. He ought to be able to put down a good amount on a new one. Maybe a GMC this time....

"Think of it as an opportunity. Maybe you can get a built-in DVD player for Liv." Gordy laughed and pulled open the passenger door, offering him a hand.

"I bet she'd love that. I'm not looking forward to the process, but the result. I have to go buy another friggin' tile saw too, and refold my clothes."

"I know exactly nothing about tile saws, but I've folded a few pairs of jeans in my time."

Getting up into the Jeep wasn't easy, but it hurt less than moving those boxes of busted tile.

Gordy even pulled the seat belt around for him so he didn't have to stretch. "Your small-business insurance will cover the saw and tile and everything else. Uh... assuming you carry it? If not, we can sue the guy when they find him."

"My insurance covers if someone sues me, honey. That's all. It's for if someone cuts themselves on my saw or trips over the tiles in the house while I'm working." But the other guy's insurance would pay eventually, right? He'd call Daddy and see if someone back home would help, if he had to.

"Liability." Gordy nodded. "Well, hopefully they find the guy before me and your momma." As they left the parking lot, Gordy drove them past Colby's truck one more time. "Do not show her pictures of that front end."

"Yeah, it's prob'ly too late. I sent them to Daddy."

They'd had their discussion early this morning, because Daddy still didn't remember about Mountain Time. He'd been pissed about the truck, tickled Colby wasn't hurt, and full of curse words about the other driver.

The thing that Daddy had said that had echoed in him, though? "Thank God y'all's little girl wasn't in the truck, huh?"

"Well, heaven help the bastard, then." Gordy snorted and put his Jeep in Park. "This could have been so much worse, cowboy. I know you're in pain, but I'll take every one of those bruises over the alternative."

Gordy surprised him with a kiss that was kind of desperate and deep and followed it with a whispered, "I love you."

He grabbed hold of Gordy's leg and held on tight. "Good, it would suck to be the only one of us in love."

"Yeah, it sure as hell would." Gordy put the Jeep in gear and pulled out. "I don't ever want to see that truck again. Let's get some food."

Gordy took him home for lunch and set him up on the couch with more ibuprofen and another bag of ice. "Turkey good?"

"Perfect. Thanks. I appreciate it. All of this. Seriously." He hadn't had a lover, a partner that... well, shit. He hadn't had it, period. That Gordon was helping him, loving on him? That was special.

"Here." A manila folder landed in his lap. "Look that over while I make your sandwich. It's from my architect. I'm renovating the back of the dining room this summer. One of the things we're talking about is this Mediterranean-style fireplace and back wall. Top to bottom tile. Wanted to see what you thought."

Gordy disappeared into the kitchen and left him with the folder.

"You gonna cook in it or just lay a fire?" Pretty. That could be fun as hell.

"Just a fire. Those plans show you the layout, where the fireplace will be on the wall and all, but the architect told me he needs to hire someone to design it. I have an idea of what I want, but no idea how to make it happen."

"I got ideas on making things happen. You just need to tell me what you want, and I'll create it."

Gordy returned from the kitchen a few minutes later and reached down to close the folder, trading it for a great big turkey sandwich on a fat, soft roll. "I was hoping you'd say that." He tossed the folder on the coffee table and sat down bedside Colby with a sandwich of his own. "I have this… dish. It's like a serving platter. I got it in Morocco right after I graduated college. It's in my office on that deep window ledge; have you seen it? You know which one I mean? It's all deep blues and red and orange and yellow? That's what I want."

"Yeah?" He knew the bowl, if not the story. He loved the whole idea of a wall that would remind Gordy of something that made him happy. With that much space and free rein, he could make something stunning. "It's doable."

"That's awesome. I'll hook you up with my general contractor, and you guys can talk. For this job, he says he'll pay you by the hour, so make sure you keep track. You'll like him. He's smart, creative, and he works his ass off. He has clients all over town, by the way. I had to wait almost a year just to talk with him about this project. Don't undersell yourself."

"You working with Mike O'Donnell or Javier Dominguez?" At Gordon's curious look, Colby shrugged. "They both use this architect, and they're the best here local. I've been trying to get in with one of them for a while."

He knew his job. He didn't work on an hourly wage; he was a fucking professional, but he'd bid it fair, and he'd get the job because Gordon wanted him doing it.

Gordon grinned at him. "Javier. And you're smarter than the average bear, Mr. McBride."

"Good deal. You let me know when you've talked to him, and I'll give him a call." He knew this. His daddy and uncle laid tile. His grampa laid tile. He laid tile.

"Will do. How's your lunch?" Gordy seemed pretty pleased with himself. "You want some chips or something?"

"Nah, this is perfect. Thank you. You make a damn good sandwich." His usually went Mrs Baird's, peanut butter, jelly, Mrs Baird's. Ta-da. "Did you know that I dressed up as a loaf of bread in high school? Handed out coupons on Sundays. Freddy the Fresh Guy. Creepy as fuck. Hot too."

Gordy laughed with his mouth full and looked like he was trying not to choke on his sandwich. "You know, I want to hear all about your high school exploits, cowboy, but that might have been too much information."

"What? It was good money. Seriously." The hardest part had been separating the coupons with the gloves on. That and the fact that he hadn't been quite grown, and the costume went down past his elbows. It had been hell trying to keep it from falling off.

"Hey, everyone's gotta make a living, right? I got my start at the drive-in at McDonald's. I rocked that uniform, I'll have you know."

"I can see it. It was the only job I ever did that wasn't for the family business. I did it for three weekends and then told my momma I'd much rather help Daddy." She hadn't even "I told you so'd" him. Much.

Gordy nodded. "Roped you right in, huh?"

"They didn't let me do tile for a long time. Hell, I cleaned job sites until I was seventeen."

"Bet you were good and hungry for the real work by then."

"Yes and no." He leaned over, trying to figure out the best way to say what he meant. "Because it was forever before I worked, and those first years? Floor tiles. Hours and hours of laying twelve-bys in straight lines. And that's boring, but Momma had let me experiment. I tiled the kitchen. Both bathrooms. Her sewing room. The fireplace. I had free range. God, I had fun."

A hundred colors and different patterns. Mosaics of everything from Jesus to bluebonnets to a giant spool of thread.

Gordy leaned to meet him and kissed him. "I can't wait to see what you do with my back wall. And the big open fireplace—it's going to be so cool, I know it."

"You've put a ton of heart into it. It's going to work." He had no doubt.

"You want to deal with that rental today, or do you want to just relax here on my couch? I can take you early in the morning after I drop off Liv at school. I have to work around noon." He looked at Colby. "Shit, I guess I'd better figure something out, huh? You won't be able to handle Olivia tomorrow."

"Sure I will." He wouldn't let that baby girl down for love or money. "Worse comes to worse, we'll run through McD's and grab dinner."

"I'm not sure you should be driving yet, Colby. Can you even get her in the Jeep? You're hurting, and your reflexes.... I'm just not sure you should be driving her."

"Well, I can walk with her if I have to." He grinned at Gordy. "Can she ride a bike? Can you?"

He totally wanted a bike. If he was living in this part of town, he'd be on it a lot.

Gordy set his plate down and turned on the couch to face Colby, grinning. "If I didn't know better, I'd say you just insinuated that I'm lazy. I'll have you know that I've got a mountain bike downstairs, but the tires are hell on asphalt. And I have no idea if she can ride a bike, but at nearly six, she should learn, I guess."

"Good thing you know me. We'll have to go biking together. I'd love that." Hell, he loved being outside in the air. He loved it here.

"That list of things we want to do together is getting long, cowboy." Gordy lifted a corner of the ice off his ribs and had a look. "That is one hell of a color. Are you sure you can handle her tomorrow? I can bring dinner up for you guys."

"She'd love that. She loves knowing you're thinking about her."

"I guess I better do it while I still can. We're getting into my busiest time of year. Patios open next week, and staff will nearly double. More waitstaff, more kitchen staff. Oscar won't be able to handle evenings on his own; it's difficult enough now."

"Well, I'll be rocking the work, but I'm always off in time to grab the girl. Maybe I'll teach her how to camp." She was old enough for that. They could go up Fridays and come back down Saturday night or Sunday morning, depending.

"Sure. I bet she'd love that. Must be great up there at night in the summer."

"It's the best. There's so much to see." He couldn't wait to show Liv Rocky Mountain National Park or the Garden of the Gods. The gorge. Snowmass. Maroon Bells. The dinosaurs at the museum and over on the Western Slope.

"You'd never know how long I've lived here, would you? I know everyone in town, but with most everything else I'm still a tourist." Gordy snorted and stood up. "Let me get these dishes."

"You want some help?" He didn't get that, but everything was new and different and magical. The air here was special.

"Nope, I want you to sit right there and rest. Pull out your phone and figure out who in town has a rental truck that'll work for you."

"I can do that." He grinned over at Gordon. "You do realize that it's two hours before Liv gets home, we're inside and alone, and neither one of us is naked?" They must be actually together-together.

"And it's taken every ounce of my restraint to keep it that way, bruised and battered cowboy. Trust me on that." Gordy came back from the kitchen with fresh ice for Colby and leaned close as he traded out the bags, then shook his head and sat on the couch again.

"Come kiss me." It didn't have to be more than that. Just a kiss. A plain ole kiss.

"I can do that." Gordy leaned in again and gave him one quick kiss and then another, then smiled and kissed him better, sweet and slow. "You better heal up quickly, cowboy." Gordy's breath tickled his ear. "The only marks I want to see on you are mine."

"Listen to you." Lord, that was hotter than the hinges of hell.

"Just thought you might like a taste of what I'm working with over here." Gordy shrugged. "Pretty much all the time. Naked or not." Gordy fell back into the couch again.

"You are the finest son of a bitch on earth, man."

Gordy laughed. "Thank you, lover. Tell me that again sometime when you can move any single part of your body, any part at all, without your face going white."

He winked, because that didn't hurt a bit. "It's true. You got my word."

"Well. Then we are legit the hottest couple on the planet." Seemed like maybe Gordy was about to kiss him again when there was a knock at the door.

Gordy looked at Colby with a shit-eating grin. "Door. You wanna get that?"

"Sure, honey. Hand me a shirt?" He grabbed the bag of ice.

"Yeah, you definitely want a shirt on before you pass out getting up off this couch." A heavy hand landed on Colby's shoulder. "Cowboy, sit your ass down. You rattled your brain yesterday. I don't care what you say."

Gordy got up and headed for the door.

Gordon tickled him. He'd never had anyone take such good care.

"I brought the paperwork you need to sign, and the guys sent soup." Oscar stood there, always so damn curious.

"Uh-huh. Soup. Come on in." Colby saw Gordy head for the kitchen out of the corner of his eye, and Oscar came right around the couch.

"Hey, McBride. Boss was right, you look like crap. How are you feeling?"

"Better than I look and way better than the truck that hit me." He grinned over at Oscar. "You been keeping out of trouble?"

"Nope. I actually showed up with trouble."

Gordon groaned. "Shit, Oscar. What now?"

Oscar grinned at them both and started emptying his pockets. "Okay, so this is arnica—Kaitlin sent it; she says it'll help the bruising go away or something. I don't know, she's all into that homeo-whatever stuff." He set the bottle down on the coffee table.

"Arnica. That's trouble?"

"Hang on. Now to the good stuff." Oscar reached into his pocket and pulled out a Ziploc bag. "One legal ounce. I brought papers and my pipe—didn't know which you'd prefer. Way better than Advil."

"You are my hero, man. I swear to God." He shot Gordy a look. "You cool with this? I'll go out on the balcony."

"I'm cool. Just make sure Liv doesn't see you and it's all good." Gordy gave Oscar a clap on the shoulder. "I should give you a fucking raise. That didn't even occur to me."

"I figured you couldn't fire me over a legal ounce, even if you turned out to be uptight." Oscar grinned and looked at Colby. "Just text me when you need more."

"You got it. I appreciate it." The green would ease his bones, make that deep ache fade.

"Hope it helps. I better run. Shift meeting in a few." Oscar leaned forward and offered Colby a hand to shake. "Sorry about your truck. That sucks."

"It was a truck. Trucks can be replaced." He knew this. He just had to remember it.

"That's the truth. Feel better. I'll check in with you later, boss."

"Thanks, Oscar." Gordy showed Oscar out. "I'll be on shift tomorrow."

Colby heard the door close, and Gordy made his way back over to the couch. "Now, that's a wise man, and a pretty good friend too. Gutsy showing up with that in front of the boss."

"Eh, it's legal. It's not that gutsy." He picked the bud, then rolled himself a joint.

"Guess he knows me pretty well anyway." Colby felt Gordon watching him. "Maybe it'll help you sleep. You could go take a nap after. I know you didn't sleep last night."

"You don't mind, honest? Because I won't do it if you have an issue." It wasn't that good for him.

"Would you stop? I don't have any issues. I'm just curious, so I'm watching."

"Ah. You ever had any?" He got the ends twisted. "You want to, we'll share some when Liv's at school and you got time."

"Just not something I ever tried. I was more of a drinker in college. Add it to the growing list of things we need to do together." Gordy gathered up Colby's ice. "I'll clean up lunch and meet you out there." He offered Colby a hand up.

Colby groaned softly, then made a beeline for the bedroom. He loved the way the room smelled like them, like he belonged there.

And he did, really. He hadn't slept hardly anywhere else since Gordy brought Little Bit home.

By the time Gordon joined him, he'd found a sunny spot on the balcony to smoke, dragged one of the metal chairs over, and was soaking up the warm and the fresh air.

"You still awake?"

"I am. I'm a happy man."

"I bet. I want you to rest when you're done, okay? Right to bed. I've got Liv and dinner. I'll even try to wash her hair right." Gordy smiled at him and leaned against the balcony rail. "We'll get you wheels in the morning."

"I love you, you know?" *Not just in a random "I love you, man" way, but for real. Like in a "I would lay down my life for you" way.*

Gordy breathed in and let it out slow. Hard to tell what all that meant—could have been as simple as Gordy sampling the fresh air. "Hard to believe, but there it is."

"Yessir." And it suited him, right down to the bone.

"Nice to see that line in your forehead disappear. It's so not you." Gordy braced both hands on the arms of Colby's chair and leaned down to kiss him right where he figured that crease had been. "I'm supposed to be the grumpy one."

"You're fine to me. A little crackly around the hard edges, that's all." And maybe not loved enough. All people needed loving.

"Mm. Try to remember that when I'm averaging four hours of sleep and Oscar is crashing on the couch on Friday nights."

Gordy reached for a little clay pot that was sitting on the windowsill. "I tried to grow herbs out here once. Forgot about them most of the time." He held the pot out. "Put that in here and let me tuck you in. Your eyes are so heavy I'm surprised you can see out of them."

He nodded, stashing his—well, stash—and taking the hand Gordon offered.

"You're adorable when you're stoned, cowboy. I like that little smile on your lips." He followed Gordy inside, and his clothes just kind of fell off somehow while Gordy was talking about something. And then it was all soft pillows and cool sheets.

"Oh…. Tell me that we'll do this together one night."

"I'm in. Sleep, Colby." Gordon kissed him, and he liked the warm lips on his temple. "I love you."

"Oh good. It would be so weird, otherwise."

Sleep came easy, the world a little gentler on the edges.

Chapter Twenty-Five

GORDON CLIMBED into his Jeep, started it, and cranked the radio. Top down, doors off, and he didn't care who he annoyed along the way. He'd drained his travel mug dry on the way to drop Liv off at day camp, and there wasn't any drive-through coffee on the way back, so Maroon 5 was going to have to do.

He waited for the light to change so he could get the hell out of this parking lot, impatiently drumming his fingers on the steering wheel. He was used to being tired in the summer. The days were long, the restaurant was busy and open for lunch and dinner all weekend, and he and Oscar would manage nearly double the staff. He was usually pretty damn happy in the summertime.

And he was happy. Mostly. But this summer he had some added stress with the indoor renovation, and although it was going well, it still ate up a chunk of his seating, and he couldn't completely mask it from the rest of the dining room, no matter how many fancy screens he put up or tapestries he hung.

And then there was Olivia. He sped down the road a little too fast and glanced at the clock on his dash again. Dropping her off every morning ate time.

What was it, Thursday? Colby would grab her later because he'd be slammed with dinner. Right? Or did they decide last week that Gordy needed to zip out and grab her because Colby needed the extra time to wrap up before the rush?

Christ on a crutch. The thought made him grin. That was his Colby talking.

He was fairly sure Colby was picking her up. Right?

He'd call but he'd never hear a damn thing on his phone with the top down. He'd have to catch Colby at the restaurant later and hope he didn't annoy his cowboy by not remembering. They'd agreed to try to keep it all business downstairs.

Maybe Gordon could text him. Yeah. That would work.

He pulled into his reserved parking spot. Colby's truck was a few spaces over. He ought to put a sign up for Colby too, but he was kind of saving that for when he asked Colby to move in officially. He wanted to ask—he'd been meaning to—but after the accident and the truck and replacing all Colby's stuff, he didn't want the cowboy to bristle at a loss of independence too.

Anyway, it's not like Colby had brought it up either.

Head in the game, James.

Right. Work. He hopped out of his Jeep and headed inside.

He could hear the guys working. Above that, Colby was singing. Loud.

That made him smile. Colby and Olivia sang all the time lately, bedtime songs or whatever was on the radio, camp songs or something that Colby would teach her up in the mountains when they went camping. Gordon loved it.

He was still a little envious maybe, maybe got a little twinge in his chest seeing how tight they were sometimes, but he was happy for them both—seemed like exactly what they both needed.

And he was doing the most he could. The only family he had left in the world was healthy and whole, right?

He hadn't checked in on the construction progress since Monday—Javier had had a polite talk with him a couple of weeks ago, suggesting that his contractors were starting to feel a little micromanaged, and he'd heard the man loud and clear. But two or three check-ins a week seemed like a reasonable compromise, and so he headed out to the main dining room to see what was up.

The space was beginning to come together, and the fireplace was, no question, going to be the centerpiece of the room. Last he'd seen it, Colby was really on to something. The colors were bright, the patterns echoing his bowl.

God, it had made him so happy he'd felt like a little kid on Christmas.

He thought about saying good morning to the guys, and to his guy, but they were working and he didn't want to interrupt. So he just walked through, slowly, pleased to see that the raised platform he wanted seemed to be going into place today, and someone was up on a tall ladder futzing with some of the new lighting too.

Javier said they'd just ordered the flooring, so the end was in sight at least, if not around the corner.

"Goddamn it, McBride! Will you shut the fuck up?" someone growled, and Colby's happy laughter rang out.

"Did someone drink a little too much? Poor baby head is pounding?"

"I will beat you to death."

"You'll sure try. My money's on me. You need aspirin? I got some."

Gordon laughed out loud. He had seen a little flash of temper maybe twice in Colby's eyes, and that was enough to convince him that a fistfight was not the way to go with that cowboy. The way the man's bicep had bunched up? Nope. Gordon wouldn't want to be on the receiving end of that front two-knuckle.

"Things are looking great in here, gentlemen." Gordon figured he'd pipe up now and then get the hell out of their way. He really couldn't be any happier.

"Hey, stranger!" Colby sounded happy as hell. "Come see your fireplace. I'm laying the last tiles."

"Yeah?" Gordon was so excited he practically skipped past the little stage and ducked under the tapestry they'd hung to mask the fireplace from the rest of the dining room.

Dust covered the tile, dimming the colors a bit, but even so—the vision made him gasp.

He took a few steps closer and ran his fingers lightly over the tile in awe, then stepped way back

to take in the whole picture. "Oh. Look at this." He
shook his head, and he knew his mouth was hanging
open, but all he could do was stare. "This is gorgeous.
Oh my God."

He glanced over at Colby and grinned at him.
No, it was more than a grin; it was a huge fucking
smile that took over his face. His whole body. "Colby,
I can't believe it."

"You like it?" Colby beamed at him. "It's going to
be one hell of a showpiece."

Colby was a fucking artist. No question.

"I love it. It's perfect. It's…." It was exactly what
he'd imagined, in fact, and he knew that he and Colby
were lovers and all, but he didn't think that was why.
Colby just listened to what he wanted and saw it too.
"Talent. It's a work of art, baby."

And if it was perfect all dusty, he might faint after
Colby polished it up.

"It totally doesn't suck." Colby's expression
was satisfied. "And I'll be finished a week before I
thought."

"Overachiever." Gordon took a quick look
around, but they were pretty well hidden where they
were. Quickly, he hooked an arm around Colby's
waist and kissed him, like they were sixteen and Dad
was in the next room.

"Mmm." Colby dove into the kiss, totally unashamed, giving him all of that passion, that need.

Christ, a kiss was never just a kiss with his lover.
Colby would just offer it up, as open to him as the
Colorado sky. And right now he had that hardworking
man thing going on that Gordon let wash right over

him. He'd said it before, but he was never immune to it.

Well. The cowboy was technically on Gordon's clock, right? Gordon pulled him closer, maybe the closest they'd been aside from sleeping in a week or more.

"Mmm." Colby bit his bottom lip, just enough to sting, and they rocked together, the heavy ridge of Colby's cock proving that he wasn't alone in needing.

Jesus Christ. And Colby knew just what he was doing too.

"I don't suppose you have a break coming up any time soon?" He slid the hand on Colby's back down to that ass and gave it a squeeze. "Like, now maybe?"

"I love breaks."

"Boss? Boss, where are you? Did you not make the seafood order, man?"

"Ah, fuck. I'm sorry," he whispered to Colby and let him go. He really didn't give a fuck if Oscar caught them lip-locked, but leg-locked seemed like a bridge too far.

"Save that for me." He gave Colby one more quick kiss and started thinking about ice water. "Over here, Oscar. What was that?"

"Seafood. The order didn't show." Oscar barely nodded to Colby, the man's face a thundercloud.

"That's impossible. Excuse me, Colby." Oscar turned on his heel and stormed off toward Gordon's office, and Gordon followed right on his heels. It wasn't the exit he wanted to be making, but if he had forgotten—

No. There was no way.

Not that he remembered one way or the other. It had been a crazy couple of weeks, and he'd been doing a lot of things on autopilot. "I'll check the computer."

"I'll call Jennie. See if I can make a backup plan. She owes us for the great porktastrophe of '14."

"I've been making piggy grunts at her at the Chamber meetings ever since." He passed Oscar and stepped into his office first, headed straight for his computer. "Okay." He moved his mouse, clicked through the receipts. Beef, chicken, pork for the saltimbocca special, even portobellos, but no fucking fish. At all. Not even the fucking shellfish.

Mother. Fucker.

"This one's on me, Oscar. Fucking hell."

"Jennie says she's got scallops and plenty of trout she can sell to us, no problem."

No problem. Right. This was a big fucking problem.

Plus, Jennie would start making fish faces at him at the next Chamber meeting. He just knew it.

"Oscar, I do appreciate your calm in the face of a complete disaster. By which I mean me, of course. Maybe we can add a polenta instead of the salmon special. Or... hm. Falafel? It's Boulder, right? We don't have a fucking ocean."

Back in Boston, beef would be a crisis. Fish you could have for a song.

"No one will even blink."

That was bullshit, but he could play it off with the patrons, no sweat.

"I'll go talk to Leslie. Someone has to have an idea."

"We."

"What?" He was going to hit something.

"We will go speak to the chef, boss, and we will fix it."

Why did Oscar have to be straight and utterly not his type? The whole Oscar-takes-charge thing was hot.

The discussion with Chef Leslie went well, and Gordon had to give himself a pat on the back for hiring such creative, capable people. That was his real superpower—not running the place or making financial decisions or even marketing, which he really enjoyed. That stuff was cake. The talent was in hiring the right mix of people and keeping them.

"I'll get on the horn with our purveyors and see if I can't fix this before the weekend. Oscar, can you head over to Jennie's?"

"On it." Oscar disappeared. All he needed was a puff of smoke and he'd have been the Wizard of fucking Oz.

Get on the horn. Seriously, the Texan was rubbing off on him. Was that even possible? Colby's way with words just stuck with him sometimes.

He spent an hour or so making calls and pulling in some of his cred. He and Oscar managed to put everything right for Saturday. They'd be a hair short Friday night if the wait kept them open late, but late-night fare was always a little scaled down anyway.

His stomach rumbled, reminding him that he'd missed lunch, and he looked at his watch. It was damn near two already. Okay, so he'd get a quick snack from Leslie and—

Almost two o'clock.

Fucking hell, he'd forgotten to ask Colby about Olivia. He took off into the restaurant to look for him.

Colby was standing in front of the fireplace, tilting his head back and forth, over and over.

Colby didn't look like he was in any hurry to get on the road, so Gordon was pretty sure that meant they'd decided he had to take over Thursday pickup. Shit. The cowboy was going to blow his top. Gordon wondered if Colby had seen him or if he could just turn around and head out the door.

He was going to be late for sure. Thank God for aftercare.

"Hon… Gordon? What's up?" Colby's words caught him on the way out.

"Oh, I was just going to tell you I was on my way to get Liv, but… you seemed so deep in thought."

Hey, that was pretty damn good. He was usually a terrible liar.

"Just looking and stretching my neck out. You need me to grab her? I think I'm going to add a row of cobalt blue to the top."

Gordon stepped up next to him and had a look. "It would frame it out nicely and also maybe set it off from the ceiling better." His cowboy wasn't anxious about being late for Liv. He was all chill and into his art. Huh.

"I think so too. I'm into it." Colby grinned at him, but there was concern in his lover's eyes. "You're running yourself ragged, man. It ain't good for you."

"That's business during the summer season. You don't remember because you wanted to spend most of last summer in the mountains." Or maybe he spent most of the summer in the mountains because Gordon was so busy. Either way, business was good then, and it was damn good right now too. Dizzying, but good.

"I forgot to order the seafood this week. How about that?"

"Oops. You'll have to sell a lot of steaks." Colby winked at him. "Did you need me to grab the beast? She was supposed to go fishing today. Maybe she caught something you can serve."

Gordon laughed. "If she did, you're cleaning it." He sighed. "You can get her? We're opening at five tonight; we're packed. It would be easier on me, but this is important too." And it was absolutely beautiful. Took him back years. He felt like he was standing in a market in Marrakech.

"I can. You can make it up to me on Sunday, spend the day up on the mountain."

He'd worked half of last Sunday, and some of Monday too. He'd have to get help. Maybe if Oscar wasn't into covering alone, he could pull Steph from Gaia and let Haley cover it alone. It didn't do half the business Delmara did on a Sunday. Location, location, location.

"Yeah. I can make that work." He gave Colby a smile. "We need some time."

"We do. Okay, mister. I'm off to fetch our girl. She'll be in for her kiss before the rush."

"Can I get one from you too?"

"Anytime, honey." Colby kissed him hard enough that he forgot to breathe. "See you later."

"You will. As much of me as possible." He was so waking that ass up no matter what time he got in.

Chapter Twenty-Six

YEAH, NO.

What a fucking night. The wait got so long it went beyond good for business and into "what the fuck is wrong with that place" territory. He hated just turning people away, but in the end, they had to or they'd be serving until three in the morning. As it was they hadn't closed the doors until one. And it was only Thursday.

He knew things were getting really hairy when he and Oscar started communicating in single-syllable words and sharp looks because they were so ready to lose it and the only forgivable person to blow up at was each other. That wouldn't have done anyone any good, and they both knew it.

God, that look in Oscar's eye, though. Kaitlin was one lucky woman.

Gordon pulled off his jacket and dropped it over the back of a chair in his living room, loosened his tie, and opened a couple of buttons at his throat. Then he hit the liquor cabinet in the kitchen and poured a couple of fingers of tequila over an ice cube before collapsing on the couch.

God, his apartment was so quiet. It was heaven.

"Uncle Gordy?" Liv stood there, staring at him, her kangaroo under her arm. "I heared a scary noise."

Gordon was surprised how seeing her there made him smile in spite of his evening. "Yeah? It was probably just me in the kitchen." He'd closed one of those cabinets pretty hard. "Come on up here and sit with me."

She crawled up into his arms and snuggled in. "I catched a fish today. Uncle Colby cooked it for us to eat for supper."

"You got to keep it? How cool is that? I was sure they'd make you toss it back. What kind of fish did you catch?" *Trout, perch, maybe a bluegill.*

He noted her switch to "supper" instead of "dinner." The cowboy was sinking into them both. He kind of liked it.

"A rainbow fish." That made sense, sort of. He'd bet it was a brown trout, but he also knew when Colby went up fishing, rainbow trout was what he brought home. Gordon would bet that Colby cooked up some of the filets in the freezer and hid whatever Liv brought home.

"I do love fish." Gordon relaxed a little, sinking deeper into the couch and letting his drink go forgotten. "Camp is good, then? You like it?"

"Uh-huh. Max and Jenny and me are Brown Bears. Miss Nancy wants Uncle Colby to come help out some day and teach us how to be cowboys."

Gordon laughed. "Does she? I bet he'd love that." Colby was a big kid at heart; he probably would.

"How's Jessica liking Colorado, pumpkin? She getting along okay?"

"Uh-huh. She misses Mommy, but this place is fun. Uncle Colby says he knows where we can go see baby bears in the spring and that we can snowshoe. He promised that Santa Claus will find me here too." She yawned hugely, her eyes heavy-lidded. "And he says that we can go to the zoo."

That was what he was getting at exactly, and he was glad to hear it was fun at least. Best thing he could hope for, really. "Yeah, Santa could find you anywhere, I promise. And the zoo will be awesome."

They'd decided to take Liv for her birthday, which was less than two weeks away now. Damn. Good to remember that. He'd get that damn day off if he had to close Delmara to do it. "You ready to sleep, sweetie? Can I tuck you back in?"

"Uh-huh, 'less you want to watch cartoons. I would watch cartoons with you and keep you company."

"Aw, you're the sweetest little girl ever." He kissed the top of her head. "But it's late, and I think we both should go to bed, don't you?"

She was such a tiny thing, and he scooped her right into his arms as he stood up, hugging her to him when she wrapped her arms around his neck. "I love you, sweetie."

"Love you!" She let him tuck her in, her unicorn nightlight making the room seem warm. He remembered turning on that nightlight the night he'd learned her bedtime routine at April's house back in Boston. That seemed like eons ago for some reason.

"Sleep tight." He kissed Jessica first and then Olivia, hit the lights, and headed for bed.

Colby was curled up around his pillow, windows wide open, wearing nothing but a pair of shorts, a dog-eared paperback in one hand.

Gordon nodded, approving of the open windows; he also loved the air in the summer. He started to strip, pulling off everything but his briefs, and went to wash up. He considered showering, he probably smelled like the kitchen, but he was just too damn tired, and Colby was too irresistible.

When he came back from the bathroom, he reached over and slid that damn dog-eared copy of *Lonesome Dove* from Colby's fingers and set it on the nightstand with a shake of his head. Colby went to the library every week with Liv and never bothered to find himself another book.

Colby smiled. "Hey, honey."

"Hey. Didn't mean to wake you." Gordon kept his voice low, matching Colby's sleepy tone, and climbed into bed with him. "I'm jealous of that pillow. Come here."

Damn, all the things he wanted to do to his cowboy that he just didn't have the energy for right now—the regret was almost painful. He opened his arms, though, and let Colby get comfy.

"Mmm. Love you, honey. Sleep good." And Colby was out again.

That man could sleep anywhere, anytime.

Hell, these days, so could he. He held Colby close and closed his eyes.

Chapter Twenty-Seven

CHRIST ON a crutch, he needed a beer.

Colby sat in a low lawn chair, watching Liv play with her stuffed animals in the tent. He'd picked her up a plastic tea set and a bunch of random games and toys to goof around with when they were out. He kept them in his toolbox.

Gordon hadn't been able to take Sunday or Monday off, so Colby had found a campsite with toilets and a goony golf course and a playground, and they'd headed out Friday night, with a plan to be home Monday night. He was ahead on the work front, and he needed some of the other guys to catch up.

He sat there, staring up into the sky, trying to understand how he'd ended up like this.

Somehow, he was a full-time dad. Monday through Friday, he went to work at 6:00 a.m., got off at four, grabbed Liv and watched her. Gordy came home at midnight, later, and…. He didn't begrudge this time, he loved Gordon and Liv, but Lord, Colby was suddenly trapped. Like caught in a net where he was in love and not wanting to rock the boat.

But what if Gordon just let him stay because Liv was there? What if this was all just convenient?

"You drinking alone, Tex?"

He looked over, grinning at the heavyset, forty-something, single mom in her pink "Survivor" hat. "Hey, Miss Linda! I was, but I'm not now. Have a seat. Fat Tire or Shiner?"

"I'll have a Shiner, thank you. No Coors? You making some money this summer?" She unfolded his second chair and sat herself down.

"Saving the Coors for when the good stuff's gone." He pulled two Shiners out without looking. "How're the twins? Murdered them yet?"

Fifteen was tough.

"Nope. I'm kind of hoping they'll kill each other and then nobody will go to jail. They're damn close to it."

"May the best one win!" They clinked their bottles together, then drank deep. "I have a couple of cupcakes."

"I have a whole roll of oatmeal cookies. I'll trade you cookies for a cupcake."

"Fair enough, ma'am." He grinned at her. "They're in with the dry goods. I'll grab them for you."

"You're on. Only I'm not getting out of this chair right now, so it'll have to wait until I have to pee." She looked over at Olivia. "How's little miss? Birthday coming up soon, you said?"

"Uh-huh. July. Gonna take her to the zoo."

"With Uncle Gordy!" She heard everything.

"Hello, Olivia. What are you up to over there?"

"Making tea for me and Jessica. Would you like some?"

"Oh, thanks, precious, but Uncle Colby gave me something to drink already."

"You're missing out!"

Linda laughed. "I am sure you're right." She leaned closer to Colby. "She's a live one, huh?"

"You know it. She's my camping kiddo." Thank God or he would be losing his fucking mind, being trapped in the apartment.

"So, Gordy—this the weekend he's meeting you up here? It'll be good to meet the man that roped you in." She grinned at him.

"He's busy. I think it'll be...." Well, late fall, but then Liv would be back in school. Lord. "Maybe next time."

He could feel her eyes on him, giving him a long look, but she just looked away again and took a swig of her beer. "Well, that sucks. Sorry, honey," she said after a bit.

"Shit happens." And at least he was outside. "You coming out next weekend? My folks are coming up and picking up my travel trailer. We're going to have a grandparent weekend."

"We're here all week. We needed a vacation, and I'm steering clear of my landlord until after payday." She laughed. "I can grab your spot for you Friday morning."

She leaned forward and looked at him again. "Shit happens, yeah. People say that." She took another sip of her beer and leaned back, gesturing toward Liv with the bottle. "Is that what you'd tell her if someone wasn't treating her right?"

"I would find whoever it was and beat them until they couldn't breathe." The idea of someone hurting his baby made his chest tight.

"Yeah, I bet you would." She nodded. "But it's okay if it's just you. You can take care of yourself."

"He is working his ass off. All the time." He had to admit, he loved his job, but he loved lots of stuff more. Gordon. Liv. His folks. The mountains. Cold beer on a hot day. Kenny Chesney music. Lots of stuff.

She nodded. "Yeah? Good for him, then. He must really need the money. I get it, mouths to feed and all."

Colby wasn't sure if she was sincere or sarcastic.

"Hey, Mom?" A matching set of blond boys came walking up, long legs in shorts, feet in flip-flops, and no shirts in sight. "Can we take the fishing poles?"

"Yes, but you don't go farther downstream than that tree bridge, and you be back long before dusk."

"Okay, Mom," they said at the same time, and ran off.

"Take water and stay together!" she shouted after them.

"Lord have mercy."

He had to wonder if he wasn't contributing enough, but it had been this bad last year. Gordon was swamped in the summer and from November to February. He knew that.

Hell, he'd stayed home Thanksgiving through Christmas last year because he didn't want to make the drive twice.

Shit, he paid for damn near all the food and lots of Liv's random stuff. He was giving back.

"Right? They're good boys mostly. But when they're not? Double trouble." She winked at him and finished her beer, then sat the empty next to her chair. "Weather is perfect up here right now."

"Lord yes. I just can't bear being trapped in the city when this is right here."

Linda was watching Liv play. Olivia had found little flat rocks, and she'd put them on her plates to serve to her tea party guests.

"You're raising her right, getting her up here every weekend. Kids get so into video games and television and whatever, they don't learn to appreciate this. I work a lot trying to raise those two on my own, but we get up here at least one night on the weekends, two when I can. I need the quiet and the peace, and they need the air and the sun. You know what I mean? Everything slows down up here."

"I do. I feel like a new person up here, a better one." He didn't have the words for it, how he knew that this was a good place, something bigger than words.

"Colby." She smiled at him. "I would be really happy to watch Olivia for the afternoon tomorrow if you wanted to get some time in with Mother Nature. You know, some quiet."

"Oh, aren't you dear as all get-out." Colby wasn't sure Gordon would be okay with that. Maybe he'd call tonight, talk with Gordy, and see what his thoughts were. "I might take you up on that."

"You should. You look like a man who could use five minutes to himself. You can tie my boys up in the back of your truck as insurance if you like." She gave him a wide grin and then started to laugh.

"Lord have mercy, that would be like that old story, the one where the kidnappers beg to be arrested and the little one given back."

"Yeah, that's about how it would work out, I'd guess."

"Uncle Colby, I'm hungry." Olivia climbed right up into his lap.

"Are you? Do you think you might need a sandwich?" He held her tight, because she was his camping girl.

"Yes, please. Peanut butter and jelly?"

"How about I go and get those cookies for dessert?"

Liv's eyes lit up. "Can I, Uncle Colby?"

"If you ask Miss Linda nicely, I guess."

Liv turned on the charm. Little girls sure knew how to get what they wanted. "May I please have one, Miss Linda?"

"You got it, sweetheart. I'll be right back." Linda picked up her empty and trotted off to her site.

"I'll get the peanut butter." Liv hopped off his lap.

"Are you having fun, ladybug?" He wanted her to love this like he did.

"Yes! It's a perfect day." She stuck her nose into a crate and dug around.

"It is. You think that we should go swimming tomorrow?"

"Yes! Please? Maybe the place with the rock I can jump off of? I liked that place." She brought him the jar of peanut butter.

"Yeah? Sure. You're quite the swimmer." And swimming guaranteed a good sleep. Thank God.

"It's fun. When is Uncle Gordon coming? Is tomorrow Sunday?"

"Tomorrow is Sunday. I don't know if he can. You know he's the busiest guy ever." He put all that shit away, all the worry and frustration. He'd look at it later.

Her face fell, and she leaned against him. "Mommy worked a lot or we'd lose the apartment. Are we gonna lose the apartment? Uncle Gordon can have my zoo money."

"Oh, baby doll." He grabbed her up, his heart hurting, but also so damn proud of her. She was a good girl, down to the bone. "Your Uncle Gordy works hard and makes good money, so do I. You don't have to stress that. We will take care of you. I swear to God."

She hugged him back hard. "You sure? You promise?"

"Yes, ma'am. We will take care of you forever. I promise."

"Okay." She kissed his cheek. "Did you find the jelly?"

"Strawberry packets." He bowed, playing with her. "Nice and safe in the cooler."

"Yay!" She bowed back, giggling at him.

It was kind of funny. Most of the time, especially around Gordy, Liv would at least try to be a little ladylike. She'd sit nicely at the table, fold her hands in her lap. But up here? Liv just sat her butt in the dirt, crossed her legs, and watched him make her sandwich.

Of course, that was why they were up here, digging in the dirt and making mud pies on the bank. She got to play with a bunch of other kids of all ages, hang out and be gross and filthy and goofy.

By the time Colby got her tucked into her sleeping bag that night, she was definitely filthy, and he figured it was a good thing they'd agreed on a swim the next day. She was full of dinner and stories and had chased Linda's boys around for a good long while playing flashlight tag with the other kids, so he was hoping she'd sleep in some in the morning.

He went back out to the fire pit. All the tents were in a loose circle, all the openings faced the inside, and all the parents could see in the—*parents*. Could he say that? He knew legally he couldn't. He was pretty sure that would be tacky to even think it. He was like a… more than a nanny, right? Sort of like the nurse in the Shakespeare play from his freshman year with less hand wringing and thees and thous.

Linda was a couple of spots to the left. Her boys were in their sleeping bags, and she was in a low chair just outside the tent. They were all reading.

Colby's eyes fell on the couple directly across the way, and he watched them for a bit. She'd said she was a school teacher, and he was… something professional. A lawyer maybe or… hell, Colby couldn't recall. They'd opened a bottle of wine and were sipping it from plastic cups and sitting close to the fire. She looked chilly, and he had his arm around her shoulders.

Sweet.

A flare of jealousy hit him, and he rolled his eyes. For fuck's sake. He was never going to have that. Even if Gordon wanted to camp, there was never going to be making googly eyes at each other around other campers. He'd wanted a family, kids, and the good Lord had arranged it, and he was repaying that with being an ungrateful shit? Fuck that. He had his life. He needed to get his fucking head out of his ass.

He nursed his beer and sent his momma a picture of Liv in the tent, in her little lime-green sleeping bag.

Sweet baby. Good day in your mountains?

Fab. Been here since yesterday. Heading back Monday. She's having a ball.

Good. We can't wait to meet her. Does she like fishing? Your daddy wants to bring her a pole.

Lord yes. Fishing. Swimming. Tea parties. You name it.

He reckoned for a kid with a messed-up momma, Liv was rocking it.

I'll tell him. He'll be tickled.

His phone vibrated in his hand, and Gordon's name popped up on the screen.

"Well, I'll be damned." He blinked and answered. "Hey, you. How goes it?"

He hadn't expected to hear from Gordon until way later.

"Hey. Good. It's a good night. Is Olivia still up? I was hoping to say good night."

"She's zonked out, sorry. She had a hard day of playing. She wore herself out." Maybe he ought to send videos of her... nah. This was the mountains. It wasn't about being plugged in.

"Ah, damn. I tried to get away earlier, but... well, I just couldn't. Obviously. Okay. I'm glad she had a good day. You guys are having fun?"

"She's a natural. We're eating PB and Js and having tea parties in the dirt." He laughed at himself. He sounded so domestic. He guessed that was normal?

"I miss that laugh, cowboy. No lie." Gordy sounded tired.

"I hear you. You working tomorrow still, or do you think...?" He wasn't sure, even if Gordy had the time, that this would be restful.

"No, baby. I'm sorry. Maybe next—" Gordon sighed. "As soon as I can."

"I get you. I warned Liv you would probably be busy. I'll distract her. We're spending the day in the water." He tried for a smile. "We'll see you for lunch on Monday."

"Oscar? Yeah. I'll be there in five." Gordon had half-covered the phone, muffling his words, but he was back with Colby in a blink. "That sounds great. Hopefully I can get wrapped up by lunch and take the rest of the day. Don't say anything to Olivia just in case."

"I won't. Get some rest, huh? I love you."

"Yeah. That's good advice. I love you too, cowboy. I do." Gordon's voice got muffled again, but Colby sure heard him loud and clear. "Oscar, I said I was coming!" He came back to Colby. "I gotta... I love you. Night, baby. Kiss Olivia for me in the morning."

"Will do. Night." He hung up the phone with a sigh.

"Dude! Tex! Come play spades with us?"

A little pod of dads waved at him, and he grinned, then shrugged. Why not. "Sure."

He moved his chair over to their fire, the folding card table, making sure he could see Liv.

A guy stood up, offered his hand. "We haven't met. I'm Ray."

"Colby. Pleased. You know these two hooligans?" Mike had a boy Liv's age, a little girl who was three, and another on the way. Brandon had a set of seven-year-old twin girls and a four-year-old boy.

"Oh, yeah. Mike and I go way back, and anyone that needs a beer knows him."

Brandon snorted. "Ray's been coming here every summer for what, four years? Five? He's over there in the RV. The wimp."

Ray shrugged. "Happy wife, happy life."

"That's a good-looking vehicle," he said, just making nice. He liked it like he did it—tent, cot, lawn chairs, cooler.

Ray shrugged. "Thanks. I want to camp; she wants her stories on TV and running water."

"Who's dealing?" Brandon set a fresh beer in front of Colby.

"On it." Mike started shuffling. "Looks like we're partners, Tex."

"Good deal. Let's kick their asses, my friend." He might not have his lover, but he had a few buds, a beer, and someone was playing vintage R&B.

Life wasn't bad. Not bad at all.

Maybe one day Gordy'd be with them too.

Chapter Twenty-Eight

GORDON GLANCED at his watch and grinned. Sure, he'd had to get up at the crack of dawn to work, but he was almost finished with the paperwork from the day before and setting up the orders for the week, and then he'd be free to spend the afternoon with his family.

He wondered when he'd started thinking about Colby in those terms. They sure didn't feel much like it, having spent four days apart, but at some point he had. Hardly mattered why or when, really. It was what it was.

He turned his mind back to the computer, determined to get this last order in and then he'd be good to go.

He heard deep laughter ringing out outside, answered by happy little giggles and a little voice going, "I will turn the hose on you, Uncle Stinky!"

Gordon chuckled. That was Colby all over, because he lived in a concrete jungle and didn't even have a hose.

He double-checked his order sheet—yes, there was the seafood order—and then he pushed back from his desk. Done. Timing couldn't have been better. He picked up his phone and texted Oscar.

Orders in, including fish. Sent Jennie champagne. Floor guys are loading in today, chimney inspector will be in tomorrow morning for new fireplace, I'll handle.

It's Monday, boss, take the damn day off.

Yep. Crew is back from mountains—signing off until tomorrow

Good man

Soft squeals sounded, followed by heavy footsteps on the outside stairs. "I'm going to get you, my pretty!"

All that goofing off just made him smile. He left his office and jogged around the corner, trying to catch up. "I hear trouble!" he called after them. He hit the steps, taking them two at a time.

"Trouble, trouble, boils and bubbles!" Colby's laugh was the finest thing he'd ever heard, and thank God he recognized it, because the man and child he encountered on the stairs had to be mud men.

"Jesus, you two look like you crawled out of the swamp." Good Lord, they looked bad, but they smelled worse. "None of that"—he waved his hand—"is going in my apartment. You can strip in the hall."

"Uncle Gordy! It rained and we runned and runned to get all the things in the truck! It was so fun!" She ran to him, arms wide.

"Hey, you. You got her? I'll unload the truck." Colby shot him a half grin and headed back down the stairs as he got an armful of disgusting child.

"I do now!"

Olivia wrapped her arms around his neck, and any hope for his shirt was lost. "We're home!"

"Yep. I missed you. The clean part of you anyway." He set her down and helped her undress, leaving everything she'd been wearing on the floor in the hall. "Come on, Miss Mess, let's get you in the tub."

Hell with the tub, she was almost six. Maybe it was time to learn about the shower.

"Maybe we should shower first, huh?"

"I used the showers at the camp. It's like raining. It's fun. Did you know Uncle Colby let me shower with my swimsuit on? He says we need another one each 'cause it's like putting on stinky slug suits."

Oh. Colby had already... well, okay. That was good, one less thing he had to teach her. Of course, it was one fewer thing that he got the chance to, also.

He shook that off. It was a shower, not her fucking high school graduation. He needed to get a grip. He wasn't going to be there for everything.

"Okay." He stuck her straight in the tub and pulled down the hand shower and turned it on, angling the spray away until it got warm. "How was swimming?"

"Oh, Uncle Gordy! You should have been there. I missed you so much. We ate weenies on a stick and played flashlight tag, and all my friends showed me how to jump off the rock and not be scared."

"Sounds like so much fun, pumpkin." But for a second he couldn't breathe because, yeah, he should have been there.

He loved his work. Delmara was insanely successful this summer, and he was so damn proud of
it, and Gaia was still the little workhorse it had been
since the day he opened it. He was going to have to
give all of this some thought, though, because being
pulled in opposite directions meant he wasn't completely enjoying anything. He took a deep breath and
turned the spray on Olivia. He wasn't there over the
weekend, but he was here right now.

The dirt sluiced off her, exposing a deep tan, Liv's
hair gone blonder than ever. By the summer's end, she
was going to be a towhead. There was a heart-shaped
sticker on her shoulder, and she stopped him when he
reached for it.

"It's supposed to be magic when we take it off.
Miss Linda said so."

"Oh, yeah? You want to take it off yourself?"
He'd have to ask Colby about Miss Linda.

"No. No, but we have to hold our breath. Magic
needs you to hold your breath."

"Oh. Okay, gotcha. So on three, we'll take a deep
breath and hold it, and then I'll pull it off. Ready?"
Gordon remembered doing this on Cape Cod as a kid.
Although he'd never had to hold his breath. That must
be the Texas version.

He rested his fingers on the sticker and started to
count. "One... two...."

He pulled it off and the heart showed up, Liv's
eyes going wide. "She's magic...."

He went right along with it. "Look at that! She so
is magic. Wait until Uncle Colby sees."

At that he grabbed a washcloth and started to
scrub her down with the bodywash. Every little inch

and every nook and cranny, watching the water in the bottom of the tub turn brown. "Yuck."

He was dreading washing her hair. She didn't like the way he did it to begin with, and right now it looked like Colby hadn't combed it in a day or so. There was a knot in the back that looked like something might be living in it.

She jabbered at him, telling him over and over that she'd missed him, that she'd colored a picture for him, that she'd told all her new friends about him.

Clearly she was much better adjusted than he was. That, and Colby must have done a damn good job of keeping her busy.

The hair washing went about as badly as he'd expected, and by the time he'd gotten her wrapped in a towel she'd stopped telling him how much she'd missed him and started giving him hell about how bad he was at the whole bath thing. He had to laugh, though, because she wasn't halfway to her room before she was singing something cheerful to herself.

Gordon shook his head and cleaned up the bathroom. The tub looked more like he'd washed a muddy dog than a child, but it cleaned up easily enough. He headed back out to see about her dirty clothes.

Colby was in the kitchen, putting things away out of a cooler that looked like it had been run over, twice.

Oh, but he was clean. Gordon got a little hint of cologne, and his nostrils flared like a Spanish bull getting ready to charge. "Damn, cowboy. You smell good."

He was only slightly surprised by the throaty growl. He'd been thinking about Colby all weekend. Longer.

"Do I now?" Colby grinned at him and stood. His lover was wearing a pair of ancient jeans and nothing else. Colby's tan was deep enough that he wanted to see where it stopped, almost desperately.

He came out here to do something. Whatever it was could wait. He changed course and headed right for Colby. "I'm not sure who that animal was that brought Olivia in a while ago, but I like this guy." He hooked a finger through one of Colby's belt loops and tugged him close, then pressed a hard kiss to Colby's lips. "Mmm."

Colby wrapped one hand around his head, diving in to kiss him back, tongue fucking his mouth.

Gordon stepped forward, forcing Colby backward until his ass hit the counter and then leaned into him, grinding their hips together. Colby was hard and needing, right there for him, and begging for more.

"Ew! No kissing! That's gross."

Colby whimpered softly.

"Jesus," Gordon whispered. It took effort to let Colby go and step away, concentration to find a smile for Liv, and every ounce of will in him to get his body to back the fuck down. Christ, his balls ached. They were going to turn to stone if he didn't get his hands on his man for real, and soon. He was so frustrated he wanted to punch something, but that wasn't Liv's fault. She hadn't seen him all weekend, and he wasn't going to give her any less than his best.

He swallowed hard and forced himself to focus on her.

"Gross? I don't think so." He scooped her up and sat her on a stool. "You want some lunch, pumpkin?"

"Uh-huh. I want chicken."

Colby dumped out the cooler. "It okay if this dries out by the door?"

Gordon had to grin at the strain in Colby's voice and then just laughed out loud. "Sure. Or you could stick it out on the balcony instead, maybe. If you need some air."

"That works." Colby winked at him as he walked by, cooler held carefully in front of him.

Hell, if they couldn't laugh, right?

"Chicken it is, sweetie. How about nuggets and broccoli?"

"I love nuggets and broccoli!"

"Well, yeah! Who doesn't?" Thank God. Lunch, courtesy of the microwave. Chef would likely not approve, but Colby would back him up. He was trying his best, but his need was real right now, and his head was still foggy. He ran his hand across the counter and had to shove away an image of taking Colby over that kitchen island—a memory from his life well before Olivia arrived. Fuck, those were some good times.

He shook his head and pulled some dinosaur-shaped nuggets out of the freezer. "You know, Liv, I think maybe Jessica needs a bath too." Olivia had her arm wrapped around the kangaroo, but even so, Gordon could tell she had hit the dirt as hard as Olivia had.

"Are you going to put her in the washer? Because that scares her."

Was there another way? "Uh, well, the thing about washers? It's kind of like you and airplanes. The more you fly, the less it will worry you, you know?"

"What if she falls apart? Can you fix her?"

"I can't, but Uncle Colby's mom is coming next weekend, and I would bet she can fix anything." She must know a thing or two with all those sisters of his. "Plus, I don't think she'll fall apart, sweetie."

"Uncle Colby says I can call them Mamaw and Papaw. Is that okay?"

Whoa.

All this playing house was one thing, but now Olivia had grandparents? He'd been thinking of them as Colby's parents, but to Colby... they were her grandparents.

Man. Shit just got real. Too fast. He took a deep breath and told himself to cool it. He wasn't in the best frame of mind—or body—for all of this at the moment. He needed a clear head to think.

"I guess, uh." But what the hell was he doing? Boyfriend, little girl, grandparents? How the fuck did he get here? "I guess you call them whatever Uncle Colby says you should."

He pulled the nuggets out of the microwave and added them to the plate with her broccoli.

Really, Gordon, what the hell? He felt a little like he was suffocating.

He set the plate in front of Olivia. "You... want some milk with that?"

"Uh-huh." She looked at him a minute, then started to eat. "Do you want one?"

"Oh, no thank you. But you're so sweet to offer." He leaned over the counter and gave her a kiss on the forehead. "Thanks, pumpkin."

"I love you, Uncle Gordy."

"I know, Liv. I know." He stepped around the counter to get closer and gave her a hug. "I love you too."

She was so smart. So fucking smart. And sensitive. She just picked up on everything. He sighed and did his best to pack it all away for later. "You know, I think there's an ice cream sandwich in the freezer."

"I like those. Lots. Wanna share? We can cut it in threes."

Colby came back through, wearing a loose T-shirt now. "I ain't hungry, Little Bit. Y'all can share it."

Gordon looked at him. "You haven't eaten."

"I'm fine as frog hair. I'll grab a bite after I sit on my butt a while."

"You want a beer?" He did. He opened up the fridge.

"Sure. Thanks." Colby grinned at Liv. "Look at you, all clean and sparkly."

"We were just discussing giving Jessica a bath in the washing machine." Gordon opened both bottles and handed one to Colby. "I was explaining that if something were to happen to her that your mom could probably fix Jessica right up."

Gordon could keep this conversation cool. Some things weren't negotiable at this point. Colby's parents were coming next weekend, and that was good. Colby needed them. He loved them. Gordon was just going to have to figure out what that meant for Olivia.

And for himself.

"She's good that way. She's looking forward to meeting y'all, so much."

Gordon didn't say anything. He couldn't. He was wound up now, and he was afraid that something he'd regret saying would come out of his mouth. He rummaged in the fridge again, looking for turkey and some cheese to make a sandwich.

His phone beeped, and he grabbed it, surprised to find a text from Colby.

U pissed because of the dirt? I'll clean it up.

Really? Texting? *No. God, no. Just keep it off my carpets. :P*

k. Left the tent in my truck. Will take it 2 the car wash 2 spray it down.

Gordon looked at him, then looked back at his phone and texted, *You told her to call them Mamaw and Papaw?*

Colby frowned down at his phone, then shot Gordon a questioning look. *Yep. She asked. That's what the kids call them.*

Christ, Colby's thumbs could fly.

like grandparents

Why did he start this? Why did Colby start this? He didn't want to do this right now.

Colby read his message, and then his lips went tight. *My bad. I'll take care of it.*

Then Colby stood and stretched, red spots on his cheeks. "You know what? I don't think I want that beer after all. I had enough up the mountain."

Goddammit. Gordon sighed. "Colby, I already told her… I said whatever you said was fine."

"It ain't no big thing." That accent was so thick it dragged on his nerves. "Really."

"Uncle Colby?"

"What, Little Bit?"

"Do you need a hug?"

"I will always take a hug from you." Colby found a smile for her, hugged her tight. "You'd best finish eating your chicken so y'all can have that ice cream."

"It actually is a big thing, *Tex*."

And there it was. He regretted it the second it was out of his mouth. *Mother. Fucker.*

"Yessir." A tiny muscle in Colby's jaw jumped, and Colby stared him down. "I tell you what, I'll see you later, Little Bit. I got to go wash the tent out and all."

"Yeah, it's stinky."

"It sure is." Colby picked up his wallet, his boots, his keys, and his cap. "Y'all have a nice lunch."

"Colby."

It was a weak effort, and he knew it wasn't going to stop his lover from walking out the door, but he wasn't quite ready to apologize, even though he knew he should. He couldn't even turn around to watch Colby go. He was caught between ashamed of himself and... something. Worry. Frustration. Fear.

It was one thing to gamble Olivia's heart alongside his own on this thing with Colby while it was just the three of them. It wasn't fair to risk her losing an entire fucking family.

Olivia looked at him, then looked at the door. "Can I please go play in my room now?"

Gordon nodded. "Yeah, pumpkin. You go ahead."

He watched her go. Way too smart, way too sensitive for her own damn good.

He cleaned up the kitchen, part of him ripping himself a new asshole and the other part wondering if it wasn't better that this happened now.

COLBY SAT in a McDonald's parking lot, sucking on a chocolate milkshake as he tried to figure out what he'd done wrong, listening to his sister scream on the phone.

"What a piece of shit! Should I come beat him? I'll fucking kill him."

"I just don't understand what I did."

"You mean besides acting like you're family?"

He chuckled, but he thought that was it. He wasn't family. He wasn't ever going to be family. He was a fuckbuddy, down at the core of it. The help that got too close, too familiar.

"What am I gonna tell Momma? I can't introduce her to Liv. She's all excited. They both are." He hadn't thought he was doing anything weird, and now everyone was going to be pissed off. God, his head hurt.

"Tell her that you broke up with the piece of shit and that the sweet little girl is collateral damage. I've been a stepmom. That's how it happens. You break up, suddenly you're the piece-of-shit whore instead of the momma."

"Wow." What would Gordon tell Liv?

"I'd tell Momma for you, but you know she'd just call you anyway."

His mind was going now. What would Gordy tell Liv, who would pick her up from day camp tomorrow, what about that damn trip to the zoo next week?

"Sister, I have to let you go. I love you." He hung up the phone and called Gordon. He needed to know what the fuck was up. Now. This wasn't right, goddamn it. He'd been good. He'd been as loving and right as he knew how to be, and if Gordon didn't like it, then fuck him.

"Hey." Gordy answered the phone so fast it didn't even ring on his end.

"What the fuck is going on? Why the hell are you so pissed at me?" Might as well start out like he could hold out.

"I'm not pissed at you. Where are you? Can you come home, please?" When Colby didn't say anything right away, Gordy went on. "Please? I don't want to do this on the phone. Liv's toast, she fell asleep right after you left. We've got some time."

"Meet me outside on the landing. I don't want to worry her." Because if he'd fucked up, it wasn't her fault. It was on him.

"Yeah. Yeah, okay. I'll be waiting." Gordy hung up on him.

He was going to beat the asshole to death with his own arm.

At this point it was rush hour, and getting across town was a pain in the ass and took an age. That was fine; let the fucker wait on him. He parked in the lot and finished his two sips of shake, then waded up the stairs and into battle.

Gordon was waiting for him at the top of the stairs and pushed away from where he'd been leaning on the railing as Colby got closer, watching him as he climbed the last few steps to the landing. "Thanks for...." He shook his head. "Look. I was out of line, Colby. You pulled out that drawl, and I got... mean."

Pulled out that drawl. No. No, that was... just him. Just being mad.

Just him.

Christ.

"No big. You want to tell me what's got you all het up?"

"Yeah. You should have asked me about this whole thing with your parents. Or—no. Not asked me, that's not what I mean. We just should have had a discussion about it."

"I didn't think I needed to. My bad." *I thought I was a part of this. My bad.*

"You're bringing people into her life that you want her to think of as her grandparents and you didn't think that bears some discussion?"

"No, Gordon. I didn't." What possible harm could it do, to have two more people love you? It wasn't like love was pie, for fuck's sake.

Gordy sighed and leaned back on the railing again, crossing his arms, looking guarded. "If things don't work out between us, it's bad enough she'd lose you. She'll also be losing anyone you bring into this relationship, Colby."

"Damn Sam, I wasn't aware we were breaking up." He'd thought he'd been gone for the weekend camping.

"Oh, come on, cowboy." Gordy sighed. "If I'm going to parent her, I have to take the long view on this one. She loves you. You know she's going to love your parents. What happens if... you know? You're building all of this up for her, and I need to know it's going to still be there. I have to ask that for her. She's lost enough."

Except he didn't think this was all about Liv. He'd bet it was about Gordy too.

"I've been right here. From the start. I was the one that held her that first night here. I'm the one that's...." Christ, every weekend. Every night. And he was just... what? A convenience until Gordon could figure out how not to deal with him? Did Gordy not want them to be together? "What more do you want from me?"

"I know, baby. I know how much you love her." Gordon shrugged. "She's the luckiest girl in the world right now." Gordon reached out, and his fingers were warm where they gripped Colby's arm. "I don't want more. I want to get a handle on what already is. What kind of father would I be if I didn't ask? If I didn't make sure?"

"I guess the kind that trusted me to do what was right by y'all." And Gordon didn't trust that, he guessed. "I'm gonna ask my folks to head out on their trip Friday. I've promised them the trailer, and they're all excited, so they'll be in town, but they don't have to come by here."

He was pretty sure he was going to end up leaving, but he'd not leave Miss Liv swinging. Not even because it was easier for Gordon.

"No. Whoa. Hang on." Gordon shifted his weight, and then he had two hands on Colby instead of just one. "Wait. Can we rewind this a bit, please? I mean, we are—or, I don't know, maybe it's me—but why can't we ever have a head-on conversation and actually understand each other? Do not change your plans with your parents."

"Why would we have? I think we said seventeen words to each other about the weather in between blow jobs before Liv showed up. You weren't into me for my blazing wit, and I know that." And didn't that sting a little? That he knew if that little girl hadn't shown up, Gordon would be happy as a pig in shit having Colby blow him in his office once or twice a month. Now half of that was on him, no question, maybe more, because he hadn't thought too terrible hard on how much that hurt his feelings, but that didn't make the saying of it any less true.

"I don't know, I think maybe I was. But you're right, I never said anything. And what about you, by the way? Liv came along, but that only had to change my life. I gave you an out. You didn't take it. And I'd assumed you were only into me for my cock up to that point. I mean, I could have lived with that, maybe, but it's not like you were asking for more."

He shrugged. "Man, I'm a basically homeless cowboy living out of my truck and a fourteen-foot travel trailer. You own two successful restaurants." He'd needed something to offer, and he'd been getting there. He had.

Gordy traced a finger along Colby's jaw. "Shit, I really am an asshole."

"I help with Liv because I love her. I love kids. I grew up surrounded by family, and I never thought anything of it. I stuck with you because I wanted to. I was making my way up to meet you face-to-face."

Gordy nodded. "Okay. Yeah. I get that. I'm sorry I made you feel that way, but I get it."

"You didn't make me anything. I know that you got to have something, some balance between you. I knew it would come." He worked hard and smart, he was damn good at his job, and he was a good man.

"Balance, or in my case overcompensation." Gordy gave him a ghost of a smile. "I never had this family thing. I had... growing up I had Emma. Dad basically just drank and slept around, Mom worked all the time. Every minute. I know it makes me sound like an ass, but I never wanted it. I didn't want a boyfriend, I didn't want a daughter. And now I don't know what I'd do without either of you. Honestly. I mean that, Colby. But I had no idea what to do with kids. I still don't, really. I'm just making shit up as I go. And I really have no idea what to do with parents who—parents like yours."

Gordy's smile grew. "So while you're thinking nothing of it, I'm panicking over here. But I might at least be getting closer to figuring out what to do with you."

"All you have to do is say. My people love kids. They'll love you. They're just folks. Good people. Hard workers. I didn't ask about what to call them because all the kids call them Mamaw and Papaw. The grandkids, the kids at church, my sisters' best friends' kids, the neighbor kids, my best friends' kids. Everyone. Momma's excited to meet Liv. Daddy found her a vanity deal and fixed it up. I didn't mean to... how does that even step on feet? You ain't said she had grandparents that she'd call the same thing."

"She doesn't. She and I are the only blood either of us has left." Gordy shrugged. "Maybe that's it. I know you love her, but she's my responsibility, and it's... it felt easier just the three of us."

"She's your blood, Gordon. She's our responsibility, and no amount of saying different will change that. That is between me and God." And, okay, he knew better. He knew a phone call and Gordy could make it to where he could never see Liv or Gordy again. But this was about hope and heart, so he was going to pretend that he wasn't even thinking on that.

"You're right." Gordy stepped close, slipped an arm around him. "You're right. She's ours. I like the sound of that much better. I wouldn't worry at all about you and God where that little girl is concerned."

"I don't." Faith, hope, and love. He knew his scripture. "Maybe you ought to believe in me a little."

Gordy's soft laugh was dark with regret. "Touché, cowboy." He wrapped that arm tighter. "I do believe in you. I'll do better, okay? I'm just... adjusting. I do trust you—with my life, with hers. With everything. I'm sorry."

"I swear to God, I wasn't trying to be evil."

"I never thought that. I just thought you… oh, forget it. God. I need to learn when to shut my mouth. There isn't an evil bone in your body, cowboy. Except maybe the ones that were gearing up to fix my jaw for me." Gordon grinned at him.

"Shut up. I didn't do it." He shifted from boot to boot. "Can I come home now, man? I need a cup of coffee."

"Keeping that between you and God too, huh? I deserved it. I know that." He reached around Colby and opened the front door. "In you go. And I think you should stay."

"I think I should too." He walked in, then met Gordy's eyes. "And I think we ought to talk about whether I'm living here. I got money for an apartment now, I been saving, but I think I've been staying with you for a while, and I want to know whether you want it to be permanent. Not long-term. Permanent."

God help him, he was using all his available shots in one afternoon.

Gordy laughed. "Yeah. That would be what I meant by stay, lover. Move in for good. Own the key. Don't stay with me, live here. Permanently park your boots."

"Oh. Good. Yes. I agree and shit. In fact, I'd love to." Was it too soon to get a kiss?

"I swear to God, one of these days it's going to be me that wears you out and not just these damn arguments and the mountain air." He scooped Colby up against him and kissed him. "I'm glad you said yes."

"Me too. I love you. I'd like to have wild passion-ate monkey sex at some point before I'm eighty."

"Do you know it's been two weeks? The last time was that thing we started in the shower, and then it got kind of dangerous…? Not that I'm counting." Gordy moved away and headed for the kitchen. Colby trailed after him and watched him set up the coffeepot. "But I'm going to get ahold of that ass soon if it means I have to give Olivia whiskey in her milk. Consider yourself warned. Maybe several times over."

"I'm ready, willing, and able." He couldn't stop his grin. "I might be willing to make you work for it. You're hot when you're fighting for it."

A knowing grin caught the corner of Gordy's lips, followed by a look that seared right into Colby's soul. "I was surprised to discover that side of you, cowboy. I used to only find your name in the dictionary under 'easy.'"

"I'm a man of hidden depths and shit." He knew that. Looked like Gordy was figuring it out too.

"Yeah? Show me." Gordy set Colby's empty cof-fee mug down hard on the counter and bolted around the kitchen island.

He took off like his ass was on fire, his boots slid-ing as he gave a certain fine son of a bitch someone to chase.

Gordy was right on his heels and rushed him through the bedroom door. "You learn that running from bears in the mountains?" Gordy paused long enough to close and lock the door behind them and then dove, catching hold of the waistband of Colby's jeans.

"Armadillos. Them bastards are mean."

Gordy wasn't winded, but his cheeks were flushed. He took a deep breath, his square shoulders lifting and his chest flaring. He tugged Colby in close enough for a quick kiss and then let him go. "Mean-er'n me?"

"They carry leprosy. Kiss me again, asshole." He had to grin.

"Uh-huh." Gordy reeled him right back in and kissed him, Gordy's tongue forcing its way past his lips.

He groaned and stepped up, needing this like he needed to breathe. "More, man."

Gordy didn't seem to have a problem with that. His hands dove under Colby's T-shirt and yanked it up and off, and then his fingers tugged roughly at Colby's jeans.

"Wanna see where this tan ends, cowboy."

"You curious to know if my butt glows in the dark?" His cock was happy as hell, so happy to get into the make-up sex part of the day.

"Off." Gordy grunted at him, their lips not more than a breath apart. "Now."

"Uhn." He tore at his belt, but he needed space between them, so he stepped back, getting his happy ass butt-naked.

As soon as he straightened up, Gordy's hands were on him again, one hooked behind his neck and the other wrapped tightly around his shaft and strok-ing slowly. Gordy's palm burned hot against his skin.

"Oh, damn." He let his head fell back for a sec-ond. He needed to tease about his tan, about playing hard to get, but first this.

"Yep. Right there in Webster's. Easy: see Colby McBride." Gordy lifted Colby's face to his and kissed him, that grip working his cock harder, faster. "Not fighting me now, are you, cowboy?" Gordy whispered to him, crowding him backward toward the bed.

"You like it when I do." He pushed up, smacking their chests together, wrestling control of the kiss right out of Gordon's hands.

Gordy grunted with it and then hummed at him approvingly. Colby had taken the kiss, but Gordy had the momentum and was able to hip-check Colby, knocking him against the bed.

He released Colby to fumble with the buttons on his shirt. Oh, excellent idea. Colby worked Gordy's belt open, undressing him so much easier.

Gordy kicked off his prissy loafers and shucked his jeans as soon as Colby had them open. The way that he raked his eyes up the length of Colby's body was Gordy to the bone, possessive and hungry.

"Been too fucking long, cowboy." He didn't move, but Colby could see it coiling in him, watched his fingers twitch.

"Yeah." He gave it his best bull rider stance, all tight ass and clenched abs.

"Look at you. Get in bed." Colby had to wonder if his lover really believed he'd go.

"Bossy old man." He grabbed hold of Gordon's cock and pulled like it was a leash. "C'mere."

Gordon bared his teeth and hissed like it hurt. No shit, maybe it did, the man was stiff as stone. "Fuck." Gordy reached out and gave one of Colby's nipples a savage twist.

"No titty twisters." Fuck, that made him burn. "Those are ornamental!"

"Bullshit. You love it." Gordy smoothed a thumb over his nipple, soothing it for a second before shouldering into Colby and knocking him back on the bed. "Still easy."

Gordy dove after him, trying to use just body weight to pin Colby down. He slid out from under, using all those years of football to get him moving. He hauled himself up and over, landing on Gordy's butt, just stopping short of howling in victory.

Gordy grunted, the sound part frustration and part determination, and how much fun was that? And hot too. Damn.

He didn't sit there for long. Gordon rolled under him onto his back and closed his fist around Colby's cock. He didn't stroke, just squeezed it tight, and then reached up with his other hand, tugging Colby down by his neck and meeting him partway with a hard kiss.

Fuck, he loved this son of a bitch. He poured everything into this kiss—his fear, his fury, his need to meet Gordon halfway, his respect and the way desire had turned into something so much more.

Gordon accepted all of it, the emotion and the urgency, and not passively. He tore his mouth away, and after a couple of panting breaths he nodded. "Yeah," he said, looking up into Colby's eyes.

Colby nodded, that ball in the pit of his stomach unraveling. Fuck yes. Gordy heard him. Finally. "Cool."

Gordy smiled at him and winked, then rolled them both onto their sides. "We're your home now, okay? Me and Liv? As much as your folks."

"Yeah. Yeah." Maybe more than. He'd loved Texas enough to leave, but he loved Gordon and Liv enough to fight to stay.

"Good. I love you." Gordy kissed him and then reached up and pulled supplies out of his nightstand. He waved the rubber in front of Colby's eyes. "And fuck, cowboy, I want this. I want you."

"You want me to ride?" Because he was all over that. There was something about Gordon watching him move, watching him close that tripped his trigger.

Oh, look at that grin. "Fuck, yeah."

"Good deal." He grabbed the slick and popped the top, slicking his fingers before handing the bottle back to Gordy. "Get ready for me. I intend to wear your saddle out."

Gordy laughed, a genuinely happy sound, and rolled on his rubber. "I can't wait to watch you try." He shifted onto his back, getting comfy. "Bring it on."

He twisted, getting his hole a little stretched and a lot slick, putting on a show at the same time.

"Pretty. That look. Jesus." Gordy got up on his elbows and went after Colby's nipple, pinching one gingerly between his front teeth and sliding his tongue across the tip.

"Fuck yeah." Lord have mercy, that made him shiver, made him push his fingers deeper. He didn't fight the moan either. Gordon deserved to hear it.

"Oh, I like that sound, cowboy. Give me more." Gordy switched to the other side, teeth clamping down harder, tongue rolling his nipple.

"Jesus." He bit the word out, then yanked his fingers free and moved to straddle Gordon's cock without any fanfare. He burned with needing this, and he'd be damned if he didn't take it.

Gordy released him and looked between their bodies. He stayed up on one elbow and reached to steady his own cock, making things a little simpler for Colby. "That's it. Come on."

He nodded once, then got with the program, grunting at the burn and scrape as the fat tip of Gordon's cock popped in.

"Uhn." Gordy puffed out a breath, and his hand shifted to Colby's hip. "Tight, baby."

He nodded, fighting to lick his lips, to move. Something. Anything. "Good."

He could feel Gordy's body tense and shift under him, and Gordy groaned, the hand on Colby's hip bruising into his skin. "Colby. Cowboy. You gotta...." His lover groaned again, the sound tight in Gordy's throat. "Move." It was an order. "Or I will."

"Promises." He chuffed out a laugh that was more moan than air, then braced himself on Gordon's broad chest and started riding.

Gordy leaned and took a kiss, and then one more before collapsing back into the comforter. "So good." He rolled his hips, matching Colby's rhythm. "Missed this. Missed you."

All Colby could do was nod, but he figured that was okay. Gordy got it.

"Are you that gone already, cowboy? God, you're beautiful." Gordy's hands slid down his sides, grabbed his ass, and Gordy rocked under him hard.

"Fuck. Do that again." That lit him up like the Fourth of July, and he wanted more. More of Gordon's cock, more of his hands. Everything.

Gordy groaned, and his fingers dug into Colby's ass, but he gave Colby what he was asking for. And not just once. Gordy gave it to him five, maybe six times over. That was what he needed, and he started to give back, driving back and down until his muscles screamed.

"Colby. Fuck!" Gordy let go of Colby's ass and for a minute went a little crazy, hips rocking and hands fucking everywhere. Finally he settled a bit, hooking one around Colby's cock and the other threading through Colby's hair. "Christ." His breath was mostly shallow panting. "What you fucking do to me."

"Love you with all I got." And that was enough.

"Man of...." Gordy interrupted himself with a groan and then went on. "Hidden depths. Right?"

"You would know." What the fuck? They were both too goddamn coherent.

Gordy laughed. "All right, cowboy. That's your eight seconds." Gordy hooked an arm around Colby's shoulders and flipped them, dumping Colby heavily on his back in the duvet and then seating himself, balls-deep, thighs tight against Colby's ass. "My turn."

Okay, that was the hottest fucking thing in history. "All yours."

"Mm-hm. Mine." Gordon bent over him and kissed him, starting out with long, measured strokes. "You keep me up-to-date, baby. I want to be one second behind you."

"One second. So fucking good." He was all over this. He ached, and the deep burn found him grabbing his cock and tugging hard.

"Shameless. I like it."

Gordy managed to keep his careful control for a bit, and Colby knew it was only with real effort. His bangs started to stick to his forehead, and his shoulders and chest grew damp as the sweat beaded up and his skin turned pink. Colby got every sound—every moan, every grunt—Gordy wasn't holding on to anything.

His balls drew in and he curled with the pressure, his shoulders lifting from the mattress as his abs went tight.

"Yeah." Gordon's hips sped, and he bent to Colby, biting at Colby's lips with his teeth.

"Soon." He was moving on pure instinct, lizard brain insisting that it was time, that the pressure needed to release.

Colby didn't need Gordy's silent nod to know his lover was with him. Gordy's hips pistoned faster, one solid jolt after another.

He mashed their lips together as he shot, pushing his cry into their kiss, the world shattering into a million pieces. Somewhere far beyond the ringing in his ears he heard Gordy shout, and it felt for a second like he might tear right in two.

Colby blinked, shook his head as he tried to put all his scattered chickens back together.

As Gordy slipped away from him he heard the groan, and then Gordy's soft laugh disappearing off to his left someplace. It could have been a minute or twenty before Gordy's weight shifted the bed again and warm lips closed over his. "Hey."

"Hey." Lord have mercy, that felt good. "Missed you, honey. Something fierce."

"I know. God, I missed you too. And this. We need this." Gordy's arm slid over his waist. "It's on me. I know. I'm… thinking about it."

"Hey, you got to do what's important to you. I get that." He wasn't blowing sunshine up Gordy's skirt, either. He understood loving what you did.

Gordy kissed him again. "I believe you do get it, cowboy, and I love you for that. But other things—people—are important now too. Not sure how to change things in the near term but...." Gordy shrugged.

"It'll work itself out." Most shit did, and the other stuff bashed at you 'til you settled it.

"It will. I'm here now, anyway. And that was well worth the wait. You were on fire."

"I wanted you." Simple as that.

"Mm. I hear that." Gordy sighed. "Too bad it's almost dinnertime. You think Liv is still asleep? We should wake her up and feed her. And I owe you a coffee." Gordy's words were all about what they should be doing, but instead of getting up, he tugged Colby into his arms.

"Shh. She's wore. We got a second to be."

"Yeah. Good. Tell me about your weekend. Oh—who is Miss Linda with the heart sticker?"

"Oh Lord. You ought to meet her. She's living up at the campground a little bit. She's late on the rent. She's got a pair of twins that are hooligans, but good boys." He smiled, stealing another kiss. "Liv was taken with her."

"Sounds... interesting for sure." Gordy shifted a bit and ran his fingers through Colby's hair. "Liv is now convinced she is also magic. You have a lot of magic friends up there?"

"I play cards with a group of guys that change every weekend. There's a younger couple that's pregnant that was there this weekend. She loves Liv." People came and went. The tourists didn't come back; the locals did.

"I wish I had your ability to make friends. People always love you."

"You work in hospitality, man. You have to make friends for a living." He just liked to talk.

Gordy snorted a laugh. "I make acquaintances for a living. I can schmooze anyone. Usually they're perfectly happy to leave it at that."

"Ooh. Come schmooze me, baby." He made kissy faces and waggled his eyebrows, looking to make Gordy laugh.

"Hey, cowboy, where you been all my life? Oh, wait. Aren't you that guy that blew me in my office? How about that?" Gordy rolled him a bit and hung over him, planting a playful kiss on his lips. "You're a nut."

"Yep, but I'm yours, and I reckon you aim to keep me."

"Damn straight. And right here too. For as long as possible."

Chapter Twenty-Nine

"HEY, YOU wanna come up? They're here." Oh, Colby sounded so damn happy.

"Hey, cowboy. That's great, I'll be right in."

"Good deal."

Gordon hung up the phone and looked at his watch. It was already after three, and Delmara opened at five. They were packed as usual with reservations right off the bat, so dinner with Colby's parents was out of the question. While that was probably expected, Colby might still frown at him.

He stood and smoothed out his dress shirt, a little dismayed by the ball of anxiety in his gut. Despite all his ambition, there were still a lot of things he'd never imagined for himself, and meeting his lover's parents was certainly among them.

His partner's parents? Were they there now? Gordon thought they were. Colby was certainly a lot more than a live-in lover.

He left his office and found Oscar to let him know what was what and then headed up the stairs to the apartment.

A big booming laugh greeted him, the sound huge, like Santa and King Kong had a Texan baby. There was no question who the man that owned the laugh was, or what Colby was going to look like in thirty years either. This was his lover, just wrinkled and a little bigger, all around.

He stepped in and closed the door behind him, suddenly feeling seventeen. He shook it off quickly; he had a first impression to make. He walked right over to Colby first and gave him a kiss on the cheek. "Hey."

"Hey. Gordon, I'd like to introduce you to Deb and Harrison—my folks."

Colby's mom was a round lady who was sitting on the floor with Liv, looking at a baby doll and a load of clothes. "Hello, Gordon. Pleased to meet you."

Gordon went to her and bent to offer her a handshake. "Really nice to meet you, Deb." He gave her a smile and straightened. "I'm so glad you guys could make it. Colby talks about you a lot."

He looked over at Colby's dad and then took a couple of steps in his direction, hand out. "Harrison."

"Gordon." Harrison shook it firmly, but not hard. "Nice place you got here."

Gordon got the feeling he'd killed the mood a little. The handshake was a far cry from the laughter as he was walking in the door. But he figured they had to be at least as apprehensive as he was. Or maybe it was that smooch on the cheek. Oh, well. Colby hadn't warned him off. "Thank you. I like it. Can't beat the commute."

"No, sir. Cole here's been telling us all about your restaurants and how nice they are. You got some damn fine tile work in there."

"Cole?"

"I'm named after Momma's oldest brother. All my people call me Cole, is all."

"Cole." Gordon grinned. Maybe if he paid attention he'd learn something. For now, he heard an opportunity to brag, and he was going to take it. "I don't suppose he told you that he's the one that did that stunning tile work for me? It's brand-new—just finished this week. It's my favorite thing about the restaurant now, that whole fireplace. Your son is a real artist."

Harrison nodded. "He did. Not that I wouldn't have known a McBride did the work. We're the best in the business."

The pride in Harrison's voice made him smile. This was a man who loved his son, believed in him.

"That's what he told me, that he learned from the best. And he's got a great rep around town." He went to Colby and stood close, bumped shoulders with him. "Hey, I have a four-top for you and Liv and your parents at six if you want to eat downstairs. No pressure, I just held it in case."

"Uncle Colby! Please! Please, I want to have reservations!" Liv ran to him, so excited. "Uncle Gordy! I will be so good!"

Colby's soft chuckle made him smile. "I think that sounds great, honey. Thank you."

Gordon scooped her up and looked at Colby. "Okay, so maybe some pressure. Sorry." It was about all he was going to be able to do for Colby's parents tonight. He should be joining them, sitting with Colby, supporting him, but maybe once they got an idea of how busy he was going to be they would forgive him for being a poor host.

"And you'll be on your best behavior, pumpkin. I have a special dessert for you if you're extra good, okay?"

"Uh-huh. I will be sparkly good. I will wear my rainbow dress and my headband."

"Wow. You'll be the prettiest girl in the room." She was already the prettiest girl in the room. He wondered at how that smile of hers made him so happy and broke his heart at the same time, every time. He gave her a squeeze, then kissed her temple and set her back down on the floor.

He glanced at Colby, thankful that his lover just got it and he didn't have to explain.

"Did Colby already offer you a beer, Harrison?"

"He didn't. He's a bad son. Offer away, my friend."

Gordon laughed. "Can I get you a beer, sir?" He didn't wait for an answer, just made his way into the kitchen. He brought one back for Colby too. "Deb, are you a beer drinker?"

She snorted. "Honey, you know how long I've been a mom? Beer is the reason they all lived to adulthood."

"Right on, Momma." Gordon bypassed Colby with a shrug and a grin and handed Colby's beer to Deb.

"I'm abused, Liv." Colby grinned at their girl, who giggled happily.

"I thought cowboys would do anything for their mommas?" Gordon headed right back to the kitchen to get his man a beer. Pretty soon he was going to have to get into his suit and make a graceful exit, but not before he made sure Colby was happy.

"We do. No question." Colby followed him, stayed close. "Thanks for the supper invite. That's cool."

"Yeah?" Gordon hooked an arm around him. "Least I can do. I'm sorry I can't eat with you, but they'll get the red-carpet treatment, and I'll stop by the table a few times. Are you sure I can't get them a hotel room for tonight?"

"They're going to stay in the trailer. Momma's convinced it's got boy funk in it."

"It probably does." Gordon gave him a quick kiss. "So did I blow it or does your dad just not know what to make of me yet?"

"He spoke to you, shook your hand, and he's coming to supper. You did fine."

"And bonus for the beer." Gordon grinned. It was what it was; he couldn't do more than be himself. "I'm going to have to get dressed. Thursdays are always super casual, so don't let anybody worry about that."

"Will do. Can I have a quick kiss? No one's gawking."

Gordon nodded. "Doesn't even have to be quick." He pulled that tight body into his and planted a good one on Colby, one that would make him want dessert later.

"Mmm." Colby leaned into him, took his kiss eagerly. "Tell me you'll be ready to give me some loving when you get done closing."

"I'm ready now, cowboy, so by closing you're going to be all I'm thinking about."

"Good."

He loved that smile on Colby's face. Loved it.

"Remember that look. It's good on you." He let Colby go, reluctantly. "Now if I don't get going, Oscar is going to have my balls." He gave Colby one more quick squeeze and then headed off to the bedroom to change.

He pulled on a dark suit and a crisp white shirt, knowing that by the end of the night it would look like he'd slept in it. But for now, he had his trendy tie and his shiny shoes and he was feeling pretty damn good about himself.

Hell, he'd met the parents and he hadn't choked.

He was on a roll.

Chapter Thirty

LORD, THIS was easier with other adults. Colby stretched out under the sun, one eye on Liv and Daddy as they goofed off in the water.

Christ on a pink sparkly crutch, Daddy was having a ball.

"She's a sweetheart." Momma sounded pleased. "Y'all are so lucky she's easygoing. She ever talk about her momma? At all?"

"It comes up." Colby's phone started to vibrate in his pocket. As convenient as it was, there was something not right about cell service in the mountains. "Hold up. You watch her, huh?"

"I will beat you, son."

Colby answered the phone without looking. "Yo."

"Hey, baby."

Colby expected to hear road noise and old-man rock on the radio, but instead he was pretty sure he heard the hum of a crowd and the sound of cutlery against china.

"Hey, you. What's up?" Like he didn't know. This was where someone didn't show or something was broke or there was a VIP. This was Gordon's life.

Gordy sighed. "We're down a chef. I have a swing, but he's going to need help and... well, Oscar's taking the floor and I've had to roll up my sleeves. I'm not going to make it out there, Colby, I'm sorry."

"Well, that sucks." He wasn't surprised, but he was disappointed. At least he hadn't told Liv Gordon was coming. "At least you're making money, right?"

Gordy snorted. "Yeah. That's exactly what I used to tell myself." The sounds in the background grew muffled. "Listen, I can't tell you that tomorrow... I mean, he's not going to be in so...."

"No worries. I'll see you Monday afternoon. Get some rest, huh?" What was he supposed to do? Be pissed the rest of his life? That was bullshit. He'd just have his love affair with the mountains every weekend.

"Colby." Gordon's voice stopped him hanging up. "I'm really sorry. I swear, I'd be there if I could. I love you."

"I know. I know. You're not in trouble." *Much.* "I love you, honey. Go work."

"Kiss Liv for me. Love you. Night." Gordon hung up and the line went silent.

He sighed, then went back to sit, knowing Momma was going to give him what for.

But Momma just sat there beside him and said nothing at all. She cut her eyes at him once, sighed a minute later. Jesus Christ, it was worse than catching hell. His shoulders hadn't relaxed since he'd hung up the phone, and he found himself wishing she'd just let him have it already.

She opened her mouth, and he winced, which made Momma roll her eyes. "So fess up, son. Your man ain't coming?"

"No, ma'am."

"He have a good reason?"

"Yes, ma'am. Work."

She sighed softly. "Well, that's a shame. I was looking forward to actually getting to know him."

"Oh, Momma. He lives for those restaurants. That's just his thing. He loves it above all else. He built it from the bottom up."

"Does he love it more than you, more than that little girl, more than the good Lord?"

Oh, for fuck's sake. "Momma. Drop it."

"You're not the little girl's daddy, Colby. You can… I don't know."

Colby turned, looked at her, full-on. "No, ma'am. I cannot. She's as much mine as anyone's, and I love her. I love him. I can't blame the man for loving his job."

She watched him for a long, long minute. Then her lips pursed and he braced himself for an ass-chewing, but what she said was, "Well, good for you, standing up for yourself."

"Uncle Colby! Are you coming swimming ever? Papaw says I look like a prune!"

"Sorry, Momma. My girl needs me." He stood up, headed for the water. "Yo. Prune girl!"

Liv shrieked happily when he jumped in, the wave splashing her. "See? Wrinkly fingers. Show Papaw how you throw me?"

"Are you ready, Papaw?"

"I am, indeed, ready, son. Show away."

Colby grinned and grabbed his girl. "Ready, Little Bit?"

"Ready."

He checked to make sure it was safe, and then he tossed her, her happy squeals filling the air.

She came down with a splash, going under, but Colby wasn't worried. This was a regular game with them now, and she was a good little swimmer. Sure enough she popped right up, laughing and kicking her feet. "Again!" she demanded as she swam back over. "Please? One more time?"

"Better you than me." Daddy waded to that sunny rock and hauled himself up next to Momma. "Do it again, Uncle Colby!"

"Traitor." He grabbed her, swung her around. "Ready? Let's go!"

Chapter Thirty-One

GORDON WAS headed west on 119 in his Jeep, top down and radio blaring. The farther he got from the city, the more he was able to relax, which was a little surreal, considering he was leaving behind a restaurant without its regular chef and down an extra set of hands.

He and Oscar had had a long meeting in his office over a good bottle of wine last night, talking into the very early hours, and this freedom was the remarkable upshot of that conversation—he was wearing shorts and a T-shirt, his sunglasses, and he was headed for his family.

He hadn't called; it was early when he left Boulder, and then, with the top down, Colby wouldn't have been able to hear him anyway. He turned the radio way down as he pulled off onto the access road that

Colby had marked for him on the map, slowed as he felt the 4x4 kick in, and headed into the trees.

The campground was busy, tents and campers dotting the sites. There was a little pool, lawn chairs, and fire pits. It was charming as hell.

Gordon took it slow down the dirt track around the outside, cautious of all the little ones running around and also trying not to kick up a lot of mess with his tires. He nodded and returned friendly waves as he went, his Jeep drawing the attention of parents keeping an eye on their kids.

How amazing was all of this? No wonder Colby loved it.

It wasn't long before he spotted Colby's trailer up ahead, and he turned down the bumpy little drive going in that direction, his smile growing as he got closer.

He could see Colby, leaning over the campfire, wearing a pair of shorts and a flannel shirt. Olivia was in Colby's mom's arms, rocking in a plastic rocking chair.

He slowed almost to a stop, just to take in that picture—the calm, the family time, his cowboy. Then he started looking around for a place to park his Jeep, settling on a spot across the lane from Colby's camp, under open sky. The less tree sap on his seats the better.

He adjusted his sunglasses, tugged on his baseball hat, and jumped out of the car.

"Uncle Gordy!" Olivia's squeal made the birds fly, the sudden sound shocking, loud and sort of wonderful.

Gordy jogged toward her, meeting her halfway, and caught her when she leapt the last two steps. "Hey, pumpkin! Having fun?"

"You came! I telled them you would. I telled them you would come." She hugged him tight. "Uncle Colby! Look! I said!"

"You did. You are brilliant." Colby walked right up to him, hugged him, offered him a kiss. "This is the best surprise ever."

He shifted Liv to his hip and lifted his cap, taking Colby's kiss and then some. "I'm a little surprised I made it myself. What a great drive, though. And this little campground is lovely."

"Isn't it? You want coffee? I was just fixin' to start the bacon. Momma made biscuits in the trailer."

"Yes, please." He gave Liv a smooch on her head and set her down, leading her by the hand back over to Colby's mom in the rocking chair. "Morning, Momma." He leaned down and kissed her cheek. *What the hell, right? In for a penny....*

"Hey, honey. Glad you could make it." She patted his cheek like she'd done it a thousand times.

"Papaw is still sleeping. He was up late playing cards."

Gordy grinned. "More bacon for me. Speaking of which, I should see if I can help. Would you mind eyeballing her for a bit?"

"Of course not. We were rocking and telling her granny secrets."

"Granny secrets?"

She nodded. "Things just between a little girl and her mamaw. Shoo. Go make food."

"Thanks." He winked at her, helping Liv back into her mamaw's lap before heading over to the fire. Colby had just finished pouring his coffee, and he took the mug. "What can I do?"

"I've got the bacon on. I was thinking a scramble with veggies in. You want to help?" Colby kept grinning at him, just beaming. Right now, right at this moment with those blue eyes shining so bright, he wouldn't care if Delmara burned to the ground.

"I do make a mean scramble." He sipped his coffee and stood close, one hand on Colby's hip, not caring a bit who was looking. "You got a pan? I'll grab the eggs."

"I do, indeed, have a pan." Colby leaned a little. "It's good to see you, sir."

He pressed his face to Colby's neck and kissed it, breathing in woodsmoke and sweat and mountain air. "You too, cowboy. I'm looking forward to a couple of days up here." A couple of days that didn't involve yet more obligations. He couldn't recall the last time he'd been away just because.

"Yeah? You can stay?" Colby moaned softly. "Oh, you have made my whole day."

"Yeah. I'm good until Tuesday morning if you are." He let Colby go and headed for the cooler. "We've got some catching up to do." He laughed. "Swimming or something, right?"

"Swimming. Sitting in the sun. Beer. Cards. Lots of relaxing together."

"However will we manage it?" Not to mention that his phone was off and locked in the glove compartment. It was almost too good to be true.

Gordon sipped his coffee and carried the eggs back to the fire. "Eggs, sir. I haven't played cards in forever. What do you guys play? Poker?"

"Depends on who's playing. Last night it was poker. Sometimes spades or hearts. They tried to teach me pinochle, but damn."

"People still play pinochle?" He'd never understood that game. He watched Colby throw some veggies in the hot frying pan and toss them around. "No marshmallows and ghost stories?"

"Marshmallows, yes. Liv is addicted to the idea of sticking food in the fire. She's not old enough for ghost stories, I don't think."

"Good, I don't know any anyway." Gordon laughed and started cracking eggs into the pan, letting his hands get in Colby's way on purpose. "I know a few horror stories, but no ghosts."

"You can whisper them into my ear tonight."

"Oh. We have to talk?" He took the spatula from Colby's fingers and scrambled the eggs in the pan.

"Not even a word." Colby turned the bacon. "She sleeps like the dead up here."

"I was thinking she'd like a sleepover in the trailer. Wouldn't that be cool?" He snorted. Liv might sleep like the dead, but he wasn't sure he could... with her... yeah, no. "Salt and stuff?" He looked back in the direction of the cooler.

"Oh, you'll love this. Check it out." Colby pulled up a tackle box, opened it, and there was salt, pepper, garlic powder, cumin, plus a variety of cooking supplies.

"Look at that!" Gordon was completely impressed. "I never would have thought of that. How brilliant." He reached for the salt and pepper and added some to the eggs. "You're a clever cowboy."

"I learned that trick from my dad." Colby pulled the bacon out of the skillet and dumped a bag of shredded potato in the grease.

"You mean the guy that would know McBride workmanship from a mile away while blindfolded?" Gordon teased.

"That would be the one. Also known as the man who wore his ass out playing with Liv yesterday."

"Took one for the team? Nothing but respect, brother." He chuckled. "Eggs are done."

"Cool. Can you pour Liv some milk?"

"Uncle Colby! Dr Pepper?"

"Nope. Aren't you the child who told me she didn't drink Coke?"

"I liked the Sprite, remember?"

"I need a decoder ring to follow your soda talk." He fished the milk out and poured some in a cup for Olivia. "Your Bostonian grandfather would have said 'no tonic with breakfast, young lady.'"

"Can you swim, Uncle Gordy?"

"No." Gordon grinned at her. "Will you teach me?"

"You can't swim?" Liv's eyes grew as big as saucers, and Gordon had to laugh.

"I can swim, pumpkin. I was teasing. But are you talking about that tiny little pool over there? Because I think it would be hard for me to swim in."

"No, Uncle Gordy." She rolled her eyes at him, and her tone was hilariously exasperated. "Over there."

He'd been swimming in some very fancy swimming pools, soaked in a couple of decadent hot tubs, but he'd never been swimming in a lake. Creek. River? Whatever that was.

"Is the water cold?"

"In the morning time it is. In the sunshine, it feels so good."

"I'm going to hold you to that. We'll go in this afternoon, okay?" He scooped some eggs onto a small plate for her. "Go sit, sweetie, so you don't drop anything." He looked at Colby. "Plate for Momma?"

"She loves bacon and potatoes. I'll trade her for some biscuits. Daddy will eat her eggs."

He helped Colby get her plate together and then sent him off with it. Biscuits sounded so good.

The rest of the morning was full of laughter. They cleaned up breakfast, he kicked a ball around with Liv for a while, and Colby showed him no mercy playing horseshoes as the day got warmer and warmer. The sun was out and shining all afternoon, but Liv had obviously absorbed some kind of Texan thick skin, because despite swimming and jumping around like a fool, Gordon never did get used to the temperature of the water.

He spotted Harrison sunning himself on a wide rock like a lizard and waded over to join him while Colby tossed Olivia around for the ninetieth time.

"You have the best spot on the river." Gordon hauled himself out, sighing as the heated rock warmed his backside.

"I do. I'm baking my bones." Harrison looked over from under his hat brim as Liv squealed. "She's having a ball."

He nodded, watching them, thinking that the day couldn't get any better. "She is. She loves him like a father."

"I'm assuming you're good with that?"

Gordon nodded, squinting over at Harrison. "I'm better than good—I want that. He wants that."

"Good. He's a good father. I'm not surprised. He loves kids."

"He really does. When I brought her home from Boston, he just stepped right up. And it wasn't even about me and him; it was all about her." It had been about him too, he knew that. He'd been a wreck, and Colby had been a rock for him. But the bottom line was Olivia had needed something Gordon didn't know how to give her and Colby did.

Harrison nodded once. "I'm glad y'all could care for her. I know it's a bitch, juggling work and family, and I did it the way that I got nine months of planning 'fore the first one showed."

"It's… hard." Gordon sighed. "I never wanted kids, honestly. Never even considered it. I wasn't set up for this, you know?"

He wasn't sure why he was suddenly confiding in Colby's dad. Maybe because it sounded like Harrison was ready to listen. "I love her, I do. I just feel like I'm always trying to catch up. And I'm… conflicted."

"How's that?" Harrison's eyes were on Colby and Liv, and that made it easier to talk.

He thought about that. Because really, right now he had everything. "Well, my restaurant was my baby, you know? It used to be my whole life. I love it. But I love those two to death. I have to let go of some of one so I can keep the other."

"That's true. I had to work hard to build my business, and about two babies in, my wife flat-out told me she wasn't doing this for her looks. I had to make some changes. I never work Sundays, and she got a sitter for Friday afternoons so we could, uh… well, let's just say we didn't stop at two little ones." Harrison wore a shit-eating grin.

Gordon laughed out loud. Loud enough that Colby turned his head. Gordon just gave him a grin and a wave.

"Oh, I know it well. Colby talks about his sisters a lot. You kept going until you got the boy." He snorted. "And you ended up with another son-in-law anyway."

He couldn't stop the train of thought, but he stopped the flow of words by biting his lips together. Shit. He'd just said that out loud, hadn't he? To Colby's father, of all people. Jesus.

"I got no problems with that, man. Cole was born gay. I know this; I prayed on it. God knows what He's doing, way more than me, and God's law is love. Y'all are our family." Harrison's lips twisted. "You might oughta run."

Gordon knew that look well. Colby looked so much like his father it was scary. Even the knowing bit of mischief in Harrison's eyes was familiar.

"Hell, I'll take crazy over nothing." Gordon smiled at him, starting to feel like family. "Thanks, Harrison. For the welcome. And… everything." Things he hadn't gotten from his own dad. Things he didn't have words for.

"Uncle Gordy! I scratched my finger!"

Colby came wading up, holding Liv up toward him. "She needs you to kiss it better, honey."

"Let me see, pumpkin." She was wearing a yellow bathing suit with ladybugs on it, and her pout was so cute he could hardly stand it.

He took her hand and leaned over for a closer look but really didn't see anything, which was exactly when it dawned on him what was going on. Somebody caught his shoulder, somebody gave him a good shove from behind, and he ended up flipping face-first into the icy water.

Oh, someone was going to pay! He bobbed up, gasping and snorting, Liv's merry laughter filling the air. He gave his head a shake and wiped his eyes, laughing right along with her. "Like father, like son? Or am I to believe that Liv cooked that one up?"

He reached for Olivia and set her carefully on the rock beside Harrison. Then he turned on Colby. "Well?"

Colby fluttered his eyelashes outrageously. "Are you accusing me of something?"

"I'm convicting you of something." He knew without having to see it for himself that Colby would easily outswim him if he didn't get hold of the cowboy now, so he dove, getting one arm around Colby's neck.

"Very nice." Colby had nothing on him, size-wise, but the man was tall and had one hell of a reach.

Gordon maneuvered around behind Colby and whispered in his ear, "Well, you know what happens when I let you run."

"Be good, honey. I'm going to have to stay in the cold water for a bit as it is."

Gordon chuckled. "Sorry, baby." He looked back at Liv. "Come in, baby girl. I bet you can't beat me to that rock!"

Liv jumped up and stuck her hands on her hips. "Can too!"

"Yeah? Ready?"

She didn't wait for his go, she just dove right in.

"Hey! I think that's cheating!" He looked at Colby, letting Liv get her head start. "Isn't that cheating?"

"She's totally cheating. She must get that from her Papaw."

"Yeah. That's exactly what I was thinking." Right. He kissed Colby's cheek. He watched Liv for another second and then dove in to chase her.

He was having so much fun.

COLBY SAT in his chair, head leaned back, beer in his hand.

This had been the perfect day.

Seriously. Steaks. Swimming. Goofing off. Cards. And now, beer.

All with Gordon to share it.

"Liv is all tucked in with Momma in the trailer. I think they both liked the idea of a sleepover." Gordon's chair creaked and groaned as he sat down. He sighed. "Mm. Fire's nice."

"It is. Supper was good, huh? Liv ate her weight in beef."

"I think I did too." Gordy scrunched down in his chair, crossed his ankles, and rested his head back. "But I earned it."

"Mm-hmm. You've been working yourself to death." This had been good for Gordon. Good for him too.

"I have, you're right. But I think Oscar and I figured it out last night, baby. We're pulling Shannon over from Gaia as a swing to assist Oscar on Fridays and Saturdays, and promoting Shannon's assistant to full weekend manager over at Gaia."

Gordon hooked his fingers into Colby's, laughing softly. "Oscar sat me down, poured me a glass of wine, and told me it was time to start acting like an owner and not a manager. He practically fired me."

"Yeah?" Colby held on, trying to figure out, practically, what that meant. "We'd love to see more of you."

"Well, I'll be around for sure Sundays and Mondays now. That was the biggest issue we wanted to resolve. We're going to switch up a few things so I can do the financial stuff and some of the orders on Friday instead of Sunday morning. The rest we still have to work out. I'd love to swing one Saturday a month."

"Wow. That's excellent. I can totally keep Mondays for you, at least most of them."

"You think? So we might get a day to ourselves sometimes? That would be incredible." Colby felt Gordon's grip tighten up. "I mean, things happen and people need time off—so there will still be some crazy weeks, but nothing like it's been. I just couldn't take your voice on the phone yesterday—and knowing that I was doing that to you."

He turned his head, met Gordy's gaze. "I can't tell you how wonderful it was, is, I mean. To share this with you."

"It feels good." Gordy held his eyes easily. "It's nice to just focus on this. You know?"

"I do. This is important to me. Being up here, under the stars. It's like being… not free, 'cause I don't feel trapped, but… maybe whole? Shit, I don't know." But he felt like this was necessary.

Gordy shrugged. "I just feel like… like I can breathe easy up here. I don't think you've ever really told me how important this is to you. I mean, I knew you loved the mountains, but you haven't explained to me why before."

"I'm not sure I know why. I just know it is. It's amazing with you."

"I agree. Guess the why doesn't matter." Gordy sipped his beer. "Hey, so your dad and I had a nice chat this afternoon. He's something, huh? I really like him."

"He's a good guy. We had our things when I was a teenager, but who doesn't?" That was part of life, wasn't it?

"He told me I was family. That was kind of a big deal to me, so." Colby thought maybe he heard a little emotion, but Gordy covered it with a sip of his beer. "Anyway, I appreciated that."

"You are. My family. I know it started weird, but it's true."

"Did it start weird? I kind of think it started truthful. I know I was pretty damn sincere." Gordy's laugh cut through the quiet campsite.

"Truthful, huh?" He liked that. He liked it a lot.

"Sure." Gordy grinned at him, the light from the fire reflecting in his eyes. "I mean, were you really looking for family the day I seduced you in my bathroom?"

"No, sir. I was looking to get off, and I spent three days kicking my own ass for blowing the first big job I'd had." Then he'd gone back for more.

Gordy's grin grew wide and lit up his face. "See? Truthful. Honest. I'm not the least bit ashamed of myself." He leaned across the arms of their camp chairs a little awkwardly and kissed Colby. "Had to start somewhere. Personally, I thought it was a damn good beginning."

"We have had some fun, huh?" How much better was it going to get?

"We have, cupcake." Gordy snickered and settled back in his chair.

"Don't make me beat you, honey." He leaned back, eyes on the flames.

"I think we should get Liv a bike for her birthday."

"I think she'd love that. She's been making noise about one." A bike, a Barbie car, and a dolphin for the bathtub.

"Yeah? Cool. Zoo on Wednesday, right? Have you got a job lined up this week? I've got time to pick one up Tuesday morning if you don't."

Listen to them, talking like normal people, like parents. "I do have a little job Tuesday. A hearth for a fireplace."

"Nice. Okay, I'm on it. And a cake I guess too. Chocolate." Gordy held his beer up and looked at the fire through it. "I'm empty."

"You want another?"

Gordy turned his head and looked at him. "I don't think so." Gordy's chair creaked and protested, and then Gordy was standing in front of him, one hand out to help him up. "I want to dance."

"What?" He stood up, taking Gordy's hand automatically.

Gordy pulled him in a little too close for dancing but placed a hand on his back, held his other hand in a dance grip and gave him a spin. "You promised you'd teach me to two-step. I'm free tonight, are you?"

"Oh, I bet you're a natural." Colby smiled and keyed up King George on his phone. "You lead or follow?"

Chapter Thirty-Two

SITTING DOWN to dinner at Delmara felt a lot like sitting in the passenger seat of your own car. Familiar, a little uncomfortable, and a totally different perspective.

"Good evening, I just wanted to stop by and welcome a VIP. Miss Olivia." Oscar smiled at Olivia and set a fancy, colorful frozen drink in front of her. "Happy sixth birthday."

Olivia bounced in her seat. "Thank you!"

"I heard these two escorted you to the zoo?"

"We saw polar bears!"

"No way." Oscar's eyes popped open wide, making Gordon grin.

"Uh-huh. They're really big."

"That is so cool."

"They have feet as big as Uncle Colby's head, and they live where it's cold and their homes are melting, so we have to recycle. Do you recycle, Oscar?"

"Of course I recycle, little girl. It's the responsible thing to do. The whole restaurant does too. Your Uncle Gordon made sure of that a long time ago."

"See?" Gordon poked Liv playfully in the arm. "I told you."

"Good." She settled back in her chair.

"Sam has your dinner order?"

"Yeah, thanks, Oscar." Gordon nodded. "We're all set."

"All right, then, enjoy." Oscar winked at Liv and hurried off to another table.

They'd seen a lot more than polar bears, but Liv had been fascinated by them. He'd been pretty impressed by the rhinos, and the basket of curly fries they'd shared at lunchtime. They'd even had their picture taken with the penguins. It came out pretty well for a first family photo.

"Been a good day, huh?" Gordon knew it had been, but he couldn't help asking.

"The best day. The best." She looked at him, frowned slightly. "Can I ask you a question?"

"Of course, pumpkin. What's up?"

"Is it okay if I miss Mommy but I can still have the best birthday? Does that make me bad?"

Gordon glanced briefly over Liv's head at Colby, swallowing down a lump in his throat. He knew by now that he ought to be ready for these questions, knew they'd keep coming, but he was still blindsided every time.

"No, baby. Not bad at all. Your mommy would want you to have the best birthday. She'd be really happy for you."

Colby's lips twisted, but he nodded at Gordon, offering him support.

"Okay." She grinned happily. "Are we doing cheers?"

"We are absolutely doing cheers." Colby picked up his beer.

"To the birthday girl." Gordon touched his wineglass to Liv's fancy drink and then to Colby's frosty beer.

"Cheers!" Liv laughed and clinked her glass with Colby's. She watched everything, her eyes wide and wondering. He'd bet anything that she was asleep before they got her upstairs in bed.

He was counting on it, in fact. He had plans for his cowboy.

Gordon leaned back in his chair and sipped his wine, trying not to look around the restaurant with too critical an eye. He'd be in the weeds tomorrow, with plenty to worry about then. He'd taken the damn day off. "First grade. That's pretty impressive, don't you think, Uncle Colby?"

"Exceptional. First grade. Six years old. Lord have mercy."

Gordon nodded as their food was set out on the table. He had decided to try the chicken; he'd eaten plenty of beef over the weekend. "You're going to have Mrs. Wilson, right? She seems nice."

Liv shrugged. "She's okay. She gives homework."

"Oh. Homework. Well, that just means you're growing up."

Homework, school bus, reading, playdates. Wouldn't be long before it became dances, dating, and a driver's license. He knew. He remembered his first day of first grade, missing front tooth and everything. Blink and he'd miss it.

He didn't plan on blinking for at least ten or twelve more years.

Olivia ended up just picking at her dinner, but her appetite improved when the cake arrived, six little candles plus one to grow on burning bright.

Colby beamed, eyes shining in the candlelight. Then he stood up, smiled wide, and made this fabulous redneck noise that shut everyone right up. "Okay, y'all. Let's everybody sing to our Olivia. She's six today."

Liv looked about as shocked as Gordon felt and twice as pleased. Jesus Christ, he loved that man. Sure, he felt equally mortified at the moment, but what the hell? She only turned six once, right? Gordon stood right up with Colby and started to sing.

The whole restaurant sang along, cheering as soon as the song ended. Liv sat there and beamed. "They singed to me!"

"They most certainly did, Little Bit." Colby sat down and grinned. "Blow out your candles."

Gordon just sat back and watched them, loving how into this Colby was and how happy it made Olivia, part of him wondering how he ever got along without this. All of it—the chaos, the fun, the frustration, and the moments like this one. To think that not long ago he would have told anyone who asked that he didn't want any part of it.

She blew her candles out, and Colby snapped pictures and cheered. Goofball. Still, it made him smile, ear to ear.

It was a good thing they didn't have to wait for a check, though, because by the time she finished her cake, Liv was leaning on Colby and her eyes were droopy. Colby scooped her right up like she didn't weigh a thing, she put her head on his shoulder, and that was pretty much all she wrote.

"Wow. I think that might be a record." Gordon followed Colby up the stairs, not even bothering to whisper.

"It was a long day. Sun and walking and polar bears, a new bike, then cake? Dude."

Dude, indeed. "That cake was fantastic too. You do know I'm going to get pranked by the waitstaff tomorrow for that rebel yell of yours." He laughed, patting Colby on the ass. "Next time I need to get someone's attention I know who to call."

"It seemed the easiest thing." Colby stood to the side and let him unlock the door.

"Well, I loved it." He pulled out his keys and opened it up, holding it for him.

"You think I should try and wake her up to get her nightgown on or just get her shoes off?"

"She petted rhinos and walked through penguin shit. Why dirty a perfectly clean nightgown?"

"Good point." Colby got her shoes and socks off, smiling as she wiggled around until she found Jessica.

Gordon hooked an arm around his hips and stood there with him, watching her get comfy. "We can just wash everything—and her—in the morning." He kissed the side of Colby's neck. "Mm. Might wash you tonight."

"I think that's an amazing plan." Colby's grin lit up his whole face, and Colby took Gordon's hand. "Lead the way."

Chapter Thirty-Three

LORD HAVE mercy, what a day.

Colby sat in his truck, trying to get the energy to walk up the stairs. He'd had a box of tiles slip out of his hand and land on his leg, tearing a strip of skin and ruining a pair of jeans. Two of the tiles had cracked on him, and of course, the motherfuckers were special order, so he ended up running into Denver to grab them.

Now he was late and sore and tired, and he wanted someone to come and carry him.

Oh, now there was a vision—his lazy ass being hauled up those steep steps.

He blinked as someone started blowing up his phone with text messages, and he was fixin' to lose it until he realized they were all from Gordy, probably sent over the last hour and they were just all coming in at once. He must have lost service at some point. The last one read:

worried now, please tell me you're okay

home. Love you. Crawling up the stairs now.

"Come on, cowboy. Get your ass moving," he told himself.

Gordon appeared at the foot of the stairs before he'd even made it across the parking lot. A couple more long strides and Gordy was right in front of him. "Hey, you. I'm not going to lie, I was pacing. Jesus, does that leg hurt? What the hell happened?"

"Sorry, honey. The messages all came through at the same time, see?" He held out his phone, but Gordon waved it away. "I dropped a box of tile and it ripped all the way down. These jeans are toast."

"Shit. You're lucky it didn't land on your foot. Are you limping? Let's take the elevator."

"I am lucky. I'm not damaged, just sore." He'd take the elevator, though. "Man, what a fucking day. And when I had plans too."

He did his damnedest not to work Mondays, but sometimes shit happened.

"It's all good, you're here now. The sitter is hanging out with Liv, and honestly, we don't have to go out if you're not up to it. I don't care if we order a pizza. I'm just happy you're home in one fucking piece." Gordy held the elevator door open for him.

"Me too. Let me clean up, and we'll go somewhere like grown-ups." He headed in, then grabbed Gordy for a kiss. "I hate that I'm running late, honey."

"I know just how that feels." Gordy took the kiss, then gave him a wink and let him go. They got inside, and he got a kiss from his girl and went to shower before it got any later.

Gordy did up the button at his throat and tightened up the knot in his tie. "There's Neosporin in the medicine cabinet. You want some help?"

"Sure. Always." Of course, there was a chance that help would end up with a really long shower. Really long.

"Oh good. How hungry are you?" Gordon laughed and followed him down the hall and past the sounds of the sitter and Olivia reading a book.

"I do love you in a suit. You make it look so good." It wasn't his favorite look on Gordy. That was jeans and a flannel shirt first thing in the morning. That look? Jesus. But this one, it was good.

"I try." Gordy slid warm hands under Colby's grubby T-shirt and tugged it off over his head. "Toss the jeans and let me look at that cut?"

"It's more of a scrape." With a bunch of nasty bruises. Thank God for steel-toed boots.

"Really? You're going to argue semantics? Take your jeans off, cowboy." Gordy grinned. "Or I could just tear them off you."

"Could you now?" He worked his belt buckle open, removed his belt, and shimmied out of his jeans.

"Well, no. Probably not, but it sounded hot. The jeans you buy are too well built." Colby watched Gordy wince when he got a better look at the scrape. "Okay, maybe that's a scrape, but it's ugly."

"It'll be sore as fuck tomorrow, but nothing's broke, thank God."

Gordy nodded. "Yeah. And thank God your truck wasn't in a ditch, because you have to know what I was thinking." Gordy took Colby's jeans and didn't quite meet his eyes. "I'm going to trash these. You get cleaned up, and then I'll help you get some stuff on that scrape. It's going to need more than a Band-Aid."

"Hey." He grabbed Gordon's arm, tugged him close. "I love you. I'm real sorry I worried you, huh?"

"You didn't worry me; I was just worried." Gordy shrugged and circled his arms around Colby. "Sorry you had a crap day. I love you. Sometimes so much it… hurts."

"I get that." He leaned in, rested their cheeks together. "You know how good it is to have you to come home to?"

Gordy sighed and just held him for a minute. "I do," he said finally. "I… oh." He laughed softly, kissed Colby's cheek, and then pulled away. "I do." He was grinning like a fool, eyes suddenly bright. "Just… hold that thought."

He scurried off toward the living room.

Colby watched, then shook his head and started cleaning up. The last thing he needed was to go into date night smelling like a rutting moose.

He heard Gordy come back into the room, heard the bedroom door close, and then Gordy appeared in the bathroom doorway. He leaned against the jamb watching Colby, arms crossed and one of those manila folder deals under one arm.

"This is not at all how I'd planned things, but it's so appropriate it's almost too good to be true."

"How's that? You look like the cat that swallowed the canary." He grabbed a towel and dried off.

"Well, the first time I cornered you in here you were a bit more clothed, but otherwise, this is pretty close." Gordy reached out and helped Colby wrap the towel around his waist and then put the folder carefully in Colby's hands. "This time I have something… slightly different for you."

"Yeah?" He grinned, pretty sure he was lost, but whatever it was, it was going to be okay. He opened up the folder, eyes going wide as Gordon knelt down. "Honey?"

"Colby McBride, I have two questions for you. And I'm kind of hoping you have just one answer." Gordy looked up at him, eyes steady and serious. "The first is will you marry me? And the second, and I'm hoping this will make up for my current lack of a ring, is in that folder. I want you to be Olivia's father. Legally. The first question is big, I know, but I feel like the second is almost more important."

Colby stood there a second, waiting for a clown to pop out of the closet and goose him. When that didn't happen and he didn't sprout wings or tentacles or nothing, he reckoned maybe it wasn't a dream, so he simply nodded. "I reckon I can more than live with that."

"You—that means *yes*, right?" Now Gordy was looking a little nervy. "Can you just… because sometimes we don't communicate so well."

"Yes. God, yes. One hundred percent with all my redneck heart, yes." That should be clear, even for a Yankee.

Gordy popped up off the floor and kissed him, crushing the folder between them. "I thought so, but you know, I was nervous and... God, I love your redneck heart." Gordy kissed him again.

Oh, this was the best proposal in history.

Colby leaned back, blinking a little as he fought to catch his breath. "Can we adopt her? That's legal? We can be her dads?"

"It's legal. I have an attorney here in Boulder, and we'll have to go to court, but I had the family attorney in Boston run the notices and do all the legal work, and whoever her sperm donor was, he's out of the picture. It's a quick hearing, a couple of signatures, and... yeah. We'll be her dads. Together."

"Good. I like that." Dads, yes, but together? He liked that most of all.

"I thought it sounded pretty damn good myself. We'll get rings. I just had this feeling that whatever I picked for myself wouldn't at all be what you'd pick out for your own finger." Gordy was holding him close, stealing kisses between their words.

"Mm-hmm. You know me, honey. Something solid and simple."

"Yeah? I might have something like that for you." Gordy took the file from him and set it on the vanity.

"Oh, darlin', you may be solid, but you're not a bit simple. You're the biggest, best challenge I ever had, swear to God."

"And you make it so easy. I hope I'm worth it, cowboy."

"Yes, sir." And together they'd be worth Liv. It worked for him, balls to bones.

"Thank you." Gordy slipped a finger into his towel, and it slid right off his hips. His lover's—his fiancé's—kiss was deep and heavy as Gordy herded him back against the vanity.

He curled his fingers into Gordy's lapels for balance, and Gordy slipped a hand between them, sliding it over Colby's abs and heading south.

"Uncle Colby? Uncle Gordy?"

Gordy broke off the kiss. "Shit! I thought I locked that door."

Colby grabbed his towel, keeping Gordy close enough to hide the inappropriate tenting. "What you need, Little Bit?"

"Good night kisses?"

"I'm on it." Gordy stretched out, snagged the closest robe, and slipped it to Colby. Then Gordy scooped Liv up and turned so her back was to him, winking over her shoulder.

"You ready for your kiss, Daddy?"

Liv's eyes lit up. "You asked him?"

"I asked him." Gordy kissed her nose.

"And I said yes, baby girl."

"My magic cowboy daddy." Liv grinned at him, and he damn near died, his chest so tight for a second that he fought to breathe.

He managed it, though, because he wasn't going to miss a second of this. "Yes, ma'am."

Gordy leaned in so Liv could give him a kiss.

"We'll celebrate in the mountains on Sunday." Gordy kissed him too. "Off to bed. Don't go anywhere, cowboy."

"Like there's anywhere I need to go, honey." After all, for the first time in longer than he'd care to remember, he was well and truly home.

A Collaborations Novel

Texas artist Tucker Williams arrives in New York City for a gallery showing of his work and finds the city blanketed in snow. He meets free-spirited underwear model Calvin McIntire on the steps of the Midtown library and is captivated by a wild beauty that manages to compete with the demons that occupy his soul and fuel his work with their lust for blood and erotic imagery.

Unable to deny a new inspiration, Tucker sublets a studio and finds the city's energy almost as addictive as Calvin.

Tucker is obsessive, barely holding on to sanity as his art consumes him, and Calvin is dealing with demons of his own, trying desperately to protect his soul in a business where only his appearance has value. They each prove to be the perfect remedy for the other's personal brand of crazy until, in the midst of stress and exhaustion, they discover that a promise Calvin needs is the one thing Tucker can't give him, and their heaven turns to purgatory.

Can both men find a path toward wholeness in Tucker's beautiful but chaotic Texas home? In order for them—and their passionate relationship—to thrive, they'll need to adapt, share their psychoses, and find a true balance between New York City and rural Texas.

www.dreamspinnerpress.com

Chapter One

TUCKER WILLIAMS leaned against the steps of the library beside the big stone lion and watched the white stuff fall out of the sky. Colder than he'd ever been in his whole life, he shivered, trying to figure out what the fuck a guy like him was doing all the way up here.

The logical part of his brain, the part not frozen solid, reminded him that he had a gallery opening tomorrow. A major opening. Right.

So he was up here touristing all by himself and freezing his nuts and his toes off and waiting to show up in his best jeans and jacket tomorrow night.

Go him.

Christ on a sparkly pink crutch, everyone here wore black, and no one smiled a bit. Surely there had to be somewhere here with friendly folks and heat.

Right on cue, one of those black-clad Yankees—this one in a black knee-length coat, black earmuffs, and chunky black boots—came trotting down the steps right past him. Like every other guy on the busy street, he was on the phone.

"That spread is mine, Michael. I want it. You make it happen. I've got the best ass of the bunch, and you know it."

The man stopped two steps below Tucker. "I'm easier to work with too. You tell them, okay? I need to get out of the weather. Who ordered this shit? Later."

Huh. Earmuffs were a thing. Go figure. Tucker had to admit, the whole pseudo-duster thing was pretty hot.

"'Scuse me, sir, but is there a decent place to get a cup of joe around here?" Tucker asked.

The guy turned his head, but Tucker couldn't get a good look at him behind the collar he'd pulled up against the weather. He was squinting against the snow, and his hair was mostly hidden under a knit hat, but it looked like it might be blond.

"There's no such thing as a bad cup of coffee in New York. You look like you're freezing your ass off, man. Come on, I'll show you." The guy just took off down the steps, and Tucker didn't have much choice but to follow.

Good Lord and butter, these folks walked like huge flocks of birds. Great big old flocks of ravens. Oh. Oh, he could—he could paint that, right now.

"Calvin." He was offered a gloved hand. Black leather, of course.

"Williams. Tucker Williams. Pleased." He pulled his hand out of his pocket and shook.

"Not from around here, I take it?" Calvin gave him wink and a grin.

Cool. This one smiled. "No, sir. I'm a bit from home, but that's obvious, I reckon."

"I'll say. In here." Calvin opened a door, and Tucker was hit with the smell of baking bread and a beautiful blast of warm air. "We're expecting a pretty good hit. How long are you in town?"

"Until Monday." Then he'd go explore somewhere else for a few days. Although, he loved that bird image….

"Well, if you haven't been in the city in a snowstorm before, and it looks to me like you haven't…." Calvin laughed. "You should know that you can't get a cab in the snow. Ever. Don't even bother trying. Get some boots and take the subway. Just coffee? I'm gonna hang out for a bit and eat something." Calvin pulled off his earmuffs and squinted at the menu. "Large almond-milk latte with an extra shot and the vegetarian chili… and…?" He looked at Tucker.

"Triple espresso and whatever y'all have that's the darkest chocolate." No way he was going underground to get on a train. No way on earth.

"Mmm, chocolate. That's one way to warm up." Calvin pulled off his gloves and then fished a credit card out of his pocket. "On me. Well, on my agent. It's a work day." He held his card up to the reader until it beeped, and the card disappeared into his pocket again. "I'm gonna grab a seat. You headed back out there?"

"I think I'll just sit a minute. Defrost." Eventually he'd figure out how to get back to his hotel.

"Do that." Calvin glanced over his shoulder as he headed for a table, and this time Tucker saw a flash of bright green eyes as they caught the light. "Tell me why you're up here in this shitty weather?"

"I have a thing I have to be at Saturday evening. Everyone told me to come up a few days early and explore. What kind of agent?" He had one too. Her name was Marge. She was something else.

"Oh, Michael. He's a talent guy." Calvin stuffed his gloves into his pockets. "So you came out in this weather just to visit the library? Did you get a picture with the lions, because that's a thing. Patience and Fortitude."

"No, sir." It was a cool library, though, and he'd spent a couple of happy hours in the 750s, just looking. Sort of like he was just looking at Mr. Pretty here. "Are you from here?"

Their order arrived, and Calvin waited to answer. "I grew up in Vermont. But I'm from here now. Got here when I was seventeen."

"Wow. I wasn't ready for something like this at seventeen." He wasn't ready for it now, he didn't think. Although that motion…. Tucker wondered if a guy could rent a studio space for, like, a week. Just to paint.

Calvin looked at him. "Oh. Did I say I was ready?" He laughed and picked up his latte. "No, I had a job, but I wasn't anything close to ready for this town. I adapted pretty quick, though. It's home now." He sipped his latte and then spooned up some "chili." Didn't seem like a great combination.

Shit, he was fairly sure that vegetarian chili was a crime against nature, but he was a stranger in a strange fucking land, so he didn't remark none on it.

"Where are you staying? Oh—that's nosy, right? You don't have to answer that. Sorry. I was just making small talk." Calvin giggled.

Yeah, Tucker was pretty sure that qualified as a giggle.

"How's your chocolate?"

"Dark." He licked his fork and hummed, the bitter and sweet exploding over his tongue. "Possibly the best piece of whatever-the-fuck fancy-assed piece of cake I've ever had."

Calvin put his spoon down. "You're good at that."

"At eating?" He'd hope so. Lord knew, he'd done it for years.

"No, the tongue thing. With your fork. Licking." Calvin braced his elbow on the table and his chin in his palm, eyes narrow and a wicked smile on his lips. "Do that again."

"Listen to you." Lord have mercy. That was hotter than the hinges of hell. Damn, how did that... how did something like that even happen?

"Yes, listen to me." Calvin sounded playful, and he shifted, picked up his latte, and took a sip. "Do it again, Mr. Williams? Please?"

"Well, since you asked so pretty." *Lord, please don't let me get my ass kicked here*. He took another bite, his cheeks lit on fucking fire. He licked his lips clean, then managed to meet Calvin's eyes. "Ta-da?"

Calvin laughed and applauded, the sound pure happy. "Oh. That was lovely! *So* hot. You're a riot, Tucker. I'm glad I pulled you out of the snow." Didn't seem like he was too worried about people overhearing, but then he leaned in closer. "Also, I think your cheeks are warm enough to melt that shit right off the sidewalk."

"Y'think? Shit marthy. I can't believe this mess." That he was flirting like he knew this guy, like this feller knew him from Job.

"Wait until tomorrow morning. Might be eight or nine inches." Calvin leaned back again and dug into his chili. "Might even be a foot. Hard to get around in this weather. Personally, I like to stay in bed all day."

"Eight or nine inches, huh?" He couldn't have stopped his expression if he'd tried.

"Mmm. Last I checked." Calvin's look was absolutely deadpan. "The weatherman doesn't always get it right, though. Sometimes it's a better idea to check out the radar for yourself, you know?" He took another bite and winked. "That might be carrying the metaphor a bit too far."

He had to laugh, had to, because not only was that true, but he hadn't expected to meet someone to flirt with shamelessly while on one of his wanders.

Calvin laughed with him. He got up to put his bowl in a rack by the garbage cans, and when he came back, still giggling, he shrugged off his coat and hung it over the back of his chair. "Warm finally." He had on a tight green sweater that left almost nothing to the imagination. Every ridge and line of his chest was plainly obvious, and the fabric stretched across broad shoulders.

Pretty, pretty. Tucker liked that Calvin wore a color. The green suited him to the bone.

He could eat that fine son of a bitch up, yessir.

"In all seriousness, shit's gonna close tomorrow. But the Empire State will be open and the World Trade Center, if you're looking for a view and some local history. I've never been up to catch the view in the snow. I bet it's pretty cool. You won't have the same pictures as everyone else, anyway."

Calvin's phone started ringing. "Excuse me a sec?" He pulled the phone out of his coat pocket. "A-yo. Hey. No, I want the—well, you know my angle, whoever will pay me more. Oh, I've never heard that joke before, Michael. *Ever*. Yes, go with Calvin. Thanks, man." He hung up. "Sorry."

"No worries. I don't mean to be keeping you from anything. Honest." A man had to work.

"You're keeping me from going insane in this snow. Keep up the good work." Calvin sipped his latte again. "My agent thinks Calvin Klein jokes are funny. You can keep me from that any day."

"Calvin Klein jokes? Like the drawers?" Those were still a thing? Lord have mercy. "Or don't they do perfume too?"

Calvin laughed. "Cologne. And yes, they do that too, but you don't get paid as well as you do for the underwear ads. Is that what you mean by drawers? They do jeans too, if that's what drawers are."

"Yessir. I mean tighty-whities. Is that what you do? Model?"

"Yeah. Sorry I didn't say that earlier. Sometimes people get… sometimes they forget they're talking to a real person when you tell them, so I like to hold off a bit." Calvin winked.

"No worries. I work with models, every now and again." For the most part, he found them patient as fuck.

"Yeah?" Calvin was flirting again. "What did you not say you do again?"

"I'm a painter—not houses."

"Okay, not houses. What do you paint? Land-scapes? People? Abstract stuff? I love art that you have to look at and think about."

"Uh. It's sorta… it's a little weird." He didn't tell a soul at home about the paintings that he was show-ing here. Not a soul.

"This is New York, my friend. We make *weird* an art form all the time. But it's cool. You don't have to tell me. I'm nosy. I just ask questions."

"I sorta make a living painting about horror, sex. Right now, birds. I'm very into birds." He didn't know why he did either, but he did, and he was, apparently, damn good at it.

"Horror and sex and birds." Calvin nodded, looking thoughtful. "Can't quite picture it. But birds are probably great subjects. They're so aloof and knowing."

"Yeah? Cool." Okay, so Calvin didn't run scream-ing or tell him he was going to hell; that was a plus.

"You have a pic on your phone? I'll show you mine if you show me yours."

"Fair enough." Did he? Lord, yes. His phone was his goddamn life. He scrolled through, finding the al-bum of his paintings.

"Deal." It took Calvin about three seconds to pull up a picture of himself on a rooftop wearing a pair of blue boxer-briefs with DIESEL printed on the wide black waistband and a white tank top that he was lifting up around his ribs with one hand. City office buildings were blurred in the background. "No laughing."

"Well, look at that. You have a nice heinie." He could tap that, no question. "Was it hot up there?"

"Fuck, yeah. It was like working in a frying pan. They would spray the roof with a hose to cool it off, and it would dry in three seconds, and then they had about fifteen seconds before I started screaming." Calvin laughed.

"Lord. You got some balls, I swear. I got nothing but respect for the work y'all do." He personally thought posing was hell. He didn't do still. Ever.

"Well, thank you." Calvin beamed at him. "I had ice cream that day as a reward, so it wasn't that bad. Okay, your turn."

He pulled up one of his demon series—a fierce horned beast appearing from between white feathers, the mouth promising pure decadence.

"Oh. Oh my." Calvin reached out and took the phone from him to get a closer look. "Fuck, man. This is way hotter than 'horror and sex and birds' sounded. I mean, Jesus. Look at him. *You* do this? You look way more… I mean, not like *this*. I would never have guessed. Wow."

"No one does. That's probably good, hmm?"

Calvin flicked his eyes from the phone to Tucker's face. "Yes and no. I mean, you should look how you want to look, but man, the artist that does *this* work? With a body like yours? You could seriously rock something… way darker."

"I tend to work buck naked. Saves clothes." Wait. Did he say that? Out loud?

Calvin's eyes popped open wide, and he started to laugh. Hard. Loud enough that people looked over at them, and he had to wave his hand to apologize because he seemed to be having trouble breathing.

He managed to just drink his coffee, keeping a mostly straight face. This guy let folks take his pictures in his skivvies; working naked was nothing.

Calvin silently handed Tucker back the phone, fanning himself with his other hand. He finally got a deep breath and puffed it out, grinning. "Jesus Christ. I don't know what I was expecting you to say, but it wasn't that. But that's cool; I do some of my best work naked too. I just don't get paid for *that*." He winked and picked up his coffee. "Shit, my sides hurt."

"When you get it from laughing, that's okay, I think." He pocketed his phone and finished up his sweet. So rich and good.

Calvin blushed. "I'm sorry. I'm not laughing at you. Honest, I'm not. I'm laughing at how stupid I am for looking at a fairly clean-cut, good-looking Texan, and... I don't know. I got it all wrong, obviously, and for some reason that makes me absurdly happy." The blush and a little humility made Calvin look younger, sweeter.

He grinned, that smile charming the hell out of him. "Shit, honey. I'm just tickled you didn't ask if I was an axe murderer."

Calvin's eyebrows twitched. "I figured that would be rude since you hadn't asked me that question yet." He finished off the last of his coffee, tipping the cup up high to get the last drop.

"Rumor is you folks have all the axe murderers you need."

"More muggers and thieves than axe murderers, actually. I don't think I know anyone that hasn't been robbed at some point. Especially people who look like tourists." Calvin laughed. "You better watch your wallet."

He arched one eyebrow. He didn't think he'd take real kindly to that. Of course, who the fuck did? Seriously. No one just threw themselves in front of someone and said, *"Fuck with me!"* right? Right.

"I do, but thank you. I appreciate that warning."

"For what it's worth, crime usually goes way down in the snow." Calvin slid his empty cup a couple of inches away. "I am all out of coffee."

He leaned around the table and checked out Tucker's boots. "Are those waterproof?"

"They do okay, yeah." More waterproof than cold proof, for sure.

"Good. Come on." Calvin stood up, looking more like a model now that Tucker knew he was one, and pulled on his coat. "Sorry. Unless you have plans, of course."

"Plans? I have to be at the gallery Saturday night. That's my plan."

"That's it? God, the things I could do with you for two days." Calvin brushed a little too close as he stepped around Tucker and didn't even pretend it was an accident.

They headed back out into the snow and retraced their steps to the library. The white stuff was starting to pile up, maybe three or four inches now.

Calvin didn't say much on the short trip, but as he got close to the library, he poked Tucker with an elbow. "You're gonna love this."

He heard voices and laughter as they rounded the corner of the big building and headed into the little park next to it, where a small crowd of people was having one big snowball fight.

"You ready?" Calvin took a few steps backward and then started to run.

It took Tucker a second, but he figured what the hell? He hadn't wanted to play so bad in a long damn time.

Tucker gave chase, a redneck yell filling the air.

JODI PAYNE spent too many years in New York and San Francisco stage-managing classical plays, edgy fringe work, and the occasional musical. She therefore is overdramatic, takes herself way too seriously, and has been known to randomly break out in song. Her men are imperfect but genuine, stubborn but likeable, often kinky, and frequently their own worst enemies. They are characters you can't help but fall in love with while they stumble along the path to their happily ever after.

For those looking to get on her good side, Jodi's addictions include nonfat lattes, Malbec, and tequila however you pour it. She's also obsessed with Shakespeare and Broadway musicals. She can be found wearing sock monkey gloves while typing when it's cold, and on the beach enjoying the sun and the ocean when it's hot. When she's not writing and/or vacuuming sand out of her laptop, Jodi mentors queer youth and will drop everything for live music. Jodi lives near New York City with her beautiful wife, and together they are mothers of dragons (cleverly disguised as children) and slaves to an enormous polydactyl cat.

Website: www.jodipayne.net

Email: jodipaynewrites@gmail.com

Facebook: www.facebook.com/payne.jodi

FB Author Group: www.facebook.com/groups/jodisgents

Twitter: @JodiPayne

Instagram: @jodipayne1800

Goodreads: www.goodreads.com/author/show/267617.Jodi_Payne

BA TORTUGA, Texan to the bone and an unrepentant Daddy's Girl, spends her days with her basset hounds, getting tattooed, texting her sisters, and eating Mexican food. When she's not doing that, she's writing. She spends her days off watching rodeo, knitting, and surfing Pinterest in the name of research. BA's personal saviors include her wife, Julia Talbot, her best friend, Sean Michael, and coffee. Lots of coffee. Really good coffee.

Having written everything from fist-fighting rednecks to hard-core cowboys to werewolves, BA does her damnedest to tell the stories of her heart, which was raised in Northeast Texas, but has heard the call of the high desert and lives in the Sandias. With books ranging from hard-hitting GLBT romance, to fiery ménages, to the most traditional of love stories, BA refuses to be pigeonholed by anyone but the voices in her head.

Website: www.batortuga.com
Blog: batortuga.blogspot.com
Facebook: www.facebook.com/batortuga
Twitter: @batortuga

DREAMSPUN
DESIRES

COWBOY IN
THE CROSSHAIRS

BA Tortuga

Where the West is still
wild... and weird.